THE LITTLE SLEEP

A HOLT PAPERBACK

HENRY HOLT AND COMPANY   NEW YORK

A Novel

THE LITTLE SLEEP

PAUL TREMBLAY

Holt Paperbacks
Henry Holt and Company, LLC
Publishers since 1866
175 Fifth Avenue
New York, New York 10010
www.henryholt.com

Library of Congress Cataloging-in-Publication Data

Tremblay, Paul.
  The little sleep : a novel / Paul Tremblay.—1st ed.
    p.   cm.
  ISBN-13: 978-0-8050-8849-6
  ISBN-10: 0-8050-8849-0
  1. Private investigators—Fiction.   2. South Boston (Boston, Mass.)—Fiction.
3. Narcolepsy—Fiction.   4. Extortion—Fiction.   I. Title.
  PS3620.R445L58   2009
  813'.6—dc22   2008008855

Henry Holt books are available for special promotions and premiums.
For details contact: Director, Special Markets.

First Edition 2009

Designed by Linda Kosarin

Printed in the United States of America

1 3 5 7 9 10 8 6 4 2

For Lisa, Cole, and Emma

I was more intrigued by a situation where the mystery is solved by the exposition and understanding of a single character, always well in advance, rather than by the slow and sometimes long-winded concatenation of circumstances.

—RAYMOND CHANDLER

*I smell smoke
that comes from a gun
named extinction.*

—THE PIXIES (*from "The Sad Punk"*)

THE LITTLE SLEEP

ONE

It's about two o'clock in the afternoon, early March. In South Boston that means a cold hard rain that ruins any memories of the sun. Doesn't matter, because I'm in my office, wearing a twenty-year-old thrift-store wool suit. It's brown but not in the brown-is-the-new-black way. My shoes are Doc Martens, black like my socks. I'm not neat and clean or shaved. I am sober but don't feel sober.

There's a woman sitting on the opposite side of my desk. I don't remember her coming in, but I know who she is: Jennifer Times, a flavor-of-the-second local celebrity, singing contestant on *American Star*, daughter of the Suffolk County DA, and she might be older than my suit. Pretty and brunette, lips that are worked out, pumped up. She's tall and her legs go from the north of Maine all the way down to Boston, but she sits like she's small, all compact, a closed book. She wears a white T-shirt and a knee-length skirt. She looks too spring for March, not that I care.

I wear a fedora, trying too hard to be anachronistic or iconoclastic, not sure which. It's dark in my office. The door is closed, the blinds drawn over the bay window. Someone should turn on a light.

I say, "Shouldn't you be in Hollywood? Not that I watch, but the little birdies tell me you're a finalist, and the live competition starts tomorrow night."

She says, "They sent me home to do a promotional shoot at a mall and at my old high school." I like that she talks about her high school as if it were eons removed, instead of mere months.

"Lucky you."

She doesn't smile. Everything is serious. She says, "I need your help, Mr. Genevich," and she pulls her white-gloved hands out of her lap.

I say, "I don't trust hands that wear gloves."

She looks at me like I chose the worst possible words, like I missed the whole point of her story, the story I haven't heard yet. She takes off her right glove and her fingers are individually wrapped in bandages, but it's a bad wrap job, gauze coming undone and sticking out, Christmas presents wrapped in old tissue paper.

She says, "I need you to find out who has my fingers."

I think about opening the shades; maybe some light wouldn't be so bad. I think about clearing my desk of empty soda cans. I think about canceling the Southie lease, too many people double-parking in front of my office/apartment building. I think about the ever-expanding doomed universe. And all of it makes more sense than what she said.

"Say that again."

Her blue eyes stay fixed on me, like she's the one trying to figure out who is telling the truth. She says, "I woke up like this yesterday. Someone stole my fingers and replaced them with these." She holds her hand out to me as if I can take it away from her and inspect it.

"May I?" I gently take her hand, and I lift up the bandage on her index finger and find a ring of angry red stitches. She takes her hand back from me quick, like if I hold on to it too long I might decide to keep those replacement digits of hers.

"Look, Ms. Times, circumstantial evidence to the contrary and all that, but I don't think what you described is exactly possible." I point at her hand. I'm telling her that her hand is impossible. "Granted, my subscription to *Mad Scientist Weekly* did run out. Too many words, not enough pictures."

She says, "It doesn't matter what you think is possible, Mr. Genevich, because I'll only be paying you to find answers to my questions." Her voice is hard as pavement. I get the sense that she isn't used to people telling her no.

I gather the loose papers on my desk, stack them, and then push them over the edge and into the trash can. I want a cigarette but I don't know where I put my pack. "How and why did you find me?" I talk slow. Every letter and syllable has to be in its place.

"Does it matter?" She talks quick and to the point. She wants to tell me more, tell me everything about every thing, but she's holding something back. Or maybe she's just impatient with me, like everyone else.

I say, "I don't do much fieldwork anymore, Ms. Times. Early retirement, so early it happened almost before I got the job. See this computer?" I turn the flat-screen monitor toward her. An infinite network of Escheresque pipes fills the screen-saver pixels. "That's what I do. I research. I do genealogies, find abandoned properties, check the status of out-of-state warrants, and find lost addresses. I search databases and, when desperate, which is all the time, I troll Craigslist and eBay and want ads. I'm no action hero. I find stuff in the Internet ether. Something tells me your fingers won't be in there."

She says, "I'll pay you ten thousand just for trying." She places a check on my desk. I assume it's a check. It's green and rectangular.

"What, no manila envelope bulging with unmarked bills?"

"I'll pay you another fifty thousand if you find out who has my fingers."

I am about to say something sharp and clever about her allowance from Daddy, but I blink my eyes and she is gone.

TWO

Right after I come to is always the worst, when the questions about dreams and reality seem fair game, when I don't know which is which. Jennifer Times is gone and my head is full of murk. I try to push the murk to the corners of my consciousness, but it squeezes out and leaks away, mercury in a closed fist. That murk, it's always there. It's both a threat and a promise. I am narcoleptic.

How long was I asleep? My office is dark, but it's always dark. I have the sense that a lot of time has passed. Or maybe just a little. I have no way of knowing. I generally don't remember to check and set my watch as I'm passing out. Time can't be measured anyway, only guessed at, and my guesses are usually wrong, which doesn't speak well for a guy in my line of work. But I get by.

I paw around my desk and find a pack of cigarettes behind the phone, right where I left them. I light one. It's warm, white, and lethal. I'd like to say that smoking keeps me awake, clears the head, all that good stuff normally associated with nicotine and carcinogens, but it doesn't. Smoking is just something I do to help pass the time in the dark, between sleeps.

On my desk there is no green and rectangular ten-thousand-dollar check. Too bad, I'd quickly grown fond of the little fella. There is a manila envelope, and on my notepad are gouges and scratches in ink, an EKG output of a faulty heart. My notepad is yellow like the warning traffic light.

I lean back in my chair, looking for a new vantage point, a different way to see. My chair complains. The squawking springs tease me and my sedentary existence. No one likes a wiseass. It might be time for a new chair.

Okay, Jennifer Times. I conclude the stuff about her missing fingers was part of a hypnogogic hallucination, which is one of the many pithy symptoms of narcolepsy. It's a vivid dream that occurs when my narcoleptic brain is partially awake, or partially asleep, as if there is a difference.

I pick up the manila envelope and remove its contents: two black-and-white photos, with accompanying negatives.

Photo 1: Jennifer Times sitting on a bed. Shoulder-length hair obscures most of her face. There's a close-lipped smile that peeks through, and it's wary of the camera and, by proxy, me. She's wearing a white T-shirt and a dark-colored pleated skirt. It's hiked above her knees. Her knees have scabs and bruises. Her arms are long and closed in tight, like a mantis.

Photo 2: Jennifer Times sitting on a bed. She's topless and wearing only white panties. She sits on her folded legs, feet under her buttocks, hands resting on her thighs. Her skin is bleached white, and she is folded. Origami. Arms are at her side and they push her small breasts together. Her eyes are closed and head tilted back. A light fixture shines directly above her head, washing her face in white light. Ligature in her neck is visible, as are more than a few ribs. The smile from the first photo has become something else, a grimace maybe.

The photos are curled, a bit washed and faded. They feel old and heavy with passed time. They're imperfect. These photos are like my memories.

I put the photos side by side on my desktop. On the lip of the Coke-can ashtray my cigarette is all ash, burnt down to the filter. I just lit it, but that's how time works for me. My constant enemy, it attacks whenever I'm not looking.

All right. Focus. It's a simple blackmail case. Some entrepreneur wants Jennifer to invest in his private cause or these photos go public and then she gets the gong, the hook, voted off the island on *American Star*.

But why would a blackmailer send the negatives? The photos have likely been digitized and reside on a hard drive or two somewhere. Still, her—and now me—being in possession of the negatives is troubling. There's more here, and less, of course, since I don't remember any of our conversation besides the finger stuff, so I light another cigarette.

The Jennifer in the photos doesn't look exactly like the Jennifer I've seen on TV or the one who visited my office. The difference is hard to describe, but it's there, like the difference in taste between butter and margarine. I look at the photos again. It could be her; the Jennifer from a few years ago, from high school, the Jennifer from before professional makeup teams and personal stylists. Or maybe the photo Jennifer is margarine instead of butter.

I pick up my notepad. There is writing only on that top page. I was dutifully taking notes while asleep. Automatic behavior. Like tying your shoes. Like driving and listening to the radio instead of actually driving, getting there without getting there. Not that I drive anymore.

During micro-sleeps, my narcoleptic brain will keep my body moving, keep it churning through some familiar task, and I won't have any memory of it. These acts belong to my secret life. I've woken up to find e-mails written and sent, soup cans stacked on my desk, peeled wallpaper in my bedroom, pantry items stuffed inside the refrigerator, magazines and books with their covers torn off.

Here's the top page of my notepad:

Most of it is likely junk, including my doodle arrows. The narcoleptic me is rarely accurate in his automatic behavior. The numbers don't add up to any type of phone number or contact information. But there's SOUTH SHORE PLAZA, Jennifer's public mall appearance. She and I need to talk. I get the hunch that this blackmail case is about as simple as quantum physics.

THREE

All my mornings disappear eventually. Today, some of it disappeared while I was on the phone. I tried to reach Times via her agency. No luck. I couldn't get past the secretary without disclosing too much information, not that I'm in possession of a bucketful of info, and I've always had a hard time with improv.

I did ferret out that my automatic self was wrong about the South Shore Plaza. There's just no trusting that guy. Times's mall meet-and-greet is at Copley Plaza, downtown Boston, this afternoon.

It's later than I wanted it to be, it's still raining, my black coffee is somehow hazelnut, and the line to see Times is longer than the Charles River. I hate hazelnut. The other coffee I'm carrying is loaded with cream and sugar. It's a cup of candy not fit for consumption, which is fine, because I don't intend to drink it.

Copley is cavernous, brightly lit in golden tones and ceramic tile, and caters to the high-end designer consumer. No Dollar Store here, but it's still just a mall, and its speakers pump out *American Star* promo ads and tunes sung by Times. I think I prefer the old-school Muzak.

There are kids everywhere. They wait in line and they lean over the railings on the upper levels. Escalators are full in every direction. There's even a pint-sized pack of punks splashing in the fountain, taking other people's dimes and quarters. Everyone screams and waves and takes pictures. They hold up posters and signs, the *i*'s dotted with hearts, *love* spelled *luv*. Times is getting more mall worship than Santa and the Easter Bunny combined.

Because waiting in lines is detrimental to my tenuous conscious state, I walk toward the front. I growl some words that might sound like *Excuse me*.

I'm not a huge guy, but kids and their reluctant parents move out of my way. They do so because I walk with an obvious purpose, with authority. It's an easy trick. A person carrying two coffees has important places to go. Or, just as likely, people let me by because they're afraid of the hairy guy wearing a fedora and trench coat, the guy who's here without a kid and has a voice deeper than the pit of despair. Hey, whatever works.

I'm only ten or so people from the front of the line, far enough away not to be cutting in plain view of the cops and security guards circling Times and her entourage, but close enough that my wait will be mercifully brief. So I stop and step in front of a father-daughter tandem.

The father wears a Bruins hockey jersey and he's built like a puck, so the shirt works for him. His daughter is a mini-puck in jeans and a pink T plastered with Times's cheery face. This will be the greatest moment of her life until she forgets about it tomorrow.

I hold out the second coffee, my DO-NOT-STOP-AT-GO pass, and say, "Ms. Times wanted me to get her a coffee. Thanks, pal." My voice is a receding glacier.

The hockey puck nods and says, "Go ahead," and pulls his daughter against his hip, away from me. At least somebody is thinking of the children.

No one in our immediate vicinity questions my new existence at the front of the line. There are grumbles of disapproval from farther back, but nothing that needs to be addressed. Those grumblers only complain because they're far enough away from me to be safe, to be anonymous. If they were in the puck's shoes, they wouldn't say boo. Most people are cowards.

I sip my coffee and stain my mustache and smell hazelnut. God-damn hazelnut. I want to light a cigarette and chew on the smoke, scorch that awful taste out of my mouth, but that's not going to fly here. At least the coffee is still hot.

The line moves with its regimented torpor, like all lines do, and my wait won't be long, but my lights are dimming a bit already, an encroaching numbness to the excitement and bustle around me. Thoughts about what I'm going to say to Times can't seem to find a foothold. I cradle the coffees in the crook of an arm, reach inside a pocket, and pinch my thigh. Then I regroup, shake my head, and take another sip of the 'nut. All keep-me-awake tricks that sometimes work and sometimes don't.

I scan the crowd, trying to find a focus. If I lock eyes with someone, they look away quick. Folks around me are thinking, *If he really got her coffee, why is he waiting in line at all?* It's too late for any kind of revolt, and I'm next. Two bodyguards, each with heads the size of Easter Island statues, flank Times, though they're set back a lunge or two. The background distance is there to encourage a ten-second intimate moment with every fan.

My turn. Maybe she'll John Hancock the brim of my hat, or my hand. I'll never wash it again.

Times sits at a table with stacks of glossy head shots, blue Sharpie in hand, her hair pulled back into a tight ponytail, showing off the crabapple cheekbones. She wears jeans, a long-sleeve Red Sox shirt, and very little makeup. All hints of sexuality have been neutralized; a nonthreatening just-a-sweet-young-American-girl-in-a-mall look.

She's probably not going to be wild about seeing me here. No probably about it. And I'm not exactly sure how I'm going to come out of this impromptu tête-à-tête in a positive light. She is my employer and I'll be admitting, in not so many words, that I was asleep on the job before it even started.

I step up to the plate and extend the candy coffee out to her, a gift from one of the magi, the defective one, the one who's broken. No frankincense or myrrh from this guy.

I say, "Thought you might need a coffee." A good opener for the uncomfortable revelations to come, and it reinforces that I'm willing to work for her.

She opens the curtain on her practiced, polished smile. One thousand watts. It's an egalitarian smile too. Everyone has been getting that flash of teeth and gums. There's not a hint of recognition in her face. Her smile says I'm faceless, like everyone else. She's already a pro at this. I'm the one who's amateur hour.

She says, "I don't drink coffee, but thank you, that's so nice." One of the Easter Island statues moves in and takes the coffee. Maybe he'll analyze it, afraid of death by hazelnut and cream and sugar. I can't think of a worse way to go.

I try to be quiet and discreet, but my voice doesn't have those settings. Check the manual. "Sorry to do this here, you as conquering local hero and all that stuff, but I dropped by because I need your direct phone line. Your agency treated me like a refugee when I tried to call earlier." It isn't smooth. It's bumpy and full of potholes, but I'll explain if she asks.

"Why were you calling my agency?" She looks over both her shoulders. That twin-generator smile has gone, replaced with a help-me look. The giant heads stir, angry pagan gods, awake and looking to smite somebody's ass. They exchange nonverbal communication cues, signs that the muscle-bound and intellectually challenged understand by instinct: puffed-out chests, clenched jaws, tightened fists.

Is Times serious or putting on a public show, acting like she doesn't know me because she's not supposed to know me? Either way, this isn't good. This is already going worse than I imagined.

My head sweats under the hat. Beard and hazelnut mustache itch. Being stressed out won't exactly help me avoid some of my condition's less pleasant symptoms. But I sally forth.

I say, "I was trying to call you because I had some questions about your case, Ms. Times." I use her name in a formal but familiar way, reassuring and reestablishing my professional status.

"Case?"

"Yeah, the case. Your case."

She doesn't say anything.

I lean in to try a conspiratorial whisper, but she slides back in her seat, and it's too loud in here anyway, with all the chattering and screaming. Can't say I practice our culture's celebrity worship, and it's downright inconvenient right now. This place is the monkey house. I lose my cool. "Christ. You know, what was inside that manila envelope you left me certainly wasn't a set of Christmas cards."

All right, I'm not doing well here. Wrong line of questions, no tact. Okay, she clearly doesn't want to talk about it, or talk to me in public. I should've known that.

She says, "I don't understand."

I've been standing here too long. Everyone is staring at us, at me. Nothing is right. We're failing to communicate. It's only a matter of time before someone comes over to break up our verbal clinch.

"Fine. Just sign me a *picture*," I say, and pause, waiting to see if my pointed word has any effect on her. Nothing. She appears to be confused. She appears to be sincere in not knowing who I am. I add, "And I'll leave." It's weak. An after-afterthought.

Her mouth is open and she shrinks into a tightened defensive posture. She looks scared. She looks like the girl in the first photo, the clothed girl. Does she still have those bruises and scabs on her knees?

"My mistake. Sorry to bother you," I say, and reach into my coat for a business card. I'll just leave it on the table and walk away. Yeah, she contacted me first, which means she likely has my number, but I have to do something to save face, to make me feel like something other than a stalker.

I pull out the card between two nicotine-stained fingers and drop it on the table. The statues animate and land their heavy hands on each of my shoulders. There's too much weight and pressure, underlining the banner headline I'M ALREADY FUCKING THIS UP COMPLETELY. I've angered the pagan gods with my ineptitude. I don't blame them.

I guess I'm leaving now, and without an autograph. As the statues escort me toward one of Copley's many exits, I have enough leisure time to consider the case and what comes next. A cab ride to my office, more phone calls to Jennifer's agency, Internet searches. A multimedia plan B, whatever that is.

Four

Chapter 147: Section 24. Applications; qualifications of applicants

An application for a license to engage in the private detective business or a license to engage in the business of watch, guard, or patrol agency shall be filed with the colonel of the state police on forms furnished by him, and statements of fact therein shall be under oath of the applicant.

George and I dropped out of Curry College together, each with three semesters of criminal justice under our belts. We didn't like where it was going. We spent our last weekend in the dorm skimming the yellow pages, fishing for do-it-yourself career advice. At the end of the weekend, we closed our eyes and made our choices.

I picked private investigation. I figured my mother, Ellen, who would not be pleased about my dropping out, might eventually be receptive given that a PI was somewhat related to my brief collegiate studies. I was right.

Eight years ago I got my license. According to Massachusetts law, having fulfilled the outlined requirements and submitted the fifty-dollar application fee makes me, officially, Mark Genevich, Private Detective.

> Such application shall include a certification by each of three reputable citizens of the commonwealth residing in the community in which the applicant resides or has a place of business, or in which the applicant proposes to conduct his business—

Eight years ago I was sitting in the passenger seat of George's van, hurtling back to South Boston from Foxwoods, one of the Connecticut reservation casinos.

George was an upper-middle-class black kid from suburban New Jersey, but he pretended to be from Boston. He wore a Sox hat and talked with a fake accent when we were out at a bar. He played Keno and bought scratch tickets. He told bar patrons that he was from Southie and he was Black Irish. More often than not, people believed him.

George's yellow-pages career was a start-up rug cleaning business. I cleaned rugs for him on the weekends. He had only one machine and its exhaust smelled like wet dog. After getting my private detective's license, I was going to share my Southie office and charge him a ridiculously small rent. I could do that because Ellen owned the building. Still does.

The rug business name was Carpet Warriors. His white van had a pumped-up cartoon version of himself in standard superhero garb: tight red spandex, muscles bulging over other muscles, CW on his chest plate, and a yellow cape. Our buddy Juan-Miguel did the stenciling. George was not really a superhero. He was tall and lanky, his limbs like thin tree branches, always swaying in some breeze. Before getting into his Carpet Warrior van, George would strike a pose in front of his buff superhero doppelgänger and announce, "Never fear, the Carpet Warrior is here," reveling in the innuendo.

George was twenty-two years old. I was twenty-one. At Foxwoods, I played roulette and he played at the tables: blackjack and poker. We lost a shitload of money. In the van, we didn't talk until he said, "We blew ten rugs' worth." We laughed. His laugh was always louder than mine and more infectious. We might've been drunk, we might've been fine.

A tire blew out. I heard it go and felt the sudden drop. The van careened into a drainage ditch and rolled around like a dog trying to pick up a dead squirrel's musk. Everything was dark. I don't remember seeing anything. The seat belt wasn't tight against my chest because I wasn't wearing one. My face broke the passenger's side window and was messed up worse than a Picasso, everything exaggerated and in the wrong spots. Nose and septum pulverized, my flesh as remolded clay that didn't set where it was supposed to.

I broke the window but my body stayed in the van. George's didn't. He went out the windshield, ahead of the van, but he didn't fly far. Like I said, he wasn't a superhero. The van fishtailed sideways, then rolled right over him. George died. I miss him.

—that he has personally known the applicant for at least three years,
that he has read the application and believes each of the statements
made therein to be true, that he is not related to the applicant by
blood or marriage—

After the accident and the surgeries, I grew a beard to hide my damaged face. My left eye is now a little lower than my right, and smaller. I'm always winking at you, but you don't know why. Too bad the beard never covers my eyes. The fedora—I wear it low—comes close.

Postrecovery, I lived with Juan-Miguel and another college buddy in the Southie apartment above my office. My narcolepsy symptoms started as soon as I got back from the hospital, a creeping crawling terror from a bad horror flick. I was Michael Landon turning into the teenage werewolf. I was always tired and had no energy, and I fell asleep while working on the computer or watching TV or eating breakfast or on the phone with potential clients. So I rarely answered the phone and tried to communicate solely by e-mail. I stopped going out unless it was to drink, which made everything worse. I know, hard to believe alcohol didn't make it all better.

Juan-Miguel came home one night to find me half inside the tub, pants down around my ankles, hairy ass in the air. I'd fallen asleep on the toilet and pitched into the tub. I told him I was passed out drunk. Might've been true.

When I was supposed to be sleeping, I didn't sleep well. I had paralyzing nightmares and waking dreams, or I wandered the apartment like the Phantom of the Opera, man turned monster. I emptied the fridge and lit cigarettes I didn't smoke. They left their marks.

Worst of all, I somnambulated into the TV room, freed myself from pants and underwear, lifted up a couch cushion, and let the urine flow. Apparently I wasn't even considerate enough to put the seat down after. I pissed on our couch every other week. I was worse than a goddamn cat.

—and that the applicant is honest and of good moral character.

I denied it all, of course. I wasn't asleep on the couch. If I was, it was because I drank too much. I wasn't doing any of those horrible, crazy things. It wasn't possible. That wasn't me even if my roommates saw me. They were lying to me. They were pulling cruel practical jokes that weren't at all practical. They were leaving lit cigarettes on the kitchen table and on my bedspread. One of them had a cat and they weren't admitting it. The cat was pissing on the couch, not me. I wasn't some animal that wasn't house trained, for chrissakes.

The kicker was that I believed my own denials. The truth was too embarrassing and devastating. I argued with my roommates all the time. Argument became part of my character. Nothing they said was true or right, even the mundane proclamations that had nothing to do with me or my narcoleptic actions. The only way I could consistently deny my new symptoms and odd behavior was to deny everything. I became even more of a recluse, holed up in my room until the asleep me would unleash himself, a midnight, couch-pissin' Kraken. My roommates moved out within the year.

Narcolepsy is not a behavioral disorder. It's neurological. It's physical. Routine helps, but it's no cure. Nothing is. There's no pattern to the symptoms. I tried prescription drugs, but the chemical stimulants resulted in paranoia and wild mood swings. My heart raced like a hummingbird's, and the insomnia worsened. So I stopped. Other than the coffee I'm not supposed to drink and the cigarettes I'm not supposed to smoke, I'm au naturel.

Eight years ago I got my private detective's license and narcolepsy. I now live alone with both.

That said, I'm waking up, and there's someone in my apartment, and that someone is yelling at me.

FIVE

Sleep is heavy. It has mass. Sometimes it has supreme mass. Sleep as a singularity. There's no moving or denying or escaping. Sometimes sleep is light too. I've been able to walk under its weight. It can be light enough to dream through, but more often than not it's the heavy kind. It's the ocean and you're pinned to the bottom of the seafloor.

". . . on fire? Jesus Christ! Wake the hell up, Mark!"

The impossible weight lifts away. I resurface too fast and get the bends. Muscles twitch and my heart pushes past my throat and into my head where it doesn't belong, making everything hurt.

It's Ellen, my mother. She stands in the doorway of the living room, wearing frilly blue oversized clown pants and a T that reads

LITHUANIA. The shirt is an old favorite of hers, something she wears too often. The clown pants I've never seen before. I hope this means I'm having another hypnogogic hallucination.

I'm sitting on the couch. My mouth is still open because I was asleep with it that way. I blink and mash the back of my hand into my eyes, pushing and squeezing the sleep out. I have my cell phone in my right hand. On my left side is smoke and heat.

The couch is smoking, cigarette and everything. It's a nasty habit the couch can't seem to break. The couch doesn't heed surgeon generals' warnings. Maybe it should try the patch.

I lift my left leg and twist away from the smoke, but the cigarette butt rolls after me, leaving a trail of red ash. In the cushion there's a dime-sized hole, the circumference red and still burning. I'd say it's just one blemish, but the reality is my couch has acne.

I pick up the butt. It's too hot and I drop it on the floor. I pat the couch cushion. Red ashes go black and there's more smoke.

I say, "I wasn't sleeping. I wasn't smoking." Ellen knows what I mean when I'm lying: I don't want to talk about it, and even if I did want to talk about it nothing would change.

She shakes her head and says, "You're gonna burn yourself up one of these days, Mark. I don't know why I bother." Her admonishment is by rote, perfunctory. We can get on with our day, now that it's out of the way.

I make my greeting a subtle dig at her for no good reason other than I'm embarrassed. "Good to see you too, Ellen. Shut the door on the way out." At least this time she didn't find me asleep with my pants around my ankles and an Edward Penishands porno on the TV.

Ellen stays at my apartment a couple of nights a week. If pressed, she maintains she stays here because she wants to play Keno and eat at the Italian American and L Street Diner with her sister and friends. She won't admit to being my de facto caregiver. She's the underwriter of my less-than-successful private detecting business and the landlord who doesn't want her property, the brownstone she inherited from her parents, to burn to the ground. I can't blame her.

Ellen is Southie born and bred and, like every other lifelong resident, she knows everything about everybody. Gentrification has toned down the small-town we-are-Southie vibe a bit, but it's still here. She starts right in on some local dirt, mid-story, assuming I know what she's talking about when I don't.

"Davy T said he knew she was lying the whole time. He told me weeks ago. He could just tell she was lying. Do you know when someone's lying, Mark? They say you watch the eyes. Up and left means recall, down and right means they're making stuff up. Or it's the other way around. I don't know. You should take a class in that. You could find a class online, I bet."

Davy T is the centuries-old Greek who owns the pizza joint next door. That's the only part of her monologue that registers with me. I check my cell phone, no messages. It has been a full day since Jennifer's mall appearance.

Ellen says, "Anyway, Davy T knew. It'll be all over the news tonight. They found her out. She was making it all up: the cancer, her foundation, everything. What kind of person does that?" Ellen crosses the room as she talks, her clown pants merrily swishing away. She opens my windows and waves her hands. The smoke obeys and swirls in the fresh air. Magic. Must be the pants. "Maybe you should've been on that case, Mark. You could've solved that, don't you think? You could've saved folks a lot of money and aggravation."

To avoid discussing my condition or me burning up with the apartment, Ellen defaults into details of already solved cases that presumably I could've tackled; as if I've ever worked on a case that involved anything more than tapping keys in front of my computer or being a ghost at a library or a town hall registrar.

Still patting the couch like I can replace the burned and missing upholstery with my Midas touch, I say, "Sure thing, Ellen." Truth is, my confidence and self-esteem are fighting it out in the subbasement, seeing which can be lower.

Jennifer hasn't returned any of my calls to the agency. I fell asleep up here, waiting for a callback. Waiting for something to get me going, because I have nothing. I don't know how she was contacted by the blackmailer, if the pictures were mailed or left on a doorstop, if there had been earlier contact or contact since. It's kind of hard to start a case without a client, or at least a client that will talk to you.

I say, "So what's with the Bozo the Clown getup?"

Ellen walks into the kitchen. "I was shooting some kid's portrait today and the little bastard wouldn't stop crying until I put the pants on." When Ellen isn't her force-of-nature self in my apartment, she lives in the old family bungalow in Osterville, a small tourist haven on the Cape. In downtown Osterville she has a photography studio and antiques shop. She shoots kids, weddings, graduation pictures. Nothing fancy. She's been doing it since my father died.

"Wouldn't a red nose and a horn get the job done? Maybe one of those flowers that shoots out water. You need to rely on cliché a little more."

"What, you're an expert now? I got the shots." She plays with her clown pants, pulling them up at the knee, making mini circus tents. "I need to change." Ellen abruptly disappears into my bedroom and shuts the door.

I pick up the cigarette butt off the floor and try to tidy things up a bit, putting dirty glasses and dishes in the sink, stacking magazines, moving dust around. I eyeball the couch to make sure it's not still burning.

I check my cell phone again, even though I've already checked for messages. Why wouldn't she call me back? If this is supposed to be some super-special double-secret case, it's not going to work out. The sleeping me should've told her thanks-but-no-thanks when she dumped those pictures on me. The sleeping me is just so irresponsible on my behalf.

Earlier, I did a cursory Web search, reading blogs and message boards, finding no hint or threat of the existence of the photos, or a stalker, or a potential blackmailer. Everything from her camp seems as controlled and wholesome as can be. No one has even posted fake nudes of Jennifer yet, which is usually an instantaneous Internet occurrence once there's a new female celebrity. I don't get the lack of buzz. The irony is that if I posted the pictures, I'd likely be helping her career, but I'm not her agent.

Ellen emerges from the bedroom. Her shoulder-length gray hair is tied up and she has on her black-framed glasses, thick lenses that enlarge her eyes. She's still wearing the clown pants but has on a gray sweatshirt over LITHUANIA.

I say, "Are you going to take my picture later? Maybe tie me up some balloon animals? I want a giraffe, a blue one."

She says, "Everyone at the Lithuanian Club will get a kick out of the pants. And they are comfortable. Nice and roomy." She walks by and punches my shoulder. "So, should we do something for dinner?" Ellen never makes dinner a declarative statement. She's earnest in the illusion of a choice being offered. It's not that I can't say no. I never have a reason to do so.

I say, "Something sounds delicious, Ellen." I have a gut feeling the case is slipping away, and if I let it get away I'll be screwing up something important. This is my shot, my chance to be something more than Ellen's charity-case son who works on glorified have-you-seen-my-lost-puppy cases and sleeps his days away in front of his computer.

So let's skip from plan B down to plan X. I know that Jennifer's father, the DA, grew up in Southie and is around the same age as Ellen. Maybe, a long-shot maybe, she knows something about Jennifer, the first bread crumb in the trail.

I say, "Hey, do you still watch *American Star?*" Plan X: asking Ellen delicate no-I'm-not-working-on-anything-really questions to defibrillate my dying case. I don't have a plan Y or Z.

Ellen looks at me funny, like I stepped in something and she's not sure if she should admit she smells it. She says, "You're kidding, right? I don't miss a show. Never have missed a show in five seasons."

I know that, of course. She's obsessed with *American Star.* She watched the first two seasons from Osterville and still had me tape all the episodes here.

She says, "Why do you ask? Are you telling me that you're finally watching it too?"

I shrug. Shoulders don't lie. My fedora doesn't hide enough of my hairy face. It's the proverbial only-a-mother-could-love face because the mug was reshuffled partway through the game. Ellen hasn't once suggested that I shave. That means what it means.

I say, "The show is kind of hard to avoid now. I had it on the other night, but I fell asleep." Ellen is waiting for more, so I add, "Been hearing stuff about the local girl. She's the DA's kid right?"

Ellen smiles. "I might be crazy, but it sounds like you're pumping me for information. If you got something to ask, just come out and ask it. I'll help. You know I want to help."

I can't. I can't let her know that I'm working on a case that potentially involves extensive fieldwork. Leaving the apartment and going out by myself. There will be no dealing with any of that conversation. She wants to be supportive only as long as I'm safe in the apartment.

I say, "Nothing like that. Just having a conversation, Ellen. For someone who wears clown pants, you're tightly wound."

Ellen goes into the kitchen and roots around in the freezer. She says, "Yes, she's his daughter. She's—what, about ten years younger than you?"

Might as well be fifty years younger. "Yeah, I guess so."

Ellen says, "There's nothing good in there," and closes the freezer. "I didn't have time to pick up anything. We'll have to go out. At least I'm dressed for it, right?"

I stand in the kitchen doorway, holding up the frame. "Isn't DA Times from Southie originally?" A softball question, one I know she can't resist.

"Hell yeah, he's from Southie. He still owns a brownstone at the end of East Broadway. He doesn't stay there anymore though. He rents it out."

"Do you know him at all?"

"I know him well. Or knew him well, anyway. Billy Times and your father were close, used to pal around as kids. They lived in the same building in Harbor Point."

She hits the softball out of the park. Her answer isn't what I was expecting. Not at all. I talk even slower than normal, making sure I don't mess anything up, stacking the words on the kitchen table like bricks, making a wall; maybe it'll protect me. "Really? You never told me that before."

Ellen says, "Come on. I've told you that before."

"No. You haven't." I'm not offering subterfuge here. I'm more likely to find Spanish doubloons in a handful of loose change than get nuggets of info concerning my father, Tim, from Ellen. She's miserly with it, hoards it all for herself. I stopped asking questions a long time ago.

"That can't be right." Ellen is trying for a light, jovial, fluffy-banter tone, but it's faltering. "You just forgot." She adds that last bit as an afterthought, each word decreasing in volume. The sentence runs out of gas, sputters, and shuts off. The sentence goes to sleep. Everything goes to sleep if you wait long enough.

Now, what she said is not fair. Yeah, I forget stuff all the time, but she can't pass off years of silence and daddy awkwardness on the narcoleptic me like that. I'd call her on the cheap shot, but that's another argument I don't want right now. Need that primed pump to keep spilling. I say, "Cute. So Tim and the DA were BFFs and wore each other's varsity jackets?"

"Yes, actually, they were best friends but no jackets." Ellen laughs, but I'm not quite sure why. Nothing is that funny. "Those two used to be inseparable, always causing trouble. Nothing big, you know, typical Southie boys who thought they were tougher than they were." She waves her hand, like she's clearing the air of more smoke. Further details won't be forthcoming unless I keep pecking away at her.

Okay. This goes a long way toward explaining how Jennifer Times landed in my office with her slide show. Her daddy can't take the case because people talk, word gets out, media sniffing around the DA, especially with his flavor-of-the-minute daughter smiling and primping all over the airwaves. So Daddy DA has Jennifer take her blackmail case, which is as sticky and messy as an ice cream cone on a summer Sunday, to an unknown lower-than-low profile investigator in South Boston, family friend and all that, a schlub willing to do all kinds of favors and keep things quiet with a capital Q, all in the name of his own dear old dad. This makes sense, but the only problem is I don't know any of this. I'm guessing. Maybe I was told a few days ago while the doctor wasn't in. Or maybe I wasn't told anything. Maybe . . .

"Hey, Mark!"

"What?" My body catches itself in mid-slide against the wall. Heavy feet move to get my weight back over them. They're neither graceful nor quiet. They kick a kitchen chair and clap against the hardwood floor. Don't know what my feet have against the floor, but they're always trying to get away.

Ellen is now sitting at the kitchen table, smoking one of my cigarettes. She says, "You were getting ready to go out, Mark." She won't say *sleep*. Not around me.

As difficult as it is to cobble together some dignity after almost falling asleep mid-conversation, I try to patch it up. I've had a lot of practice. I say, "Would the DA recognize the Genevich name, you think?"

"Of course. There's no way he'd forget your father." Ellen leans forward fast, stubs out her cigarette like she's killing a pesky ant. She's adding everything together and doesn't like the sum. She's going to tell me about it too. "Why do you care? What's going on here, Mark? There's something you're not telling me. You better not be messing around with stuff that requires involvement with the DA. Leave that shit to the people who carry guns."

"Relax. There's nothing going on. It's just this all might be useful information. I'm supposed to ask questions for a living, right? Besides, a guy in my line of work having a potential family friend in the big office could help my cause."

Ellen stands up. Chair falls down. She's not buying any of it. "What cause?"

I like that she's so riled up, on edge. She doesn't know for sure I'm working on a case, but even she can sense something big is going on. It's real. It's legit. And thanks to her, I finally have my breadcrumb trail, or at least one crumb. I sit down at the table, take off my hat, run my fingers through my thinning hair.

"I was speaking figuratively, Ellen. My general cause. Or someday, when I have a cause." I wink, which is a mistake. My face doesn't have a wink setting anymore.

"You're being awful strange tonight." She says it to the table. I'm supposed to hear her but not give anything back. Fair enough.

Worry lines march all around Ellen's face, and not in formation. She taps the all-but-empty pack of cigarettes with her wedding ring. Tim Genevich is twenty-five years dead, and Ellen still wears the ring. Does she wear it out of habit, superstition, or true indefinable loss, so the loss is right there in plain sight, her life's pain waving around for anyone to see? The ring as her dead husband, as Tim. My father on her hand.

I lean over and snatch the last cigarette out of the pack. Ellen stops tapping with Tim. I light up and inhale as much smoke as I can, then I take in a little more. Exhale, and then I do some reiterating, just to be clear in our communication.

I say, "Don't worry, Clowny. I have no cause. The DA and I are just gonna get acquainted."

SIX

Tim was a landscaper, caretaker, winterizer of summer cottages, and a handyman, and he died on the job. He was in the basement of someone else's summer home, fighting through cobwebs and checking fuses and the sump pump, when he had an explosion in his brain, an aneurysm. I guess us Genevich boys don't have a lot of luck in the brain department.

Three days passed and no one found him. He didn't keep an appointment book or anything like that, and he left his car at our house and rode his bike to work that morning, so Ellen had no idea where he was. He was an official missing person. Got his name in the paper, and for a few days everyone knew who Tim Genevich was.

The owners of the cottage found him when they came down to the Cape for Memorial Day weekend. The basement bulkhead was open. Tim was lying facedown on the dirt floor. He had a fuse in his hand. I was five years old, and while I'm told I was at the funeral and wake, I don't remember any of it.

I don't remember much of Tim. Memories of him have faded to the edges, where recollection and wish fulfillment blur, or they have been replaced, co-opted by images from pictures. I hate pictures.

Too much time has passed since my own brain-related accident, too many sleeps between. Every time I sleep—doesn't matter how long I'm out—puts more unconscious space between myself and the events I experienced, because every time I wake up it's a new day. Those fraudulent extra days, weeks, years add up. So while my everyday time shrinks, it also gets longer. I'm Billy Pilgrim and Rip Van Winkle at the same time, and Tim died one hundred years ago.

That said, I do have a recurring dream of my father. He's in our backyard in Osterville. He puts tools back in the shed, then emerges with a hand trowel. Tim was shorter than Ellen, a little bent, and he loved flannel. At least, that's what he looks like in my dreams.

Tim won't let me go in the shed. I'm too young. There are too many tools, too many ways to hurt myself. I need to be protected. He gives me a brown paper bag, grocery-sized, and a pat on the head. He encourages me to sing songs while we walk around the yard picking up dog shit. We don't have a dog, but all the neighborhood dogs congregate here. Tim guesses a dog's name every time he picks up some shit. The biggest poops apparently come from a dog named Cleo.

The song I always sing, in my dreams and my memories, is "Take Me Out to the Ball Game." Tim then sings it back to me with different lyrics, mixing in his dog names and poop and words that rhyme with poop. He doesn't say *shit* around the five-year-old me, at least not on purpose. The dream me, the memory me—that kid is the same even if he never really existed, and *that* kid laughs at the silly improvised song but then sings "Ball Game" correctly, restoring balance and harmony to the universe.

Our two-bedroom bungalow is on a hill and the front yard has a noticeable slant, so we have to stand lopsided to keep from falling. We clean the yard, then we walk behind the shed to the cyclone-fenced area of weeds, tall grass, and pricker bushes that gives way to a grove of trees between our property and the next summer home about half a block away. Tim takes the paper bag from me, it's heavy with shit, and he dumps it out, same spot every time. He says "Bombs away" or "Natural fertilizer" or something else that's supposed to make a five-year-old boy laugh.

Then we walk to the shed. Tim opens the doors. Inside are the shiny and sharp tools and machines, teeth everywhere, and I want to touch it all, want to feel the bite. He hangs up the trowel and folds the paper bag. We'll reuse both again, next weekend and in the next dream. Tim stands in the doorway and says, "So, kid, whaddaya think?"

Sometimes I ask for a lemonade or ice cream or soda. Sometimes, if I'm aware I'm in the dream again, I ask him questions. He always answers, and I remember the brief conversation after waking up, but that memory lasts only for a little while, an ice cube melting in a drink. Then it's utterly forgotten, crushed under the weight of all those little sleeps to come.

Seven

William "Billy" Times has been the Suffolk County DA for ten years. He's a wildly popular and visible favorite son. All the local news shows are doing spots featuring Billy and his *American Star* daughter. He hosts now-legendary bimonthly Sunday brunch fund-raisers—the proceeds going to homeless shelters—at a restaurant called Amrheins in South Boston. All the local celebs and politicians show their faces at least once a year at the brunches.

Although I am Tim Genevich's kid, I haven't been on the brunch guest list yet. That said, Tim's name did manage to get me a one-on-one audience with DA Times at his office today. What a pal, that Tim.

I fell asleep in the cab. It cost me an extra twenty bucks in drive-around time. I stayed awake long enough to be eventually dumped at 1 Bulfinch Place. Nice government digs for the DA. Location, location, location. It's between the ugly concrete slabs of Government Center and Haymarket T stop, but a short walk from cobblestones, Faneuil Hall Marketplace, and the two-story granite columns and copper dome of Quincy Market, where you can eat at one of its seventeen overpriced restaurants. It's all very colonial.

Despite naptime, I'm here early when I can't ever be early. Early means being trapped in a waiting room, sitting in plush chairs or couches, anesthetizing Muzak tones washing over me, fluffing my pillow. An embarrassingly large selection of inane and soulless entertainment magazines, magazines filled with fraudulent and beautiful people, is the only proffered stimulus. That environment is enough to put a non-narcoleptic in a coma, so I don't stand a chance. I won't be early.

I stalk around the sidewalk and the pigeons hate me. I don't take it personally, thick skin and all that. I dump some more nicotine and caffeine into my bloodstream. The hope is that filling up with leaded will keep all my pistons firing while in the DA's office. Hope is a desperate man's currency.

I call the DA's secretary and tell her I'm outside the building, enjoying a rare March sunlight appearance, and I ask when the DA will be ready for me. Polite as pudding, she says he's ready for me now. Well, all right. A small victory. A coping adjustment actually working is enough to buoy my spirits. I am doing this. This is going to work, and I will solve this case.

But . . .

There's a swarm of *ifs*, peskier than a cloud of gnats. The ifs: If, as I'm assuming, the DA sent me his daughter and her case, why wouldn't he contact me directly? Again, am I dealing with the ultimate closed-lips case that can't have any of his involvement? If that's right, and I'm supposed to be Mr. Hush Hush, Mr. Not Seen and Not Heard, why am I so easily granted counsel with the public counsel? He certainly seemed eager to meet with me when I called, booking a next-day face-to-face appointment.

There are more ifs, and they're stressing my system. Stress, like time, is a mortal enemy. Stress can be one of my triggers, the grease in the wheel of my more disruptive narcoleptic symptoms. I could use another cigarette or three to choke myself awake, freshen up in the smoke.

I step out of the elevator and walk toward the DA's office. Bright hallways filled with suits of two types: bureaucrats and people carrying guns. The bullets and briefcases in the hallway make me a little edgy.

The DA's waiting area is stark and bright. Modern. Antiseptic. Very we-get-shit-done in its décor. Wooden chairs and glass-topped tables framed in silver metal, and all the window shades are up. No shadows here.

There are two men waiting in the room and they are linebacker big. They wear dark suits and talk on cell phones, the kind that sit inside the cup of your ear. The receiver is literally surrounded by the wearer's flesh; it's almost penetrative. The phones look like blood-swollen robot ticks.

The men are actively not looking at me. Sure, I'm paranoid, but when I enter a room people always look at me. They map out my lopsided features and bushy beard and anachronistic attire. Every-one is my cartographer. I'm not making this up. Even when I display narcoleptic symptoms in public and the cartographers are now truly frightened of me and try not to look, they still look. Furtive glances, stealing and storing final images, completing the map, fodder for their brush-with-unwashed-humanity dinner-party anecdotes. I'm always the punch line.

Instead of the direct path to the secretary's desk, I take the long cut, eyeing the framed citations on the walls, walking past the windows pretending to crane my neck for a better view of Haymarket. Those two guys won't look at me, which means they're here to watch me. I'm already sick of irony.

The secretary says, "Mr. Genevich?"

I've been identified. Tagged.

The two men still don't look up. One guy is shaved bald, though the stubble is thick enough to chew up a razor. The other guy has red hair, cut tight up against his moon-sized brain box. Freckles and craters all over his face. They talk into their phones and listen at alternating intervals like they're speaking to each other, kids with their twenty-first-century can-and-string act.

I say, "That's me." This doesn't bode well for my meeting with the DA. Why does he need Thunder and Thumper to get their eye-ful of me?

The secretary says, "The DA is ready for you now." She stays seated behind her desk. She's Ellen's age and wears eye shadow the color of pool-cue chalk. I wonder if she wears clown pants too.

I say, "I guess that's what we'll find out." It feels like the thing to say, but the line lands like a dropped carton of eggs.

His secretary points me past her desk, and I head into an office with an open door. I walk in too fast.

DA William Times sits behind a buffet-style oak desk. The thing spans the width of the room. A twin-engine Cessna could land on top of it. He says, "Mark Genevich. Come on in. Wow, I can't believe it. Tim's kid all grown up. Pleasure to finally meet you." The DA walks out from behind his desk, hand thrust out like a bayonet.

I'm not quite sure of protocol here. How he's supposed to be greeted. What sort of verbal genuflection I'm supposed to give him. I try on, "Thanks for giving me the time, Mr. DA."

DA Times is as big as the two goons in the waiting room. I'm thinking he might've banged out a few hundred push-ups before I came in, just to complete his muscle-beach look. He has on gray slacks and a tight blue dress shirt; both have never seen a wrinkle. His hair is pepper-gray, cut tight and neat. White straight teeth. His whole look screams public opinion and pollsters and handlers. We have so much in common.

We cross the divide of his office and finally shake hands. His grip is a carnival strength test and he rings the bell. He says, "Please, call me Billy, and have a seat."

"Thanks." I don't take off my hat or coat, but I do pull out the manila envelope. I sit. The chair is a soft leather bog, and I sink to a full eye level below the DA and his island-nation desk. I wait as he positions himself. He might need a compass.

He says, "So, how's Ellen doing?"

He's not going to ask about my face, about what happened to me. He's polite and well mannered and makes me feel even more broken. We can play at the small talk, though. That's fine. Maybe it'll help me get a good foothold before we climb into the uncomfortable stuff. Daddy and his daughter.

I say, "Ellen's fine. She has a good time."

"Do you guys live in Southie again? She still owns that building on the corner of Dorchester and Broadway, right?"

I say, "Yeah, she owns it. I live there, but Ellen part-times Southie now."

"God, I haven't talked to her in years. I have to have you guys down at the next Sunday brunch. I'd love to chat with her."

I'm not quite sure what to say. I come up with, "That'd be just fine, Billy," real slow, and it sounds as awkward as I feel. I'm flummoxed. I was expecting anger on the DA's part, that he'd go all Hulk, you-wouldn't-like-me-when-I'm-angry, yell-scream-bite-scratch and bring in the goons because I wasn't doing my job, wasn't keeping things quiet by showing up at Jennifer's public appearance and now at his office.

He says, "So what can I help you with, Mark?"

Our meeting is young, the conversation still in we're-all-friends-here mode, but I already know he did not contact me. He did not suggest his daughter contact me. He has no idea why I'm here.

Need to play this straight, no funny stuff, no winks and nods. My winks tend to turn into fully shut eyes. "Not sure if you're aware, Billy, but I'm a private investigator."

The DA is still smiling. "Oh, yeah? How long have you been doing that?"

"Eight years, give or take." I pause because I don't know what to say next.

He jumps right in. "No kidding. I probably have a copy of your license somewhere in this building." He laughs. Is that a threat? A harmless attempt at humor? Humor is never harmless.

Maybe this was a mistake. Maybe I'm not ready for this and should've stayed in my apartment behind my desk and forgotten about everything. I'm getting a bad feeling. Not the gut this time. It's more tangible, physical. There's a small hum, a vibration building up, my hands tremble on the envelope a little bit. My system needle is twitching into the red. Danger Will Robinson. It's the same feeling I get before cataplectic attacks.

Cataplexy, like other narcolepsy symptoms, is REM sleep bullying its way into the awake state. Cataplexy is complete and total loss of bodily control. Muscles stop working, I can't even talk, and I melt to the floor, down for the count but not out. I'm not asleep. I'm conscious but can't move and can't speak, paralyzed. Cataplexy is the worst part of my nightmare.

I don't have cataplexy often; the most recent event was that time after Ellen found me asleep in front of a porno. She walked into the apartment and I woke up with my pants around my ankles. She wasn't upset or hiding her face or anything like that, she was laughing. She could've walked in and found me playing with the world's cutest kitten and had the same response, which made it worse, made it seem like she was expecting to find me like that. I was so overwhelmingly embarrassed and ashamed, the emotions were a Category-5 hurricane on my system, and cataplexy hit while I was quickly trying to pull up my pants and put everything away. My strings cut and I dropped to the floor, heavier than a dead body, landing on my cheap came-in-a-box coffee table and smashing it, all my stuff still out and about. Ellen shut off the television without commenting upon a scene involving Edward Penishands and three of his most acrobatic female neighbors. She pulled up my underwear and pants, buttoned my fly, and prepared dinner in the kitchen while I recovered from the attack. Took about twenty minutes to come back completely, to be able to walk into the kitchen under my own power. We ate stir-fry. A little salty but decent, otherwise.

Too much time has passed since the DA last spoke, because his vote-for-me smile is gone and he's leaning on his desk. He says, "Did you bring me something? What's in the envelope, Mark?"

Okay, another new strategy, and yeah, I'm making all this up as I go. If this is going to work, I can't let myself think too much. I'm going to read lines, play a part, and maybe it will keep the emotions from sabotage, keep those symptoms on the bench no matter how much the narcoleptic me wants in the game.

I say, "Your daughter, Jennifer, came into my office the other morning and hired me to solve a little problem." My hands sweat on the envelope, leaving wet marks.

The DA straightens and looks around the room briefly. He repeats my line back to me. "Jennifer came into your office with a problem." The line sounds good.

"Yup. Left me this package too. She didn't tell you anything about this?"

The DA holds up his hands. "You have me at a loss, Mark, because this is all news to me."

In concert with our everything-is-happy intro conversation, I think he's telling the truth, which complicates matters. Why would Jennifer not tell her DA daddy about the pictures and then come see me, of all PIs? Was it dumb blind luck that landed her in my office? I don't buy it. She and this case were dropped in my sleeping lap for a reason.

I say, "I came here because I had assumed you sent her to see me. To have me, a relation of an old family friend, deal with the situation away from prying public eyes."

"Jesus, Mark, just tell me what you're talking about. Is Jennifer in danger? What's going on?"

If he really hasn't sent Jennifer to me, then I've screwed up, big time. It's going to be very difficult to skip-to-my-Lou out of here without showing him the pictures, and I can't say too much, don't want to put any words into Jennifer's mouth. I don't want the case to be taken away from me.

I say, "I've made a mistake. If you didn't send Jennifer to me, I shouldn't be here. Client confidentiality and all that." I stand up. My legs are water-starved tree roots.

The DA stands and darts around his desk to stop me. He moves fast, and I'm no Artful Dodger. He says, "Wait! You can't come in here and drop a bomb about Jennifer and then just leave."

"Tell it to the goons you have waiting for me outside." I say it, even though I know it doesn't add up. One plus one is three.

"What?" He shakes his head, resetting. "Let's start again. Jennifer. What's wrong? You have to tell me if she's in any danger. You know, I can probably help here." He opens his arms, displaying his office, showing off his grand criminal justice empire.

My system-overload feeling is still there. My hands keep up with
their tremors, twitching to some hidden beat, and my mouth is dry.
This can't happen now. Not now, can't be now.

I say, "Let's sit again, and you can take a look." I have to sit. At
least if I have an attack I'll be sitting.

We sit. The chair is a hug and my body reacts accordingly; the
tremors cease but crushing fatigue rolls in like a tide. It's undeniable.

New plan. I don't care that I'm breaking client confidentiality.
Given the clientele, I doubt word of my etiquette breach will get out
and ruin my little business, taint my street cred. I want to see the
DA's reaction. I want to know why she'd drop these photos on my
desk and not on Daddy's.

I yawn big, showing off the fillings, sucking in all the air. The
DA looks at me like I pissed in the dinner wine. I shrug and say,
"Sorry, it's not you, it's me."

I open the envelope and hand him the two photos. Definitely
taking a chance on bringing him the originals. I didn't think to make
copies; the negatives are in my desk. Anyway, I want to see what his
reaction is to the real photos, not copies.

The DA takes the pictures, looks at them, and sinks into his chair.
The pictures are a punch to his stonewall stomach. He loses all his
air. I feel a little bad for him. Gotta be tough to have someone else's
past walk in the door and drop nudie pictures of your kid in your lap.

He holds up both photos side by side and is careful to hold them
so that they cover his face. He sees something.

The DA says, "Who gave you these pictures?"

"I told you. Jennifer. Try to stay with me, here."

"Who sent them to her?"

"I don't know yet. That's the case. I'm good, but I do need a little time to work my mojo." I meant to say magic, but it came out mojo.

He says, "Who else has seen these?"

"No idea." This is a rare occasion where telling the truth is easy as Sunday morning.

"Have you shown them to anyone?"

"No, of course not. What kind of private investigator do you think I am?"

He looks at the photos again, then me. The look is a fist cracking knuckles. He says, "I have no idea what's going on here, Mark, but the woman in these pictures is clearly not Jennifer."

Not the response I was looking for. I squirm in my seat, which is suddenly hot. I'm bacon and someone turned on the griddle. I fight off another yawn and push it down somewhere inside me, but it's still there and will find its way out eventually. I have bigger problems than a yawn. I ask, "What makes you say that?"

"It's not her, Mark." All hint of politics gone from his voice. He's accusing me of something. He's in attack mode, getting ready to lawyer me up. This isn't good.

I say, "It's her. Jennifer was the one who brought me the goddamn photos. Why would she need me if the photos aren't of her?" I'm getting mad, which is not the right response here. Shouldn't be ready to throw a tantrum because someone wants to tell me there's no Tooth Fairy.

The DA focuses. I'm his courtroom. He says, "There are physical inconsistencies. Jennifer has a mole on her collarbone, no mole here—"

I interrupt. "That's easy to Photoshop. You should know that."

He holds up a stop hand. "Her hair is all wrong. In the photo there's too much curl to it, and it doesn't look like a wig. That's not Jennifer's smile; the teeth are too big. This woman is smaller and skinnier than Jennifer. There's a resemblance, but it's clearly not Jennifer, Mark. I'm positive."

All right. What next? I say, "Can I have the photos back?" Christ, I'm asking permission. I'm a pathetic Oliver Twist, begging for table scraps.

The DA doesn't give them to me right away, and my insides drop into my shoes. I'm not getting the photos back—or my insides. I couldn't possibly have fucked things up any worse if I had a manual and followed the step-by-step instructions on how to screw the pooch.

He does hand the pictures over. I take an eyeful. The hair, her smile, all of it, all wrong. He's right. It's not her. My big mistake is getting bigger. I scratch my beard, then put the photos away. I need an exit strategy.

The DA stands again, walks to his window, then turns toward me, eyebrows arched. Maybe he's really seeing me, the broken man, for the first time. He says, "What are you up to, Mark?"

"I told you what was up, DA. Nothing funny on my end. Can't vouch for your daughter, though."

His hands go from inside his pockets to folded across his chest. He's a statue made of granite. I'm an abandoned rag doll.

"Maybe we should just call Jennifer, then, to straighten everything out," he says, pulling out his cell phone and poking at a few buttons before getting my permission.

"Let's. A fine idea." I yawn, my head getting murky, its natural state. I'm afraid of this phone call. I'll only get to hear his end of the conversation.

He says, "Hi, sweetie. It's Dad. . . . I know, but I need a quick honest answer to a potentially difficult question. . . . I know, great way to start a phone call. . . . So, did you hire a Mark Genevich? . . . Mark Genevich, he's a private detective. . . . He's here in my office, and he claims you went to his Southie office and hired him—says you gave him some photos. . . . What? . . . Oh, he did? . . . Okay, okay, no. . . . Don't worry, Jennifer. Nothing I can't take care of. I have to go. . . . Good luck tonight. You were great last night and I'm sure you'll make it through to next week. . . . Love you too."

I think I need to find my own attack mode. The problem is I'm toothless. I say, "You two have such a swell relationship and all, but if she said she's never met me, she's lying."

"Jennifer said you showed up in the autograph line at Copley the other day, claimed to be working on her case, and left your card."

"I sure did."

"She also said she'd never seen you before Copley."

I yawn again. The DA doesn't like it. There's nothing I can do about that. I say, "I have her signed contract back at my office." Complete bluff. He knows it too.

He walks around to the front of the desk and sits on the top. One leg on the floor, one leg off. A DA flamingo. He says, "Blackmail is a felony, Mark." He drops the hard-guy act momentarily and morphs into pity mode. He holds out his hands as if to say, *Look at you, you're a walking shipwreck, unsalvageable.* "If you need money or help, Mark, I can help you out, but this isn't the way to go about it."

I laugh. It's an ugly sound. "Thanks for the offer, DA, but I get by. And I'm not blackmailing anyone. If I were, would I be dumb enough to do it while sitting in your office? Give me a little credit."

"Okay, okay, but Mark, try to take my point of view here. You are presenting me an odd set of circumstances, to say the least. You come out of nowhere, telling me that my daughter hired you on the basis of photos that aren't of Jennifer. Are we on the same page so far?"

I nod. I yawn. The murk is getting used to my chair. The conversation is getting fuzzy. I need to move around, literally put myself on my toes. I stand up and wander behind the chair, pretending to stretch my back.

He says, "Jennifer denies having ever met you before you showed up at Copley. What is it exactly you want me to believe?"

Good question. I want to hear the answer too. I say, "I don't know what to tell you. Kids lie to their parents all the time, especially when they're in trouble. Maybe she's met some bad people. Maybe she's embarrassed, doesn't want Daddy to know that someone sent her a threat, some nude photos that look a lot like her, enough so that if released into the wild many folks would believe it's her in the pictures." I say it all, but I don't really believe it. There's something missing. What's missing is me. Why am I the one with these pictures?

He says, "No one would believe that woman was Jennifer."

I shrug. "Sure they would. Presented in the proper light; people want to believe the worst."

The DA has his chiseled face in hand, another pose, and says, "I'll have another talk with her later, but right now I believe her, not you."

It's not a shock, but it stings. To be dismissed so easily. I fire back with a double-barrel dose of healthy paranoia. "That's fine. I believe me over both of you. Tell me, DA, how do I know that Jennifer was really the person on the other end of that phone call?"

He rolls his eyes, gets up off the desk, and walks to his office door, holds it open. He says, "Okay, I think our meeting is done. If I hear or see anything more about these photos of yours, don't be surprised if you find me in your Southie office, warrant in hand."

"I guess this means no brunch." I adjust my hat and slip the envelope inside my coat. "I'm only looking out for your daughter's best interests because I was hired to."

There's nothing more to be said. We're all out of words. I walk out of the office. He shuts the door behind me. I tighten my coat, the envelope pressed up against my chest. The secretary has her head down, computer keys clicking.

The goons aren't in the waiting room. Maybe they were never here. Maybe, like Jennifer's mole, they've been Photoshopped out. The room is too empty. No chairs are askew, all the magazines are in a pile, nothing out of place, but it's staged, a crime scene without a body.

I'm alone again, with a client who denies such status and with photos that aren't of her. I'm alone again, with nothing, and I just want to sit and think, but my head is a mess, trying to put together a jigsaw puzzle that's suddenly missing all but a few pieces. I need to call a cab, go back to the office, begin at the beginning, focus on those few pieces I do have, and see if I can't force them to fit together.

EIGHT

After my DA meeting I sat at my office desk and looked at the photos again, searching for clues I might've missed. I didn't see any. In the first photo, the one with the fully clothed Jennifer, there was a bookcase that holds ten books. I couldn't read any of the slimmer titles, but there was one fat hardcover with LIT written big and white across the bottom of the spine. Library book probably. In the second photo, the camera is angled up, and I see only the ceiling and the wall and the topless Jennifer.

I locked the photos with the negatives in my office desk and slept the rest of the afternoon away on my apartment couch. I dreamed my usual Dad-in-the-backyard dream. There was still a lot of shit to clean up. No one called and woke me. No one missed my conscious presence. I'm used to it and don't take it personally anymore.

Now it's two o'clock in the morning. I've been wandering and haunting my own apartment, a ghost without the clanging chains. I can't sleep. I already said I was sick of irony, but it's a narcoleptic's lot.

I turn on the VCR and watch two taped *American Star* episodes, last night's and tonight's, the one I slept through. First show has a disco-night theme. Jennifer Times sings "I Will Survive." She sings well enough, right notes and right key, but she moves stiffly, her hips are rusty hinges and her feet don't want to stay in one spot, a colt walking in a field full of holes. The judges call her on it. The British guy says she was icy and robotic, a mannequin barely come to life. The people in the audience boo the judge even though he's correct. Truth is usually greeted with disdain.

Jennifer doesn't take the criticism well and fires back at the judges. She whines and is rude and short in dismissing the critiques. She turns and tilts her head, rolls her eyes, hands on her hips, stops just short of stomping a foot on the floor. She leaves the stage with, "I thought I was great and they did too," pointing to the audience. She gets a lukewarm cheer.

Jennifer forgot it's not about the song you sing or the words you have to say; it's always about the performance, how you present your public self. She could've come off as a hero if she argued with the judges correctly, mixing self-deprecation, humility, and humor with confidence and determination. Maybe she should've hired me as a coach instead of her PI.

As the vote-off show queues up next on my tape, I fire up my laptop and check out the Internet message boards and blogosphere reaction. Jennifer was universally ripped and often referred to as a privileged brat. There will be no recovering from that. The show's voters agreed with the brat tag, and Jennifer is the first finalist knocked out of *American Star*. A quick THE END to that singing career, I guess. Jennifer doesn't take the news on the vote-off show well either. Instead of gracious smiles and hand-waving, we get the nationally televised equivalent of a kid storming out of her parents' room after a scolding. While I think Jennifer handled her fifteen minutes of fame poorly, I do sympathize with her. Sometimes you just can't win.

Maybe this means she'll return my calls when she gets back to Boston. Maybe she'll apologize for lying to her father, for making my public self appear to be a lunatic. My performance in her daddy's office needed her help, and she threw me tomatoes instead of roses. Or maybe she won't call me and the case is dead, now that she's off the show.

I shut off the VCR and laptop and wander back to bed. Insomnia is there waiting for me. The sheets and comforter feel all wrong, full of points and angles somehow. The pillow is not soft enough; it's too hard. I'm Goldilocks in my own house.

The awake me can't help but rerun everything in my mashed-up head. Yeah, I'm stubborn, but I have to try and see Jennifer one more time, somehow straighten out all that's been bent out of shape and put the case to bed, so to speak.

NINE

The phone rings; it sounds far away, in the next universe. I lift my head off my desk, an incredible feat of strength, and wipe my face. Leftover fried rice trapped in my beard and mustache fall onto the Styrofoam plate that had been my pillow. The rice bounces off and onto the desktop and on my lap. I need to make a note to vacuum later.

It has been two days since my meeting with the DA. My office phone has rung only once. It was NANNING WOK double-checking my order because the woman wasn't sure if I'd said General Gao or Kung Pao. The General, of course, as if there was any question.

I spent those two days getting nowhere with Jennifer's case. Her agency doesn't return my calls, and I don't know when her next public appearance is. I haven't looked at the photos since locking them in my desk. I wanted them to find their own way out, somehow, before I thought about them again. Doing nothing with them couldn't be any worse than my previous attempts at doing something.

The phone is still ringing. Someone insisting that we talk. Fine. Be that way. I pick it up.

I say, "Mark Genevich," my name bubbling up from the depths, sounding worse for the trip.

"Have you found it yet?" A male voice. He sounds older. His voice is deep, heavy with time, like mine.

I'm disappointed. I was really hoping it'd be Jennifer. Instead, it's a client that I've been shirking. I have two abandoned property searches that I've put on hold since the Times case came walking in my door.

I say, "No, I haven't found anything yet. Need more time." I should just hang up and put my face back into the leftover fried rice.

"I don't think we have more time, kid. There's a red car driving around my house. It's been by four times this afternoon already. Fuck!"

Maybe I'm dreaming and I'll wake up on my couch or reawake with my face in Chinese food to start it all over again. Maybe this is my old buddy Juan-Miguel putting me on, playing a joke. When we lived together he'd call in shit like this. I decide to play along with the caller a bit longer, gather more information before I make a hasty conclusion; it's how I have to live my everyday life. That said, this guy's voice has a kernel of sincerity that's undeniable.

I say, "Relax. Calm down. Red cars won't bother you if you don't bother them."

"There're two people in that red car. They know. They know about the pictures somehow. Shit! They're driving by again, and they slow down in front of my house every time. You didn't show anyone those pictures yet, did you? You can't until you find—"

I drop the phone, of course. It slides out of my greasy hands and bounces off my foot. Goddamn it! At least I know I'm awake. I'm awake because I'm usually competent in my dreams and hallucinations.

I pick up the phone. "Sorry, dropped you for a second. I'm still here." I stand up, walk across the room, and shut the door to my office. No one's in the hallway, of course, but Ellen could walk in unannounced at any time. "No. I didn't show anyone anything." It's easier to lie because I don't know who I'm talking to.

He says, "I shouldn't have given you those pictures. I don't know what I think I was doing, who I'd be helping. It was dumb. Now we're both fucked. Should've just kept sitting on it like the old hen that I am. This is so screwed up. Shouldn't have done anything. . . ." His words fall into odd rhythms, stops and starts mixed with letters that he holds too long. He slurs his *s*'s. He's been drinking. It's not helping his paranoia—or mine. His voice fades out as he's talking to either himself or someone else in the room with him; the phone must be dropping away from his mouth. I'm losing him. I have to keep him talking, even if it isn't to me.

I say, "Hey, pull it together. It'll be all right once I find"—yeah, find what?—"it." So I'm not so smooth on my end. I pace around my office and look for something that'll help me. Nothing's here. Hopefully he doesn't process my hesitation.

He says, "You need to hurry up. I don't want to say anything more. If they're driving around my house, it probably means they're listening in too, the fuckers."

He and I have seen too many of the same movies. I'm ready to agree with him. I have so many questions to ask this guy, starting with the introductory-level *Who are you?* but I have to pretend I know what's going on.

I say, "All right, all right. But before you hang up, I think we need to talk again. Face-to-face. It'll help us sort all this out, trust me. We'll both feel better about it."

"Not your office. I can't come to Southie again. I'm not going anywhere, not right now. I'm staying here, with my doors locked."

An espresso-like jolt rushes through my system. He's been here before. I say, "Okay, I'll come to you. Give me your address."

He does, but he doesn't give me his name. No matter. Address only. I write it down. Goddamn, he lives on the Cape, in Osterville, not far from where Ellen lives and where my childhood homestead still stands. Now pieces are fitting together where they shouldn't, square pegs in round holes.

I tell him I'll be there tomorrow. He hangs up, and that's it. The office and phone are quiet again. More old fried rice, looking like mouse turds, is on the desk and on the floor. I'm breathing heavy. I pull out a cigarette and start a fire.

I unlock my drawer and take out the photos. I try on a new set of eyes and look at the girl in the photos. Maybe she's not Times. And the photos: the matte and shading is faded and yellowing in spots. The photos are old, but how old?

Okay, slow down. I know now that Jennifer was never in my office. Even her presence was part and parcel of the whole hypnogogic hallucination. But why would I dream her into my office while asleep during phone guy's little visit? Did I conjure her solely because of the resemblance in the photos? Did her name come up in our initial meeting? Is he just some crazed fan of *American Star*? Maybe he's a would-be blackmailer, but that doesn't feel right. Is he telling the truth about being watched?

He didn't want me to show the pictures to anyone until I found something, and I already showed them to the DA. Oops. Why did phone guy, presumably from Osterville, choose me? Does he know me or Ellen? What am I supposed to find? My note about South Shore Plaza. Red car, Osterville, and a drunk on the Cape.

I think I've falsely harassed Jennifer Times and her DA father. I really don't know anything about this case, and there's still rice in my beard, but at least I have a client now. Yeah, tomorrow I'll make the little road trip to the Cape and then a house call, but I'm not getting paid enough for this.

TEN

I'm in Ellen's little green car. It's fifteen years old. The passenger seat is no longer conducive to my very particular posture, which is somewhere between question mark and Quasimodo. Lower back and legs report extreme discomfort. It's enough to keep me awake, which is miserable because I keep nodding off but not staying asleep.

We're cruising down Route 3 south, headed toward the Cape. It's off-season and the traffic isn't bad, but Ellen maintains a running monologue about how awful the traffic always is and how nobody knows how to drive. Meanwhile, she's tailgating the car in front of us and we're close enough that I can see what radio station he's tuned to.

I still have a driver's license but no car. Renewing the license isn't an issue for me. Driving is. I haven't driven in six years.

Last night I told Ellen that I needed to go to the Osterville library to help with a genealogical search and was pressed for time. She didn't ask for further details. She knew I wouldn't give any. When she picked me up this morning, she didn't ask questions about why all the toilet paper was unrolled and wrapped around my kitchen table—King Tut's table now—and why the apartment door was unlocked but my bedroom door was locked. She knew the narcoleptic me went for an evening stroll with the apartment to himself.

My eyes are closed; we're somewhere between Norwell and Marshfield, I think.

Ellen says, "Are you awake?"

I just want to sit and sleep, or think about what I'm going to say to the mystery client in Osterville. The names associated with the address are Brendan and Janice Sullivan. I was able to ferret out that much online.

I say, "No. I'm asleep and dreaming that you're wearing the clown pants again."

"Stop it. I just didn't want to stuff them into my night bag and get them all wrinkly. Those wrinkles don't come out. You'd think that wouldn't happen with polyester. Anyway, they're comfy driving pants."

I say, "I guess I'm awake then."

She says, "Good. You'll never guess who called me last night."

"You're right."

"Guess."

I pull my fedora farther over my eyes and grind around in my seat, trying to find an impossible position of comfort. I say, "A state lottery commission agent. You've been winning too much on scratch tickets."

"Hardly," she says, and slaps my thigh. "Your new pal Billy Times called."

She might as well have hit me in the groin instead of my thigh. I sit up and crush my fedora between forehead and car ceiling. I resettle and try to play off my fish-caught-on-a-line spasm as a posture adjustment. I say, "Never heard of him."

"Come on, Mark. I know you visited him earlier in the week. He told me."

"Since I'm awake-awake, I might as well be smoking. Mind?"

"Yes. I try not to smoke in the car."

"Good." I light up.

She sighs and opens her window a crack. "I'm a little impressed you went all the way in town to the DA's office." She says it like it was so far away I needed a passport. A condescending cheap shot, but I probably deserve it.

I say, "I had to hire a Sherpa, but I managed."

"I didn't think you were serious the other day with the whole DA-as-family-friend talk." She stops, waiting for me to fill in the blanks. I can't fill those blanks in, not even for myself. She thinks I have something going on. I do, but I'm not going to tell her about it. She wouldn't like it. She certainly wouldn't be transporting me down to the Cape to chat with Sullivan.

I say, "I'm always serious, Ellen." All right, I need to know it all. I need to know why the DA called my mommy. It'll hang over me the whole time I'm in Osterville if I don't ask. "So why'd he call you?"

"Actually, he invited me to one of his Sunday brunches. Isn't that neat?"

"How nice. I'm sure your friends will be excited to hear you've become a socialite. You'll be the talk of Thursday night bingo at the Lithuanian Club." Ellen doesn't say anything, so I add, "Come on, Ellen, you're as bad a liar as I am. What did he want?"

"I'm not lying."

"Ellen. Your clown pants puff out bigger when you're lying. Come on, spill it."

She hits me again. "He did invite me. And, he asked questions about you. Asked if you were okay. He said your meeting was very odd and he got the sense you were struggling."

"Struggling? More proof politicians have no sense."

"Yes, struggling. That's the exact word he used."

"So what'd you tell him?"

Ellen sighs and moves her hands around while talking. Someone should be driving. "I told him you were fine, but I mentioned the accident and how you had narcolepsy now. I stressed that you're doing fine, though." She lilts with each biographical phrase, singing the song of me. It's a dirge she's sung many times before. She performs it well.

"Jesus, Ellen. Thanks a lot. Did you tell him I don't like pickles or ketchup, I pick my nose, and I wet the bed as a kid?"

She says, "What's wrong with you? He was just concerned, that's all. Did you want me to lie or make something up?"

"No. Telling him I was fine would've been enough. He doesn't need to hear my sob story."

"I don't understand why this upsets you."

"If I ever need him for a case, he'll never take me seriously now."

"Of course he will. No one holds narcolepsy against you."

"Come on, Ellen. Everyone does. No one really believes I have anything medically wrong with me. They think I'm lazy or just *odd*, like the DA said." I stop talking but I could go on: most people think I really could keep from falling asleep if I wanted to, if I just focused, like narcolepsy is some algebraic equation I could solve if I worked at it hard enough, did all the homework. I'm a bad joke. A punch line. I'm Beetle Bailey, a cartoon character falling asleep at the switch for laughs. I might as well be wearing her goddamn clown pants.

"I don't think that about you, Mark." She's mad at me and my pity party. I don't blame her.

I inhale the cigarette down to the filter, more ash in my lap than in the ashtray. Yeah, I'm nervous about my meeting with Sullivan, and I'm taking it out on Ellen and myself.

I say, "You're right. I know you don't, Clowny. I'm your *American Star*."

ELEVEN

Ellen drops me at the Osterville Free Library. It's a one-level brick building with white molding, trim, and columns. The Parthenon it's not. Ellen has a couple of family-portrait photo shoots and a meeting with a prospective wedding client, so I have three hours to myself.

I make an appearance inside the small library, wander the stacks for a bit, avoid story time and the children's wing, and check out a slim history of Osterville written and self-published by some local schmoe who probably has more cats than rooms in his house, not that I'm judging anyone. If Ellen comes back to the library before me, I can tell her I went for a read and a stroll. She might believe it or she might not.

The Sullivan house is two miles away from the library according to my Mapquest printout. The old Genevich homestead is on the other side of town, right off Route 28 and closer to downtown, so I'm not very familiar with this section of Osterville. This part of town has larger and pricier homes. No bungalows. No clapboard. These are summer homes for the well-well-to-do, mixed in with slightly more modest houses for folks who live here year-round. According to the map, most of my walk is down Wianno Avenue, left onto Crystal Lake Road, and then a quick right onto Rambler Road. Easy as A, B, and then C.

It's an overcast day with gusty ocean winds. The fedora quivers on my head, thinking about making a break for it. It's a quiet day otherwise. Only a handful of cars pass me on Wianno. None of them are red.

The exercise is good for my head, but the rest of my body thinks it's torture. Cranky knees and ankles carry the scars of the accident too. I walk as slowly as I talk.

While on my little hike, I try to focus on the case. On what it is I'm supposed to find. And it is a *what*, not a *who*. On the phone, Sullivan asked if I had found *it* yet.

Thoughts of the DA and Jennifer Times nag at me. I guess I should call the DA and apologize for the confusion, for thinking he was involved with sending me the photos. Apologize for my mistake. But it hasn't felt exactly like a mistake.

Sullivan's ringing question, *You didn't show the pictures to anyone, did you?*, was the same thing the DA asked me when he first saw the pictures. He didn't come right out with *It's not Jennifer.* He asked if anyone else had seen the pictures. I didn't think anything of it earlier because I'd assumed he didn't want his nude daughter subject to roving packs of prying eyes. Now, I'm not so sure.

Something's not right there. It's why he called Ellen too.

I turn onto Crystal Lake Road, and there are blue and red lights filtering through the trees ahead, and right there is Rambler Road. It's blocked to traffic by a police car. There are more flashing lights and the occasional chirp of a siren. Sullivan's house. I think the worst. It's easy to think the worst when it always happens. Crystal Lake Road loops around to the other end of Rambler via Barnard Road, but I bet that end is blocked off too.

I stuff my map into a pocket and walk toward the roadblock. There's one cop, leaning on the hood of the car, arms crossed over his chest. He's skinny, a straw that isn't stirring any drink. He wears sunglasses despite the overcast day. I tip my hat. Surprise, surprise, I get to pass without answering his questions three.

Fifty yards or so beyond the roadblock are two more police cars parked on the side of the road. The homes on Rambler don't crowd each other; groves of trees help everyone keep their distance.

The Rambler Road locals must all be at work. There are no rubbernecking neighbors on lawns, dressed in robes and slippers and sipping their home-brewed coffee. There's just me.

My left ankle is swelling up, rebelling against the sock, but I make it to the other cop cars. They're parked next to a black mailbox with *Sullivan* stenciled in golden cursive. The Sullivan home is set back from the road. If it were summer, the place would be difficult to see from the street because of the trees that surround it and flank its L-shaped gravel driveway, but it's March and there are no leaves or blooms. I see everything through the empty branches. The house is big and white, with a two-car garage. The exterior shows signs of wear, missing shingles and peeling paint.

There's a clearing and a small grassy patch at the end of the gravel driveway. Two more cop cars are parked on the grass. An ambulance cozies up to Sullivan's front door with its back doors open. A blue SUV sits in the driveway, the only civilian car on or around the property.

"Can I help you?" Another cop. He suddenly appears next to the mailbox and me. Neat trick. This one is my size and build, but no beard and no mangled face. Nobody's perfect.

I say, "Depends. Can you tell me if Brendan is okay?"

He says, "Sorry, I don't know anything. Move along." He's not wearing sunglasses. He doesn't look at me but past me. I've been dismissed, if considered at all.

He doesn't like me. I can tell. It's okay because the feeling is mutual. I say, "I guess you can't help me, then. I don't suppose you're going to let me walk up there and find someone who will actually, you know, help me?"

He sways on his feet, an impatient boxer listening to the referee's instructions, waiting for me to crawl out of my corner. He lets me get through my slow I'm-running-out-of-batteries spiel. He doesn't interrupt. I guess he deserves an iota of credit for that.

He says, "Why are you still here? Move along."

I hold up my hands. "Just a concerned acquaintance of the Sullivans out for a walk. I saw the lights and figured I'd check in and be neighborly."

Nothing from angry cop.

I say, "Well, you just keep on protecting the people, officer." I consider showing my PI ID and pushing back some more, but it would produce nothing but a migraine headache for me. Whatever happened at the Sullivan house isn't good, and I probably don't want to be connected to it. At least not right now. The last thing I need is to have to answer a bunch of Barney Fife questions *downtown*, and calling Mommy to pick me up at the police station would ruin the whole vibe for everyone involved. I'm more afraid of having to answer Ellen's questions than theirs. She's tougher.

My craven need for information will have to wait. I tell myself that patience will work best here and I'll find out what happened eventually. It's the only play I have right now.

I slowly walk away, exaggerate my limp, maybe give the cop some Keyser Söze thoughts. I'm aimed at the other end of Rambler, figuring to loop around to Wianno Avenue and back to the library. I have the time now, and not having to walk past the same set of cops is a good idea.

Then, through the trees, I see a stretcher brought out of the Sullivan house. It's holding a body with a white sheet over it. The stretcher's metallic legs are like the barren tree branches. They look dead, unfit to carry life and too flimsy to carry any weight.

Twelve

Back on Wianno and getting physically fatigued fast. Joints tighten and demand that I stop moving. I don't walk this kind of distance regularly—or at all. This is my marathon.

Been waiting and listening for the ambulance and cop cars to pass. Nothing yet. They must've taken a different route.

I might be a half mile from the library now. A car approaches from behind. Its wheels grind salt and sand left over from the winter. The salt and sand have nowhere to go, I suppose. The car slows down and pulls onto the sidewalk ahead of me. It's in my path. It's a red car, something American and muscular, not at all practical, and that tells you all you need to know about the driver of such a thing.

Whoever it is has to wait until I drag my limping-for-real ass up to them. Drama and tension happen naturally sometimes.

I mosey up to the car. The front windows are rolled down, engine still on, its idling is somewhere between a growl and a clearing throat. There's a thick arm hanging out the window, tapping the door, tapping to someone's favorite song. Not mine.

The driver says, "Hey there, Genevich. What's that you're carrying around?" The driver is the redheaded goon from the DA's office. The passenger is his bald buddy. It's sweet how they stick together, even this far from their natural habitat.

I say, "A book. Ever seen one before? Truth be known, I just look at the pictures." I hold it up. I don't have any secrets.

The passenger goon, Baldy, says, "Oh, he's a funny guy. I love funny guys. They make everything more fun."

I say, "That's quite the expressive vocabulary you got there. I can see why your buddy lets you talk." They both have their cell phones in their ears. Maybe they're surgical implants. I point and add, "Those phones will give you cancer. Be careful."

"Thanks for the tip," the redhead says. "What are you doing down on the Cape? For a retard who can't drive, you sure do get around." He laughs. It's forced and goofy.

I don't say anything. The goons go all sit-and-stare on me, dogs pointing at some dead animal floating in the water.

The library is in the visible distance. The clouds part a bit, a tear in the overcast fabric, and the sun shines on the library's white flagpole. I'm on a main road, middle of the day. I convince myself that I'm safe, so I decide to keep up the chatter.

I say, "I like the Cape this time of year. Think I'll play a little mini-golf later. Take advantage of the off-season touristy stuff. Want to play? Five bucks a hole until the windmill. Then it's ten."

Baldy says, "We'll pass, Mushface." He's breathing heavy, practically frothing. His chin juts out, a thick slab of granite, a section of the Great Wall of China. It seems to be growing bigger with each breath.

I say, "Now, now. No need to get personal, boys. This has been fun, but I think I'll continue on my afternoon constitutional, if you don't mind."

I resume my walk. I have goons from the DA's office tailing me in a red car, Sullivan's surveying red car. Nothing is coincidence. Everything is connected.

They follow me. The engine revs, mechanical authority, a thousand angry voices. Clouds of exhaust punctuate the vehicular threats. The roars fill me, then pool in the back of my head. I want to turn to see how close they are, but I won't.

They pull up next to me again, but we all keep moving. Nobody is the leader. The car creeps farther onto the sidewalk, cutting into my path. There's a chest-high stone wall to my left. I might run out of space soon, sandwiched between metal and rock, that proverbial hard place.

Redhead says, "We weren't done talking yet. Leaving us like that was kind of rude, Genevich."

"Yeah, well, Miss Manners I ain't."

Their car edges closer. Heat from the engine block turns loose my sweat. I'm going to keep walking. I won't be the one to flinch in this game of chicken. No way. Not after that retard crack.

Redhead says, "I hope you didn't come all the way down here to talk to Brendan Sullivan."

Baldy finishes the thought. "Yeah, wasted trip, Genevich. He's got nothing to say. Never did."

I'm not safe. I never was. Safety is the big disguise. I keep walking. Straight line. That's what courage is: dumbass perseverance. The library flagpole is my bearing, my shining beacon. I'm done talking. Just walking.

Redhead says, "I can make this simple for you, Genevich. You can make us go away by giving us those photos."

My eyes stay on the flagpole. It's covered in white vines and white roses.

"Yeah, give us the photos, and then you can have a little nap."

"Or a big one."

"It's time to be smart, here."

"We don't play games."

"Ask Brendan."

Baldy says, "Oh, wait a minute, he can't ask Brendan."

The negatives are still in my desk but the manila envelope and photos are inside my jacket. I wanted to make Sullivan look at them again. I wanted to see his eyes seeing the photos. I can't explain what information it would've given me, but it would've been something. Maybe everything.

Redhead says, "Be a smart retard, Genevich. Give us the photos."

I can pretend the photos are inside my library book and, when Redhead reaches for it, smack him in the face with it, knock him silly. Maybe it'll buy me enough time to get to the library. Maybe it won't. I wouldn't mind paying the missing book fee if it worked.

I don't give them anything, feet on pavement, playing it cool when everything is too hot. Their engine revs loud enough to crack the sidewalk under me but I just keep on going. My eyes are locked on the library and its flagpole, the flagpole with vines made of white roses, and those roses are now blooming and growing bigger, just like the smoking and growling threat next to me.

THIRTEEN

I'm falling but not falling. I'm not falling because I am sitting, but I am falling because I am leaning and sliding, sliding down. My right hand shoots out and slaps against wood. It wasn't expecting wood and I wasn't expecting any of this. Adrenaline. Fear. My heart is a trapped rabbit and it frantically kicks the walls with oversized hind legs. Disoriented is a brain comparing short-term memories to what the senses currently report and believing neither.

Goons, the DA's goons. Sitting on a bench. Surgical implants. A bench. Red car. Feet planted in grass. Walking. Falling, sliding. A stone wall. White flagpole on my direct left, and there are no vines or blooming roses. . . .

I blink and stare and look. If I was an owl I'd spin my head like a top and cover all 360 degrees, make sure there're no holes in what I see. Okay. I'm sitting on a bench, the lone bench in front of the library.

My legs hurt. They won't bend at the knee without complaining. I did the walk. Pain is my proof. My next thought is about time. How much I hate it, and how desperate I am to know how much of it has passed.

Here comes Ellen. Her little green car pulls into the library lot. I'll stay here, wait for her, and reboot from my latest system crash, but there'll be files missing. There always are.

I feel inside my jacket. The manila envelope. I peek inside and the photos are still there.

Ellen has mercifully changed out of her clown pants and into old carpenter jeans, faded, like my memories. She also has on a gray sweatshirt, part of her bingo attire. It makes her look older and tired, tired from all the extra years of hands-on mothering. I won't tell her that maybe the clown pants are the way to go.

Ellen says, "Have you been out here long?"

I wonder if she knows how awful a question that is to ask. I could say *not long* and be correct; it's relative. I haven't been out here asleep on this bench for long when you compare it to the amount of time I've existed with narcolepsy, if you compare it to the life span of a galaxy. Or I could say *not long, not long at all, just got here.*

I say, "I don't know."

Ellen ignores my response and its implications. She adjusts her monstrous bag on her right shoulder. She usually complains about that shoulder killing her, but she won't switch the bag over to her left. I don't know anyone else who exclusively uses her right shoulder for load bearing.

She says, "Did you get some work done? Get everything you need?"

I say, "Some work done. Still more to do." Still groggy. Speaking only in phrases is the ointment. For now, my words are too heavy for complex construction.

"That's good. Though you look a little empty-handed."

I had taken out the little Osterville history book. I check and pat the bench and my coat. It's gone.

Ellen says, "What's the matter?"

Maybe I hit the redheaded goon with the book after all, assuming there were real goons in the first place. I could verify some of my previous extracurricular activities. Go inside and ask if I had checked out that book, but I won't. An answer of *no* would do too much damage to me. I'd rather just believe what I want to believe. It's always easier that way.

I say, "Nothing. I think I left a book inside." I stand up and try not to wince. I'm going to have a hard time walking to the car.

She says, "What's wrong now, Mark?"

Everything. I need to go back to Southie, try to put distance between me, the maybe goons, and whatever happened at the Sullivan house. I also need to give Ellen an answer, an excuse, something that won't lead to a trip full of follow-up questions. "Nothing. My body is protesting another drive in your torture chamber."

"Want me to get your book?"

"No. It wasn't any good."

Fourteen

Back home. It's five o'clock. I've been gone for only half a day, but our little excursion to the Cape and back has left me with a weeklong family-vacation-type hangover. I just don't have a cheesy T-shirt, sunburn, and disposable camera full of disposable memories to show for it.

My office phone blinks. A red light. I have a voice-mail message. Let's get right to it.

"Hello—um, Mr. Genevich? This is Jennifer Times. I got your number from your card that you left me?" Her statements are questions. She's unsure of what she's doing. That makes two of us. "I think we need to meet and talk. Please call me back as soon as you can." She leaves her number, and the message ends with a beep.

I won't call her right away. I need the meanings and possibilities to have their way with me for a bit. Just like I need a hot shower to untie my muscles; they're double-knotted.

First I'll check my e-mail. I turn on the computer. The hard drive makes its noises, its crude impersonation of life. The monitor glows, increasing in brightness until the desktop is visible. Same as it was yesterday and the day before. There's no e-mail. Then I do a quick search for any stories about Brendan Sullivan and Osterville and murder. Nothing comes up.

Maybe I should call Sullivan's house. Don't know if that's a good idea. Not sure if I'm ready to have my name popping up on police radar screens, if he was in fact murdered. There's still too much I don't know, too many questions I couldn't answer, but the call is the chance I probably have to take at some point. I should call. Call his house now. Might not have been him I saw being taken out of the house. What I saw might not have even happened.

Screw it. I pick up the phone and dial Jennifer Times instead. Sullivan can wait. The shower can wait. It'll be good to have things to look forward to.

One ring. "Hello?"

"Jennifer, it's Mark Genevich returning your call." I'm all business, even if she's not the client and not in the photos anymore. Let her do the talking. I don't need her. She called me.

"Hi, yeah, thanks for calling me back. So, I was thinking we should meet and talk?" Still with statements that are questions. Maybe being forced from the spotlight has left her withered, without confidence. Maybe it's just my perception. For all I know she's a confident young woman, an aspiring celebrity, and she's only reflecting my constant state of insecurity because I want her to. It's what we all want from our celebrities. We want them to tell us something we don't know about ourselves when they can't.

Suddenly I'm Mr. Popular. I say, "I can do that. You pick the place." I assume that she doesn't want to come to my office. Otherwise, she would've offered.

"Can we meet for dinner at Amrheins later tonight? Seven P.M.?"

Of course. The DA's pet restaurant. "I can do that too. But make it seven-thirty." I don't need the extra half hour. Sure, it'll give me a safety net, never know when that ever-elusive thief, lost time, might strike, but I said seven-thirty because I want to exert some of my own conscious will upon the situation. For once.

She says, "Okay."

There's silence. It's big enough to span the unknown distance between us. I say, "See you tonight, then, Jennifer." I'm not going to ask why she wants to meet with me or ask her what DA Daddy told her. There'll be plenty of time for the tough questions later. I'm not going to force this. I don't need to. I'm not used to the power position. I'll try not to let it go to my head.

Fifteen

A constant stream of traffic passes by like schools of fish, the sheer number of vehicles relentless and numbing. I'm standing on East Broadway, only a block from the Broadway Red Line T stop. Seven-thirty has become seven-forty-five. It's all right. My cigarette is finished. Society always arrives late.

Amrheins is an Irish restaurant. Has its own parking lot, big enough for fifty-plus cars. The lot itself has to be worth a small fortune in real estate. The restaurant is big. It has three sections. Bar section is the middle, dining areas on the left and right. The right side of the restaurant is elevated. Everything is kept suitably dark for the patrons.

I check in with the maître d'. He's a short young guy in a white dress shirt and black pants. The bright ink from his sleeve tattoos is visible through the shirt's thin cloth, their stories hinted at but hidden. He doesn't talk, only motions at the elevated section with his head.

Jennifer is alone, sitting at a table for two tucked away in a corner, as far from the entrance as possible. She sees me and nods. It takes me a dragonfly's life to limp across the restaurant to our table. She has on a jean jacket, open and rolled up to the elbows. Light blue shirt. Her hair is tied up, off her face, and she wears glasses. The glasses are enough to turn her into Clark Kent and successfully disguise her Superman, but I know it's her.

I say, "Sorry I'm late, Jennifer." I try to think of something witty to explain my lateness, but I figure my hangdog reappearance is enough. My clothes look slept in because they are. I never did take that hot shower. I can't even keep appointments with myself.

She says, "That's okay." The tablecloth is green. An unlit tea-light candle floats in a glass bowl. The melted wax makes tentacles. It's a floating inkblot I can't read, a portent for the evening. Maybe I should just sit my ass down. Jennifer sips from a glass of sparkling water, or maybe soda. A person can get lost trying to figure out all the details.

The place is half full, or half empty, the point of view hinging on how our meeting fares. I do sit. My back is turned to the rest of the restaurant. I'm not comfortable with my seating. Don't want my back to Southie because the place is full of goons. One such goon might have red hair, freckles, and a phone in his ear, and he might have a bald buddy. Yeah, it has occurred to me that this dinner could be a setup. I slide my heavy wooden chair loudly toward Jennifer's side of the table.

I say, "I like being able to see what I want to see, which is everything." I'm still fiddling with my chair and position. Jennifer makes a hand gesture and a waiter materializes instantly.

Jennifer orders mango turkey tips with pineapple salsa, then turns to me and says, "Sorry, but I can't stay long. He'll wait while you look at the menu, all right?"

The waiter nods at me. That's all I get from the staff. Head movements.

I suppose I deserve being put on the food spot for being late. I make it easy on everyone and order without looking at the menu. "Shepherd's pie and a coffee, and make sure my mug is always full."

The waiter has his errand, clicks his heels, and returns from whence he came. I say, "So, Ms. Times, here we are." Not exactly the best opening line, but it'll have to do, creepy-older-man vibe notwithstanding.

She says, "I have some questions," then stops. Her spine is telephone-pole straight. It makes me uncomfortable.

I say, "I have many answers. Ask me the questions and we'll see if any of my answers match up."

Her hands are on the table and folded over each other. She could be holding a firefly trapped in her hands or a coin she plans to make disappear. She has all her own fingers, no bandages or scars. Not that I expected differently, of course. She says, "I've never been to your office, Mr. Genevich. Why did you go to my father's office and tell him I hired you?" Her delivery is clinical, rehearsed. She must've practiced her questions with a mirror or with DA Daddy.

Doesn't matter. I tell her. I just flat out tell her everything, the truth along with my mistakes and lies. Can't have truth without lies. First I give an introduction to my wonderful world of narcolepsy. How it started. How it won't stop. Then fast-forward to our supposed meeting in my office. Her missing fingers and the hypnogogic hallucination. She's listening. I'm believing. Believing that if I open up and share my truths, maybe she'll share hers. It's the only chance I have of getting anything meaningful out of this meeting. I give her the highlights from the trip to the DA's minus the photos of her stand-in. She only needs to know I thought she was being blackmailed. Not over what. Finally, I tell her that the real client called me yesterday. I leave out the Cape, red car, and goons. I'm not going to give it all away.

She says, "Well, I'm glad you're admitting that I was never in your office." She unfolds her hands; the firefly is free to go. She reaches for her drink. "But do you know why you hallucinated me into your office?"

"You and *American Star* were impossible to avoid around here. Believe me, I tried. The local rags and news stations pumped out daily features and updates." I stop and Jennifer doesn't say anything. So I add, "That, and I'm your biggest fan. I never missed a show and called in to vote every night, unless I fell asleep first."

I laugh. She doesn't.

She says, "Is it because the woman in the pictures you showed to my father looks like me?"

The questions are piling up fast, adding up, stressing my system again. Not sure if I can keep up. I can keep telling myself I'm in control of this particular situation, but I know better. Luckily, the waiter picks the perfect time to return with my coffee. It's hot enough to melt skin. My belly fills with lava. Perfect.

I say, "So, your father told you about the pictures, I assume. It's nice that you guys can share like that."

She nods. "Did you bring them?"

I don't say anything right away because I don't know what I should say. Experience offers me nothing here because I have none. "I think I have those Kodak moments on me, yeah." The pictures never leave me now. They've taken root inside my coat.

"Will you show them to me?"

I say, "I don't think so. You're not my client." I say that, but I'm going to show them to her. Just want to know how much she'll push.

"I think you owe me. Don't you?" It's the first appearance of that privileged attitude I saw on TV. Can't say I like it. She says it with a face as straight as her spine, which is still as straight as a telephone pole. See, everything is connected.

I say, "No. I don't owe you anything other than a sorry-for-the-inconvenience." My coffee mug is empty despite my explicit instructions. That's inconvenient.

She says, "I want to see her. It's why I called you and it's why I'm here, Mr. Genevich. Nothing else. This is it. Our paths will never cross again after this." Jennifer takes off her glasses and wipes the lenses with her napkin, then puts them back on. Disguise intact. "I would like to see her. Please."

I know the DA put her up to this. It's too obvious. Now I just have to figure out the potential risk/reward of showing her the photos. I smile instead of yawning. It probably comes out all lopsided and crooked, a crack in a glass. I say, "Am I supposed to just pull out the photos here, in the middle of a restaurant?"

She says, "Yeah, why not? There's nobody over here. You're practically sitting in my lap, so it's not like anyone could see."

Hard to argue with that. I open my coat and produce the envelope, which has taken quite a beating. The manila is going all flaky on me, its structural integrity close to being compromised. Nothing lasts forever. I take out the pictures and hand the first one to her, the one with clothes.

Jennifer says, "Wow. She does look like me. Not exactly, but enough to be weird. Aren't there more?" She holds out a hand.

"I'll trade you. New for old."

She rolls her eyes but I don't care. Now I'm the spoiled brat who won't share. I make the international gimme-gimme-gimme sign with my hand and fingers. She gimmes. I put the second picture in her hand.

She says, "What did my father say when he saw these?"

"He said it wasn't you. I asked for proof. He said no mole. Hair and teeth were wrong." I leave out the part where he asked me if anyone else had seen the photos. I'm saving that for myself until I figure out what to do with it.

She says, "She's too skinny to be me. Her breasts are smaller too." Jennifer gives back the photo.

"My girlfriend used to say that all the time." I try to sound nonchalant but come off desperate instead. I rub my beard. It sounds awful loud. Awful and loud.

Jennifer says, "Your girlfriend sounds like a keeper," and gives me a pity smile. Thanks, but no thanks.

I say, "Nah, not really. Barely remember her." I reach for my cigarettes, but then I remember I can't smoke in here. Memory slower than the hand. Back to the beard.

Jennifer says, "But you remember she talked about her small breasts?"

I can't tell how much fun she's having at my expense. Doesn't matter, I suppose. I can pretend I'm out having a harmless conversation. Pretend that I didn't lose my face and then the last eight years of my life to little sleeps. I say, "Yeah. That, and I liked how she read books."

I'm sure Jennifer isn't expecting me to go here, a tangent running wildly into my personal territory, but she plays along. She says, "Should I be afraid to ask?"

"She wrote all over her books. She circled and highlighted words and phrases, drew pictures between the lines, and wrote down descriptions of the emotions she experienced in the margins. So when she went back to reread the book, she only looked at the pictures and the notes."

"That's odd. And certainly memorable."

I say, "I remember it because it's where I live now. In the margins." I don't think Jennifer realizes how honest I am being here. Maybe she does and finds it embarrassing. I'm like a friend admitting some reprehensible bit of behavior that forever warps and taints the relationship. Only I'm not a friend. I think I understand her obvious discomfort. Strangers are supposed to lie.

She steers the conversation back to her turf. "Do you swear no one is trying to use those to blackmail me? If those pictures end up on the Internet somehow, you'll have one pissed-off DA knocking on your door."

I tell her, "You're in the clear," though I don't really believe it. There's some connection. I mean, she's here, in front of me right now. That's more than I can say for any other aspect, potential or otherwise, of this case. An awkward silence has its way.

I say, "Glad we settled that. I can sleep now." I laugh at my own joke. I laugh too hard. It shakes our table. It's a laugh a prisoner might direct at the warden who just made a meal out of the cell key.

"Who do you think it is?" she says.

I stop myself from saying *If I knew, I wouldn't be here with you,* but I don't want her to take it personally. Yeah, that's a bad joke. I know this case is a lot more serious than blackmail and nudie pics, and it scares the hell out of me. I tell her, "Don't know yet."

"So you don't know who's in the pictures and you didn't know who sent the pictures?"

I say, "I know who sent them to me now."

"That's right. The convenient phone call."

"There was nothing convenient about the phone call."

"Still sounds like a tough case."

"Nothing's ever easy. But I'll figure it all out."

"Will you?"

"Yes."

The verbal volley is fast and everything gets returned. I manage to push out every one of my lead-heavy words.

She leans back in her chair, crosses her arms over her chest. "Those pictures felt old to me, like they were taken a long time ago."

"Probably just the black-and-white." She's right, but I don't want to admit it.

Our food arrives. My shepherd's pie is molten. We eat. Our silence becomes a part of the meal, a glass of wine that doesn't add any flavor but doesn't get in the way either.

Then I decide to get in the way. "Sorry you lost, Jennifer."

"Excuse me?"

"Lost. You know, *American Star*. I thought you got screwed, although you probably gave them too much attitude. Nothing wrong with attitude, but you gotta know, the peoples, they want their stars safe, smiling, and happy. At least until they get bored with them."

Oh, she's angry. It's all over her face. The emotion looks exterior, not belonging to her. It's a mask. It's not real. She's giving me what she thinks I expect or want. Maybe I'm projecting again. I don't know anything about this woman, but I did see her on TV surrounded by fans, and we're all conditioned to believe it's validation of her goodness, her worth, even if she was the first loser. Jennifer composes herself, takes off the anger mask.

"Thanks. It's been a tough few days, but I'll be fine. My agent says offers are already coming in."

Sure they are. More local mall appearances to be followed by national anthems at minor league baseball parks, and it only goes downhill from there. Her brief run as a celebrity was a mask too, or a full-body costume, one she rented instead of owned.

Seems the both of us are down, so I won't throw any more kicks her way. But I will throw her an off-speed pitch. "Did you tell your father you'd be meeting with me tonight?"

She says, "No." She doesn't use a knife, just mashes her fork into a turkey tip, splitting it in half. She's lying. That's my assumption until proven otherwise, private detective work as contrapositive.

I say, "Does your father think I'm making this all up? Does he think I'm dangerous? Should I be expecting him and a warrant at my door soon?"

Jennifer shrugs and destroys more turkey. "I don't know. He'll probably forget about it if he doesn't hear from you again. He was pretty pissed about your meeting, though."

"I have that effect on some people." A canned line, one that I regret instantly. "Did he tell you that he and my father were childhood friends?"

Jennifer tilts her head. "No, he didn't. Is that true?"

Could be the old man was just too angry to bother with the cozy nostalgia trip. Could be he didn't tell her for a reason. I say, "As true as eight o'clock." Not sure what that means, but I go with it. "I don't get into the DA's office without the Southie and family-friend bit. They grew up in the Harbor Point projects and palled around. Ask him about it."

Jennifer looks at her watch. I'm the appointment that's supposed to end soon. She says, "I will. Where is your father now?"

"He died when I was five."

"I'm sorry." She looks at me, puts me under glass, and says, "Tell me what narcolepsy is like."

"I can't tell you. I'm in it all the time. No basis for comparison. I might as well ask you what not having narcolepsy is like. I certainly don't remember what I felt like before I had it, before the accident." I stop. She doesn't say anything. She was supposed to. Some dance partner she is. I can't follow if she won't lead.

I say, "Do you remember what you felt like eight years ago?"

"No. I guess I don't."

"Neither do I." I'm getting mad. I shouldn't. If I could be rational for a moment, I should appreciate her interest in the state of the narcoleptic me. Very few people share this interest.

"How often do you fall asleep?"

"Depends on the day. Good days, I can make it through with one or two planned naps. Bad days, I'm falling in and out of sleep as often as some people change channels on their TV. And then bad days become bad nights."

"Is today a good day?"

"I don't have a lot of good days. I guess that makes me a pessimist. I'd care and try to change if I had the energy."

"You can't stop yourself from falling asleep?" Another statement question, one I know everyone thinks but doesn't have the guts to ask.

"Sometimes I can; if I recognize the feelings, I can try to change what I'm doing and fight it off. Coping strategies are hit-or-miss. Usually I'm so used to getting along with my gas tank needle hovering on empty that I don't realize I'm about to go out. And then I'm out. Caught in the little sleep."

"How do you feel right now?"

I say, "Tired. Tired of everything."

Jennifer puts down her fork and stands up slowly, as if afraid a sudden movement would spook me. I'm a frail bird she doesn't want to scare away. Or a cornered and wounded animal she's afraid might attack. She says, "Thanks again for meeting me here, Mr. Genevich. I'm sorry, but I really have to go now."

I make a move to stand up. She says, "Please, stay, finish your meal. It's all taken care of. I've already put it on my father's tab."

"He won't mind?"

"No. I do it all the time." She smiles. It's her first real smile of the evening. It's okay. I've seen worse. She edges away from the table, adjusts her jean jacket and her glasses, and leaves without looking back.

I finish my dinner. How do I feel right now? I feel like I missed something, something important. I always feel that way.

Sixteen

I should go straight home and try to find out what, if anything, happened to Brendan Sullivan. But I don't. I stay and take advantage of the tab. I drink three beers, a couple or three shots of whiskey, and two more coffees. At the bar, the townies are on one side and the trendies on the other, and both groups ignore me, use me as their barrier, their Thirty-eighth Parallel.

All right. It's time to go. I'm fine, and I'm taking half the shepherd's pie home with me. It'll make a good breakfast or midnight snack. There's no difference for me.

There's a cabstand down by the Red Line stop, but I'll try and flag a ride in front of the restaurant. It's dark, late, and raining: my perpetual state. I pull up my collar, but that only redirects wind and water into my face and inside my shirt.

I raise the hand that isn't holding a cigarette at a cab, but a black limo cuts it off and pulls into the Amrheins lot, angled, an angry cross-out on a piece of paper, black limo takes the square. Droplets of water on the windshield shine under the streetlamp, making little white holes. Maybe the whiskey shots were overkill.

A rear door opens and the DA thrusts his head out. "I can give you a ride home, Genevich. Jump in."

I know there's no such thing as a free ride, but I take the invite anyway. The door closes and I'm inside the limo with the DA. So are my two friends the goons. I'm not surprised, but it's crowded in here. There are no ashtrays.

I say, "Evening, boys. Have a safe trip up from the Cape?" I blow smoke, smoke and words.

Redhead says, "Hey, retard, remember me?" He's grinning like a manic comic-strip villain, all teeth and split face, flip-top head, a talking Pez dispenser. Ellen still stuffs my Christmas stockings with Pez dispensers, usually superheroes like Spider-Man and the Hulk.

I say, "I missed you most of all." The three of them wear matching blue suits, no wrinkles, and the creases are sharp, dangerous. "Hey, you guys gonna be catering somewhere later? Or maybe you're starting a band. I got a name for you: The Dickheads. Best of luck with that." My anger feels good.

The DA has his legs crossed and hands folded over his knees. If he was any more relaxed he'd be narcoleptic. He says, "I trust you had a nice dinner with Jennifer."

Like I told Jennifer, I'm tired of everything. I knew she was lying to me. There was no appointment she had to keep. Her dinner with the sideshow freak was a little job for Daddy. She set me up, put me on a platter. The only thing missing is an apple in my mouth.

All right. I'm through playing the nice guy, the clueless schmuck. I'm nobody's fall guy. I'm nobody's cliché. I say, "Nah, the food sucked and she talked too much. I'm glad she lost. The Limey judge was right about her."

The bald goon punches me in the stomach, one for flinching. It doesn't hurt. He says, "Watch your mouth."

"Need to work on that uppercut. Saw it coming from last block," I say. The cigarette hangs off my bottom lip and I'm not controlling it anymore. Whether it's sticking around during a tough time or getting ready to abandon ship, I don't know. "Don't get me wrong, DA. The free beer was great. It'll help me sleep tonight."

Redhead laughs. "We can help you with sleep." His eyes are popping out of his head, showing too much white. He's on something serious. I get the sense that if he throws me a punch, I'll break like a porcelain doll.

The DA furrows his brow. He's so concerned. He says, "You have an odd way of expressing appreciation, Genevich."

I'm not nervous. I'm still on my first ball and nowhere near tilting. I should be nervous, though. The momentum of the evening is not in my favor. Must be the beers and booze helping me out.

I say, "I'll thank you for the ride home if I get there. Unless you're expecting something more. Sorry, but I don't put out on a first date." The interior light is on in the limo but everything is still dark. I think we're headed toward West Broadway.

The DA says, "You should be expressing appreciation for my patience. It wouldn't take more than a phone call and a few computer keystrokes to have you locked up. Or worse." He uncrosses his legs and leans toward me, a spider uncurling itself and readying to sprint down the web.

The goons sitting across from me, they're in the heel position but twitching. Hackles up. Ready to go.

The DA is bluffing. He's all talk and no chalk. Otherwise his threatening little scenario would've already happened. Nothing is going to happen. They're going to drop me at my apartment with another tough-guy act and another warning. Warnings. I'm collecting them now like stamps, or butterflies.

Then again, that's not to say that the DA can't do what he said. It'd be suicide to assume otherwise. I'm going to try this out: "Sounds like you're putting me on double-secret probation. What would my dear old dad say about you harassing his son like this? It's not very Southie of you."

He squints, eyelids putting on a mighty squeeze. I got to him. Not sure how. Can't be just the memory of my father, can it? He says, through a mouthful of teeth, "Your dad isn't around anymore, is he? Hasn't been around for a long time, not sure if you're aware."

"I'm always aware." I sound stupid. He gives me threats and doom, and I give him a self-help life-affirmation aphorism.

He says, "And don't tell me what's Southie, Genevich. You have no idea."

I hold up my hands. The DA is getting too hot. No telling what his goons might do if he starts to smoke. I say, "If you say so. Still not sure why all the fuss here. I'm not in your way now, and I haven't done anything wrong. I'm clean, as in squeaky."

He smiles. "When has that ever mattered?" His regained polished tone and delivery is a gun pointed in my face. It holds that much potential for damage. I have no chance.

The bald goon says, "Let's hurt him."

I say, "Jeez, DA, do your constituents know that you run with this kind of crowd? I'm shocked and more than a little disappointed."

He doesn't go for it. He says, "What do you say you just give me the photos, Genevich. The negatives—and don't look surprised, I know there are negatives—and any copies you might've made, digital or otherwise. Give me everything, and that'll be the end of this and any further unpleasantries."

"Or what? You'll call my mommy again?" Things are happening too fast. I add, "You don't need the photos. I've said my mea culpas. They're not of Jennifer. I told her as much during dinner. She's out of the picture, so to speak. And she's fine with it. You should be too."

The DA and the goons laugh. Apparently I'm funny. He says, "The photos, Genevich. I want them. Now is not soon enough. We can take them by force if necessary. It wouldn't bother me. The funny part is we could hold your hand and take you home, sit on your couch, and just wait for you to fall asleep."

I say nothing. His last line robs me of both cool and machismo. Not that I have any.

The DA says, "Tell our driver to turn left onto D Street, and we'll all just enjoy the ride." Redhead follows through on the instructions.

Might as well lay it all out right here. "So how is our friend Brendan Sullivan these days?"

The goons laugh. I've said something incredibly smart or stupid. Likely both.

Baldy says, "He ain't doing too good right now."

Redhead says, "He did answer our questions though, poor guy."

The DA says, "You don't even know what you're saying half the time, do you, Genevich? I suggest you cut the tough-guy PI act, leave the big-boy stuff to us big boys, and give me the photos."

The limo slows and stops. I look out the tinted window and see a Burger King. We're at the D Street intersection. The D Street projects are on the other side of the street. The buildings look like gravestones.

Baldy slaps my face. I hang on to the cigarette but things go fuzzy. I might just go out now, but I pull it together.

"The patty-cake shit is getting old, goon." I fill my lungs with smoke and it stokes a fire in my chest. I exhale a smoke ring that haloes Baldy's head, and I say, "I buried the photos on Boston Common, under the roots of a sapling. The tree will sprout pictures instead of leaves. Harvest in the fall. Good luck with that."

Baldy tries to slap me again but I catch him by the wrist and stub out my cigarette on the back of his hand. He yells. I pull him into my knee, right in the balls, and then push him over, into Redhead. The DA does nothing. He barely looks interested.

I try the limo door, expecting it to be locked, but it opens and I spill out onto the wet pavement and the other lane. Just ahead is a double-parked and idling cab. It's white with some black checkers on the panels. No driver. He must be inside the fast-food joint taking a leak. I look over my shoulder. Redhead crawls out of the limo after me. A gun is in his hand, big as a smokestack.

There's isn't much time. I scuttle around the cab and jump into the driver's seat. The steering wheel is warm and too big. There're too many places for my hands to go. They don't know what to do. The instruments in the dashboard are all in Japanese.

A bullet spiderwebs the rear passenger window. The glass bleeds and screams. Didn't think they'd shoot at me out in the open like this. Must be a mistake, but one that can't be reversed. A chain of events now set into motion until there's one conclusion: me with extra holes. I fumble for the automatic transmission shift. Goddamn it, it's on the steering wheel. It shouldn't be there. I pull on it but it doesn't move. I don't know its secret.

There are loud and fast footsteps on the pavement. Two footsteps become four and multiply rapidly until there's a whole city of footsteps running at me. Redhead appears at my window. He's yelling some crazy stuff, doesn't make any sense. Maybe he's reading the dashboard labels. The gun barrel snug against the glass doesn't have any problems communicating its message.

I'm pulling as hard as I can and the gearshift finally gives in to my demands, which weren't all that unreasonable. I drop the transmission into drive and squeal the wheels. I'm moving forward and I duck, down beneath the dash; there's another gunshot, this one sending glass snowflakes falling onto my head, and there's . . .

Seventeen

"We're here."

I come to in the back of a cab. I'm still buzzed and my mouth tastes of vomit. I bolt upright like a rake getting stepped on. The Johnny Rotten of headaches lurches and struts around my brain. God save my head.

The cab and me, we're at the corner of Dorchester and Broadway, idling in front of my office and apartment building. I want to go digging back under, into the brine, find me some real sleep, the kind that makes my body glad it's there to support me. But I won't find any in here, and I probably won't find any upstairs in my apartment.

"Don't be sleeping on me now," the cabbie says. His voice is full of *fuck you*, but he really cares about me. I can tell.

I'm awake now. I have no idea how much of the DA, the limo ride, and the goons happened. My left cheek, where Redhead slapped me, is sore and puffy. Maybe I did escape their limo and jump into this cab and then dreamed the rest. I don't know.

The cab's heat is on furnace blast. The muscles in my hands feel week. I open and close shaky fists. They're empty and tired, like me. The little sleep was and is too hard.

I pull a crumpled bill out of my pocket and throw it at the cabbie. It's not a good throw. "Keep the change." Don't know if it's enough, and don't care. Neither does he apparently.

I open a door, leave without a further exchange, and manage to land standing on the curb. The cab leaves. It was white and had black checkers on the panels. It's late. There aren't any black limos or red cars on the street. It's still dark and raining.

I need time to process the evening: what happened, what didn't happen, what any of it means. I have my keys out, but the front door to my office is open. The door is thick and heavy, probably as old as the brownstone building, and it sways in the wind and rain.

I step inside the front entryway. The stacks of local restaurant menus are all wet and turning to pulp under my feet. This isn't good. I walk into my office. I don't need to turn on a light to see that everything is all wrong, but I turn it on anyway. Never did like surprises.

Someone picked up my office and shook it around like Daddy needed a new pair of shoes and rolled snake eyes. And then the shaker took out his frustration with the undesired result on my fucking office.

Flat-screen computer monitor is not quite flat anymore and is on the floor, where my client chair used to be. That chair is huddled in the corner of the room, licking its wounds. It saw everything and is traumatized. It'll never be the same.

My file cabinet has been stripped of its contents. Its drawers are open, metal tongues saying ah, and the files spread out on the floor. My desk drawers are open and empty too. They didn't want to feel left out. I step on paper and walk over to my desk. My phone is gone. So is the hard drive and backup flash drive. I don't see my yellow notepad, the one with the narcoleptic me notes. It could be buried in here somewhere, but I doubt it. Good goddamn mercy. And Christ, the negatives, they're not in the empty drawers.

I leave the office and walk upstairs in the dark. It occurs to me that the ransackers could still be here, maybe in my apartment, waiting for me, the ransackee, to come home. I don't care. I have no weapons and I'm no brawler, but if there really are goons and they're upstairs, I'll hit as hard as I can give. And then hit them harder.

My apartment got the same treatment. Door is open. This entry was rougher. The door is splintered by the knob and hangs by one hinge. I knock it off its last thread, put it out of its misery. I turn on the lights. I'm alone, I can tell. The TV is gone and so is my laptop. CD towers, bookcases, pictures, lamps, and everything else flipped, kicked, or stomped over. Into the kitchen, and all those drawers are turned out on the floor. The dish didn't run away with the spoon.

I can't face the crime scene waiting for me in the bedroom, so I stumble back to the living room and my couch. I brush off the debris of my life and sit. Cigarette comes out next. Guess I can just use the floor for an ashtray.

I still have the pictures in my coat. I still have my cell phone. I'm going to make one personal call before letting the police know about the sledgehammer tap dance through my building.

I call Jennifer's number. Yeah, I still have that too. She doesn't answer. I wasn't expecting her to. I get her voice mail.

I say, "Hey, thanks for the setup tonight, Jennifer. I hope your dad and his boys had a great time tearing through my place. I knew that was the only reason why you'd eat dinner with me. Tell those guys sorry I didn't have anything good in the fridge for them, and that they had to leave empty-handed."

My voice sounds drunker than I thought. I'm crying too. Practically in full blubber mode, but there's no stopping my message from a bottle.

"So, yeah, I know you were lying to me the whole night. That's okay, because I lied to you too. I said I didn't remember what I felt like before my accident, before I became the narcoleptic me. I remember what it felt like. I was awake, always awake. I didn't miss anything. I could read books for more than a few pages at a time. I didn't smoke. I watched movies from start to finish in real goddamn theaters. Wouldn't even leave my seat to go to the bathroom. I stayed up late on purpose. Woke up and went to sleep when I wanted. Sleep was my pet, something I controlled, scheduled, took for walks. Sit up, roll over, lie down, stay down, give me your fucking paw. Not now. Now there's only me and everything else is on the periphery, just slightly out of reach or out of touch or out of time. I don't have a real career or a real life. Ellen supports me and I sleepwalk through the rest. I'm telling you this because I want you to know who you set up tonight. And there's more. Not done. Not yet. I remember what it was like to have a regular face, one that folks just glanced at and forgot. There's more. I remember everything I lost. That's what I remember. The loss and loss and loss. . . ."

I stop talking. Too much self-pity, even for me. I'm sure her voice mail stopped recording a long time ago. Who knows how much she got? Who knows what I actually said out loud?

I slouch onto the arm of the couch, cell phone balanced on my head. I'm listening to the digitized silence and it brings an odd comfort. My cigarette slips out of my hand. Hopefully it'll land on something that doesn't take fire personally.

The sleep is coming. I feel it. At least this time, I want it.

Eighteen

The sun shines bright, just like the ones on cereal boxes. Tim and I are in our backyard in Osterville. He's putting tools back in the shed, then emerges with a hand trowel. It's the specialized hand trowel. He locks the shed. I'm still too young to go inside. I wait by the door and receive my brown paper bag and the pat on my head. Good boy. It's time to clean up the yard again. The grass is green but there's more shit than usual to clean up.

The sky is such a light shade of blue, it looks thin, like it could tear at the slightest scratch. I don't feel like singing for Tim today, but I will. I'm a trouper. I give him a round of "Take Me Out to the Ball Game." My bag gets heavy with deposits. He names the dogs. We've all been here before.

We fill three bags' worth of crap and dump it all in the woods behind our property. Each time he dumps the bag, Tim says, "Don't come back."

We walk back to the shed and Tim opens the doors. He says, "So, kid, whaddaya think?"

I twist my foot in the grass and look down. The five-year-old me has something uncomfortable to say. "That friend of yours, Billy Times, he's been a real douche bag to me, Tim."

Tim laughs, bends to one knee, and chucks my chin with his fist. Aw shucks, Dad.

He says, "He's not all bad." He gets up and locks the shed doors. Tim picks me up and puts me on his shoulders. I'm closer to the cereal-box sun and the paper-thin sky now, close enough to destroy everything if I wanted to.

Nineteen

The South Boston Police know of me like the residents of Sesame Street know of Aloysius Snuffleupagus. They know my name and they tell exaggerated stories of my woe and comic-tragic circumstance, but only some big yellow dope believes I'm real. And I am real.

It's about 11 A.M. The morning after. Two officers, one female and one male, cop A and cop B, walk around my apartment and office. They take notes. They're dressed in their spotless blue uniforms, hats, guns, cuffs, shiny badges, the works.

I wear a hangover. It's three sizes too big. I'd take it back if I could, but it matches my rusty joints and blindingly sore muscles so well.

Okay, I'm still in my own rumpled slept-in-again uniform: work
clothes doubling as a lounge-about bathrobe. Everyone should be
so lucky.

I sit on home base, the couch, a coffee cup in one hand, a lit
cigarette in the other. There's sunlight coming through the naked
windows, trapping dust in the rays. I watch the pieces of my apartment floating there in the light. I can't float. I have to squint. I can't
squint and think at the same time.

Think, Genevich. First, I decide that yesterday really was only
one day. My aching and quivering muscles are proof of my yellow-
brick-road jaunt to Sullivan's house. No idea who the body was or, if
I'm willing to be completely honest with myself today, if there even
was a body. No computer or laptop means, for now, no way to find
out what happened. I could call Sullivan's number, but I'm not
ready to call yet. I think I can be patient. Play it a little slow, given the
current set of circumstances, which is my already broken world
breaking at my feet.

Cop A asks for my written statement. I give it to her. It has some
stray ashes on it but no burn holes. I grope for the little victories. I
told them what's missing and now they have it in writing too. They
didn't ask if I thought the break-in was related to one of my cases,
which is fine, because I haven't decided how I would answer that
question.

More from yesterday's log: The shepherd's-pie doggie bag is on
the floor, in front of my bedroom door. It's safe there. My cell phone
has my dialed numbers and incoming call history. Proof of my chats
with Jennifer right there on the glowing LCD screen, including my
late-night soliloquy. She hasn't called back. I don't expect her to.

The police haven't been very chatty or sympathetic. They didn't like that my distress call occurred more than ten hours after the actual break-in. And I think they believed the puke next to the couch and puddle of urine in the corner of the kitchen was somehow my fault. I told them it wasn't. Cop B said I smelled drunk. I said I was drunk, but the puke and piss weren't mine.

The cops leave, finally. My cigarette is dead. I'm left with a trashed office and apartment and more than a few choice items stolen. None of this is circumstantial or coincidence. The DA has a good reason to want those pictures, something more than their chance resemblance to his daughter.

Right about now I'm starting to feel a boulder of guilt roll up onto my shoulders when thinking about Sullivan and his possible or likely fate. Sullivan asked me in a panic if I had shown anyone the pictures yet without finding *it*. I did show them, and I certainly don't have *it*. I took the photos to the DA and then everything that was yesterday happened. I'm that portable Kraken again. Point me in a direction and I unleash my destruction.

"Jesus H. Christ, what happened? Mark, are you in here?"

Ellen. I haven't called her yet. Her voice is on a three-alarm pitch and frequency. It rockets up the stairwell and into my apartment. My hangover appreciates the nuances in its swells of volume.

I shout, "I'm okay and I'm up here, Ellen." I shouldn't be talking, never mind yelling.

Ellen pounds up the stairs, repeating her What-happeneds and sprinkling in some Are-you-all-rights. Maybe I should go into the kitchen and cover the urine puddle with something, but I don't think I can get up.

Ellen stands in the doorway. Her mouth is open as wide as her eyes.

I say, "I know. Friggin' unbelievable mess, isn't it?"

"My God, Mark, what happened? Why the hell didn't you call me?" She looks and sounds hurt. It's not a look I see on her often. I don't like it. It turns that maybe boulder of guilt for Sullivan into the real deal.

I still can't tell her the truth about the case, though. Telling her anything might infect her, put her in more danger than she already is just for being around me. I'm her dark cloud. I'm her walk under a ladder and her broken mirror all in one.

I say, "I went out last night, treated myself to a meal and a few drinks at Amrheins, and found the place like this when I came home. I was a little tipsy and fell asleep on the couch before I could call you or the police. For what it's worth, the police weren't too happy that I didn't call them earlier either."

"You should've called as soon as you woke up." She stands in the doorway with her arms folded across her chest.

"I'm sorry, Ellen. Really, I am." This is getting to be a little too much for me. The edges are blurring again. I put my head in my hands and let slip: "I don't know what I'm going to do."

She says, "About what? Are you in some kind of trouble?" She hikes over the rubble of my existence. There's no path and she has to climb. She makes it, though, sits next to me on the couch, and puts an arm around my shoulder.

I breathe loudly. She waits for me to stop. I say, "No, I'm fine. You know, just how am I going to clean up and get everything going again?"

She says, "We have insurance. I'll get an adjuster here within the hour. We'll get everything fixed up."

We let silence do its thing for a bit. Then I tell her what was stolen. She pulls out a cigarette for both of us. Time passes, whether I want it to or not.

Ellen gets up and says, "I'll call the insurance company, and I'll get somebody to clean this up. You go pack a bag while I make a few phone calls."

I say, "Bag? I'm not going anywhere."

Ellen knows I don't mean it. She says, "You'll stay with me while the place is fixed up. Just a couple of days, right?"

Living at home again for a couple of days. Yeah, Ellen owns this building but it's still my apartment, my place. I promised myself after the accident I'd never live in Osterville, not for day one, because Thomas Wolfe had the whole you-can't-go-home-again thing right.

"Nah, I can stay in a hotel or something."

"Don't be ridiculous, Mark."

I want to say: Look at this place. Look at me. I am ridiculous.

I say, "Couple of days. Okay. Thanks, Ellen. I owe you."

Ellen shakes her head and says, "You don't owe me anything." Her voice is real quiet, not a whisper, but the words have lost all conviction and they are empty.

I get up real slow, then groan and grumble my way to the kitchen. Ellen already has someone on her cell phone. She's a hummingbird of chatter.

Now that I'm up and semimoving, I realize a trip back to the Cape won't be all bad. Not at all. A couple of days out of Southie might turn down the heat. Maybe I can make another trip to the

Sullivan house via the Osterville library. Maybe I'll be safer down there too. Regardless of the maybe goons sighting I had down there, at least I'll be out of the DA's jurisdiction.

Instead of packing a bag, I try to be real quiet while filling the sink with hot water and prying the mop out from under my banana tree, spice rack, and wooden cutlery block. Discreet and mopping up piss generally aren't partners, but I give it my best shot. The job doesn't take long. The puke can be someone else's gig.

Ellen is still on the phone. I go into my bedroom and pack the proverbial bag. When I come out of the room, she's off the phone. I say, "Who were you calling?"

She tells me. Ellen has already rallied the local restaurateurs and some fellow members of the Lithuania Club to set up a nightly neighborhood watch, just like that. Her buddy Sean is going to print T-shirts and window stickers.

I tell her I feel safer already.

She says, "I just have to run to the bank and check in with Millie before we go south, okay?"

I hold out a be-my-guest hand and say, "That's fine. No rush." I'm so magnanimous.

Ellen studies me. I'm the lesson that never gets learned. She says, "Who do you think did this?"

"Terrorists." I adjust the duffel bag on my shoulder, but it's for show. There isn't much in it.

She lights another cigarette but doesn't offer me one. That means I'm in trouble. She says, "When I first came in here I assumed it was local punks. Vandalism and grab-the-new-TV-and-computer type of thing. I know it happens all the time. There was a break-in like this a couple of weeks ago on Gold Street, remember?"

I say, "Yeah," even though I don't.

Ellen walks toward the apartment door but doesn't take her eyes off me.

I say, "I told the police I thought it was vandals."

She says, "Did you?"

"Yeah, Ellen. I did."

She taps the broken front door gently with her foot. The door doesn't move. It's dead. "Is there anything going on that I need to know about, Mark?"

"I got absolutely nothing for you, Ellen." I say it with conviction.

TWENTY

Ellen has been in my apartment twice a week every week for
the past eight years, but I don't remember the last time I set foot in
the old family bungalow. Was it at Christmas two years ago maybe?
No, she had me down for a cookout last summer, I think. I helped
her set up her new grill. Isn't that right?

Doesn't matter, the place is the same. It's stuck in time, like me.

There're only five rooms: living room, dining room, kitchen,
and two bedrooms with a shared bathroom. There isn't a lot of furniture, and none of it is permanent. Everything is an antique that's in
rotation with other unsold antiques from Ellen's store. The rotation
usually lasts about six months. Right now, in the dining room there's

a waist-high hutch and a wooden table with only two chairs, both pushed in tight, afraid to lose track of the table. A rocking chair sits in the living room with a white wicker couch, its cushion faded and flat. Everything is too hard to sit on, nothing just right.

The most notable aspect of chez Genevich is the army of old black-and-white photos that cover the walls and sit on the hutch and the windowsills and almost anything above the floor with a flat, stable surface. There are photos of buildings in Southie and landscapes from Osterville. There are photos of obscure relatives and friends, or relatives and friends who've become obscure. Those are photos that belonged to Ellen's mother or that Ellen took herself, and mixed in—and likely more than half now—are photos of complete strangers. Ellen continually adds to her photo collection by snatching up random black-and-whites from yard sales and antiques shops.

Whenever I'm here, Ellen gives me a tour of the photos, telling me all their names, or stories if they have no names, and if no stories then where she bought them. I don't remember any of it.

None of the pictures are labeled. I don't know how she remembers who are our relatives and who are the strangers. Everyone has similar mustaches or hairstyles and they wear the same hats and jackets, T-shirts and skirts. Maybe Ellen forgets everyone and just makes up the stories on the spot, giving them all new secret histories.

I think she moves and switches the pictures around too, just like the rotating furniture. I think the picture of my apartment building was in the kitchen the last time I was here. Now it's in the living room.

Me? I'm in the kitchen. So is Ellen. It's late but not late enough.

I smoke. She sits and thinks. We drink tea, and we're surrounded by those old photos and old faces, everyone anonymous to me, everyone probably dead, maybe like Brendan Sullivan.

Ellen stirs her tea with a finger. She's quite the charming hostess. She says, "Feeling okay?"

"I'm peachy." I'm not peachy. I'm not feeling any fruit in particular. The narcoleptic me is taking over more often. The symptoms are getting worse. Dr. Heal-Thyself thinks it's the case and the face-to-faces with the Times clan, the stress of confrontation, that's setting me off. Before the photos landed on my desk like some terrorizing band of Cossacks, I had a hypnogogic hallucination maybe once a month. Now it's daily. I can't go on like this much longer. I need a vacation from the case I don't have.

Ellen adds more honey to her tea and stirs counterclockwise, as if she could reset the tea to its beginning. She licks her finger, and it sounds downright messy.

"Ever hear of a spoon, Ellen? Newest gadget going. Not too expensive, user-friendly too." I shoot smoke at her.

She wipes her hand on a napkin and says, "You don't sound peachy. You seem a little extra frazzled."

"Other than my home and office being put in a blender and set to puree, I'm just fine."

I'm growing more desperate. I'm actually contemplating telling Ellen everything. I'll tell her to avoid the DA and large men with cell phones in their ears. Maybe she could inspect my photos. She's the expert. She'd be able to tease and wiggle something out of the pictures, something I'm not seeing, or at least tell me when the photos were shot, how old they are.

She gets up from the kitchen table. Her chair's legs argue with the hardwood floors. "There's a picture I want to show you."

"Anyone who had the under on five-minutes-before-the-picture-tour is a winner," I say.

"Don't be a jerk. Come on. It's in the living room."

We walk through the dining room, past the collection of little bits of history, someone else's lost moments. All those forgotten eyes are staring at me, a houseful of Mona Lisas giving me the eye. Christ, I'm a mess. I need some sleep. Some real sleep.

Living room. We walk to one of the front windows. She plucks a photo from the windowsill. She says, "It's the only one I could find with both of them in it," and hands it to me.

Three preteen kids sit on the front stoop of an apartment building, presumably from the Harbor Point projects. It's summer in Southie. The boys have buzz cuts and gaps in their smiles and skinned knees. They all wear white socks and dark-colored sneakers, shoelaces with floppy loops.

The kid in the middle is the biggest, and he has his arms wrapped roughly around the necks of the other two boys. The kid on the right has his head craned away, trying to break out of the hug turned headlock. The kid on the left has his rabbit ears out but didn't get his hand up over his friend quick enough. The one trying to break away is my father, Tim.

I say, "I've probably seen this a hundred times but never really looked at it. That's Tim there, right?"

"That's him. He was a cutie." Ellen is talking about Tim. A Halley's Comet rare occurrence. "You looked just like him when you were a kid."

That's not true. I looked more like Ellen. Now I look like nobody.

Tim has dark brown hair, almost black. The other two kids have much lighter whiffle stubble and skin. I say, "So that's DA Times in the middle, right?"

"Yup."

Smack in the middle. The ringleader. The hierarchy of neighborhood authority is clear. The other two boys might as well have deputy badges on their T-shirts. Even back then he had his two goons.

The Tim in the picture, the kid so obviously owned by Times, does not jibe with the Tim of my dreams. Tim is a large, confident man in my dreams who can take care of himself and everyone else, especially the kid me, maybe even the narcoleptic me.

I'm embarrassed for this Tim. This is like seeing him with his pants down. This is like finding him sitting and crying in a room by himself. I don't want any part of this Tim, the Tim that DA Times obviously still remembers, given his strong-arm tactics with me.

I say, "Who's the third kid?"

Ellen says, "Brendan Sullivan. For a while there, those boys were never apart. They were practically brothers."

My stomach fills with mutant-sized butterflies. Their wings cut and slash my stomach. Neurons and synapses sputter and fire, and I can actually feel the electricity my body generates amping too high, pumping out too much wattage too soon, and the circuit breaker flips, shutting me off and down. Not a blackout, though. This is worse. I'll be awake and I'll know what's going on. This is cataplexy.

I crumble toward the floor, my head pitching forward and into Ellen's legs. She falls back into the window and sits on the sill, knocking pictures to the floor. I'm going to join them. Nothing works except my thoughts. I can't move or speak. My bulk slides down her legs and I land facedown, my nose pinned against the frame of a picture.

Ellen isn't panicking; she's seen this before. She says, "Are you all right, Mark?" repeatedly, a mantra, something to help her through my attack.

I'm not all right. I'm paralyzed. Maybe this time I won't recover. I'll be stuck like this forever, lying in Ellen's bungalow, facedown, on a photo.

She lifts my head and shoulders off the ground. One of the pictures below my face is of an old guy in a bait-and-tackle shop. I have no idea who it is or if I'm supposed to know. He's likely someone she picked up antiquing. He's been collected by Ellen. He wears a dark-colored winter hat, a turtleneck stretched tight across his chest, suspenders, and hip waders. Maybe he's going clamming, or he already went. He's looking at the camera, looking at me, and holding up something, some bit of unidentifiable fishing gear. It's pointed toward his temple, and from my prone vantage point it looks like a gun. The other picture is the one of my father, DA Times, and Brendan Sullivan, and I can't look at it without new, cresting waves of panic crashing. I'm in big trouble.

Ellen kicks the pictures away and rolls me onto my back. She feels my cheeks and snaps her fingers in front of my eyes. I see them and hear them, but I can't do anything about them.

All I can do is lie here until the circuits cool and I reboot. Thinking about Tackle Man might help. Why not? He's a ghost, and he can't hurt me or Ellen.

Tim Genevich or Billy Times or Brendan Sullivan, on the other hand? They can hurt us, and they are here now, in the bungalow and in my case.

TWENTY-ONE

Recovery. I'm sitting in the rocking chair, holding the same cup of tea I left in the kitchen. It's warm. Maybe Ellen stirred mine counterclockwise. I hope she used a spoon.

I say, "Can I see that picture of Tim again?" My voice is a cicada's first call after its seventeen-year slumber. After cicadas wake up, they live for only a day or two and then are usually eaten by something.

Ellen sits on the wicker couch with the picture pressed into her lap, protecting it from disaster. She can't protect them. She nods and hands it to me.

I get another good look at the three friends. Tim is part of the case. He has to be. He's why Sullivan sent me the pictures. Times is why Sullivan didn't want me to show the pictures to anyone without finding the *it* first, and yeah, I screwed up that part, just a wee bit. I owe it to Sullivan to see this thing through to the bitter end, probably my own bitter end. I'm going to keep swinging, keep fighting those windmills.

I say, "When did you meet Tim?" I wiggle my toes as a reassurance. For the moment, I'm back behind the controls.

Ellen and I are going to chat about Tim and the boys tonight. We never talk about Tim. He's never been the elephant in our room. He's always been bigger.

Ellen smiles. The smile is lost and far away, lips unsure of their positions. She says, "When he was twelve. Tim and his friends hung around Kelleys on Castle Island, bugging me for free ice cream. I only gave it to Tim. He wasn't as obnoxious as the other two, which wasn't saying much. The three of them were such pains in the ass back then. Hard to believe Billy became a DA."

"Can't disagree with you there." I look at the picture and focus on the Brendan Sullivan kid. Never mind Tackle Man, here's the real ghost—or, at least, the latest model. "These guys all lived in Harbor Point together, right?"

"That's right." Ellen isn't looking at me. Her arms are wound tightly around her chest, a life jacket of arms. I'm interviewing a hostile witness.

I say, "That was a rough neighborhood, right?"

"Roughest in Southie. It's where Whitey Bulger and his boys got their start."

Whitey Bulger. Not crazy about hearing Boston's most notorious— and still on the lam—gangster name getting dropped. I'm not crazy about any of this. Especially since the early-to-mid-seventies time line for Bulger's rise coincides with Tim's teen days. I say, "Did Tim know Whitey at all?"

"Everyone knew of Whitey back then, but no, Tim never talked or bragged about knowing him. Billy, though, he would talk big to all us neighborhood kids, stuff about him helping out and doing little jobs for Bulger. Tim always told me he just liked to talk. He probably hasn't changed a bit," Ellen says, and laughs, but the laugh is sad. It has pity for everyone in it, including herself. She sits on the edge of the couch. She might fall off. She wants the picture back. She's afraid of what I might do to it.

I say, "Was Times really all talk? He wasn't connected at all to Bulger? You know that for sure?"

To her credit, Ellen thinks about it. She doesn't give me the quick, pat answer. "Yes, I'm sure," she says. "There's no way he messed around with Bulger. Tim would've told me. What, you think Billy Times is dirty?" Ellen scowls at me, the idea apparently less believable to her than the shooter on the grassy knoll.

"No. I don't think anything like that."

Whitey Bulger took over the Winter Hill Gang in the mid-to-late seventies. He was smart. He didn't sell the drugs or make the loans or bankroll the bookies. He charged the local urban entrepreneurial types a Bulger fee to stay in business. He later took advantage of FBI protection and contacts to get away with everything, including murder, for decades. The Whitey Bulger name still echoes in South Boston. He's our bogeyman, which means we all know his stories.

This isn't going where I wanted it to. This isn't about Bulger. Ellen still isn't giving me any real information about Tim and his friends.

Then this question bubbles up out of nowhere. I don't like it. The answer might hurt. I say, "Wait a minute. Was this picture taken before you met Tim?"

"Oh, yeah. The boys are like nine or ten, maybe eleven. This is actually the first picture your father ever took. He used a tripod, a timer, and the whole bit. Then his uncle taught him how to develop it."

"Wait, wait, wait." This story is wrong. Ellen is the one with the uncle who taught her to develop pictures, not Tim. I rub my face. My beard resists my fingers. It has grown a year's worth in a matter of days. I feel the house of pictures around me, ready to fall. "You've always told me that you took these pictures, except for the antique buys." I manage a weak gesture at the legion of black-and-white photos that surround us.

There's this look I get all the time from other people, people who don't know me and haven't come close to earning the goddamn right to give me that look. The look is why I stopped talking to Juan-Miguel or any of my old roommates, even when they tried to keep in contact with me.

Ellen has never given me that look, even when seeing or finding me at my worst, but she's giving me that look now. Eyebrows pull down hard like they're planning on taking over her eyelids. Her mouth opens, lip curls. The goddamn look: concern trying to mask or hide scorn. Mashed potatoes spread over the lima beans. You can't hide scorn. Ellen looks at me like I'm wrong, like I'm broken. And nothing will ever be the same.

She says, "You're pulling my leg, right, Mark? Tim took those pictures—"

I jump in, a cannonball dive that'll get everyone wet. "It has been a long day, a long week, a long year, a long goddamn lifetime. I'm not pulling your leg."

She says, "I know, I know. But—"

"What do you mean, Tim took most of these? Tim didn't take pictures. He was a handyman, an odd-job guy, not a photographer. That's you. It's your job. You're the shutterbug. And goddamn it, stop fucking looking at me like that."

It's her turn to put her face in her hands, maybe try to wipe that look off her face. She must feel it. I do. She backs off. "Calm down, Mark, you're just a little confused. Tim was the photographer first, remember? When he died, I took his equipment and started my business. You know all this, Mark, don't you?"

"No. I don't know all this. You assume I know everything about Tim when you never talk about him. You tell me more about these photographs than you do about my father. That's all he is to me, an image. There's nothing there, and it's your fault for not telling me. You've never talked about Tim. Never." It all comes out and it's a mess, just like me. I know it's not fair. It's more likely that me and my broken brain have jumbled everything around, putting the bits and pieces of the past into the wrong but convenient boxes, but I'm not giving in.

I say, "This is not my fault. I did not fuck up my father's past. No one has told me anything. This is not something you can pin on me. No one told me any of this. No one. Not you." Even if it isn't true, repeat the lie enough times and it becomes true.

Ellen holds steady, battens down the hatches, and makes it through my storm. She says, "Okay, okay. I'm sorry. I just assumed you know everything about Tim. You're right, I haven't told you enough about him." She stops short, brakes squealing and coffee spilling. She doesn't believe her own words. We're both liars, trying to get our stories straight.

She lights two cigarettes and gives me one. We're tired and old. She says, "So ask away. What do you want to know?"

"Let's start with telling me about him and you and photography."

She tells me. Despite having no money and living in a project, Tim had a surprising amount of photo and film equipment. Yeah, he might've stolen some of it, but most of it came from locals who swapped their old projectors and cameras for Tim's odd jobs, and he'd scour flea markets and moving sales. He would sell pictures to locals and store owners, not charging much, just enough to buy more film, always black-and-white because it was cheaper, and Tim always insisted it looked nicer. Their first kiss happened in a makeshift dark-room. She only got into photography after they were married. She still has all of Tim's equipment and displays it in her shop. She talked through both of our cigarettes.

I say, "Let's look at more of Tim's pictures." I stand up and my legs are foal-unsteady. I'm learning to walk again.

We go on yet another tour of the pictures, but with a different road map and guide this time. We're walking through Tim's history, which has always been a secret. Ellen starts the tour subdued but gains enthusiasm as we progress. We are progressing. She shows me an aunt who lost a foot and three fingers to diabetes. There's Tackle Man again; he was a great-uncle of Tim's, a fisherman who died at sea. Almost everyone I meet is dead, but they have names.

Ellen keeps going, but I stop and hover at Great-uncle Tackle Man's photo. There's something else there. Three letters: LIT, in the photo's background, written on a small square of paper taped to the glass counter. I've seen those letters before, I think, in another photo, written on the spine of a book.

I'm still holding the photo of Tim and the gang. They're all still there, on the stairs, waiting for me patiently. I look and I look and I look, and there, on the stairs, under Tim's string-skinny legs, written in chalk, the letters are two or three inches high. LIT. I want to open the frame and run my fingers over the scene, feel the chalk.

Ellen stops in the hallway just ahead of me and walks back. "What's up, Mark?"

Trying to remain calm is difficult when my heart is an exploding grenade in my chest. I say, "Just noticing the letters LIT in these two pictures." I should've noticed them earlier. It's a scratch on a new car. It's the mole on somebody's face.

Ellen laughs and says, "That's Tim's signature. He'd hide the letters LIT, for Lithuania, somewhere in the background of almost all his pictures. Your father was never subtle."

I smile. I'm going to check all the pictures, every picture in the house, maybe every picture in Osterville, before I recheck the photos that are burning inside their manila envelope.

I pick up the next picture. It's a shot of a tall-grass meadow with one tree set back, not quite center in framing. I don't see the letters anywhere. I'm frantic looking for them. Maybe in the bark of the tree but the tree is too far away. Time as distance.

Ellen says, "Tim didn't take that one. I bought this last summer. I like how the tree isn't quite centered. Initially it has an amateur look to it, but I think the photographer did it on purpose. Gives it an eccentric feel. I like it."

"Why do you buy these antique pictures, Ellen?"

She doesn't answer right away. She pulls out her lighter but only flips it open and then closed. There's no fire. Ellen isn't comfortable because I'm asking her to be vulnerable.

She gives me time to make up her answer. Either she can't bring herself to throw away or pack up Tim's pictures so she mixes them in with antiques, hiding Tim's work in plain sight, distance by numbers instead of time; or she's pretending that Tim is still around, taking photos, the new ones she buys continuing their silent, unspoken conversation.

Ellen shrugs. "It's hard to explain. It's just a hobby, I guess. I like the way the black-and-white photos look. Aren't most hobbies hard to explain? Can a stamp collector tell you why she collects stamps?"

I say, "I don't know any stamp collectors."

It's all I can do to keep myself from pulling out the manila envelope in front of Ellen, ripping it open, and checking the photos for Tim's signature. I can't do that. I'll have to wait until she goes to bed. The less she knows, the better off she'll be. This case is getting too dangerous; or, to be more accurate, it already was dangerous and I didn't know any better.

Still, my hands vibrate with want. So instead, I snatch the lighter out of her fist and light up a cigarette. The smoke isn't black or white, but gray.

TWENTY-TWO

I'm in my bedroom, sitting at the edge of my bed, manila envelope on the bedspread. The door is shut. Ellen is watching TV. I'd check my closet for monsters, but I'm afraid I'd find one.

I open the envelope. No more monster talk. Now I'm thinking about letters, the molecules of sentences and songs, the bricks of words. Letters, man, letters. They might mean everything or nothing at all.

Letters are everywhere: the DA's waiting room with stacks of magazines and newspapers; the Osterville library, filled with dusty volumes that haven't been read in generations; Southie with its billboards and their screaming ten-feet-tall words; with stenciled script and cursive etchings on pub windows and convenience-store signage;

on the unending stream of bills and circulars filling my PO box, and the computer and the Internet and all those sites and search engines and databases and spam e-mails; television; lost pet signs; the tags on my clothing; my yellow notepad that ran away from home.

How many letters are in the whole bungalow, or the town, or the state, or the country? An infinite sum of letters forming words in every language. Someone at one time or another wrote all those letters but, unlike their bodies, their armies of letters live on, like swarms of locusts bearing long-dead messages of happiness or doom or silliness. And hell, I've only been thinking about print letters. How many letters do I speak in a day, then multiply that by a lifetime of days, then by billions of lifetimes, and add that to our written-letter count and we're drowning in an uncountable number. We're the billions of monkeys typing at the billions of typewriters.

Okay. I'm stalling when I don't have time to stall. Let's cut the infinite number down to three. I'm afraid of three letters. LIT. I'm afraid I'll see them and afraid that I won't.

First up, the topless photo. I need to reacquaint myself. I haven't looked at the pictures in days, but with all the little sleeps between viewings it feels like months. The woman looks less like Jennifer Times. The photo is now clearly over thirty-five years old. Perspective makes detective work easy. It's a hard-earned perspective.

I look. I don't find any letters. The camera is angled up, shot from a vantage point slightly below the subject. There isn't much background to the photo. Ceiling, empty wall, tips of bedposts, the top of the bookcase. The white light above the woman washes out everything that isn't the woman. I keep looking, keep staring into the light.

When I come to, I'm horizontal on the bed, legs hanging off like loose thread on clothing. The photos are on the floor. I go to the floor, crawl on my hands and knees. Maybe I should check for monsters under my bed, but I'm afraid I'd find one. I'm starting this all over again.

I pick up the fully clothed photo. She's wearing her white T-shirt and skirt. The camera angle is played straight. No ceiling light. There is nothing on the walls behind her, nothing on the bed. There's the bookcase in the left background. It holds books like a good bookcase should.

LIT is there, written on that book, across the bottom of its spine. Tim's signature. Tim's photograph.

The bungalow is quiet, the TV dead. Ellen must be asleep. I don't have a clock in my room. There are no pictures on the walls, only small shelves with assorted knickknacks. I put both photos back in the envelope and go to bed. I shut the light off but I probably won't be able to sleep. There's no one to tuck me in, and there are too many monsters in this room.

Twenty-three

It's morning, I think. The sun is out. Good for the sun. I'm walking down the hallway, the corridor of photos, Tim's memories, everything adding up to a story with some twist ending.

I can't stay here today or for the days after. I have to get out soon, back to Southie. Despite everything I learned last night, agreeing to stay here for the rest of the week is a mistake. I'd rather sleep on the rubble of my life back in Southie than spend another night here. At least then I can be a failure in my own home. And I am going to solve this case if for nothing more than to prove to myself that I can do something, something real, something that has effects, repercussions, something to leave a mark. Mark Genevich was here.

Ellen is in the kitchen sitting with what looks like a week's worth of local newspapers spread out on the table, splashy circulars all mixed in with the black-and-white text. She cradles one steaming coffee mug in her hands, and there're two more full mugs on the counter. I hope one of them is mine.

There's sunlight everywhere in the kitchen, and not enough shadow. Ellen doesn't look up. "You're not going to believe this."

I say, "Someone is having a sale on clown pants." The coffee is scalding hot, as if it knew exactly when I would be awake. That makes one of us.

Ellen throws a bit of folded-up newspaper at me. I don't catch it and it bounces off my chest.

"Hey! Watch the coffee, crazy lady." The microwave's digital clock has green digits that flash the wrong time. Ellen never sets the thing. Told you she was crazy.

She says, "I was just catching up, reading yesterday's newspaper, and found that."

I pick up the front page of the local rag. Headline: OSTERVILLE MAN COMMITS SUICIDE. Included is a head shot, and the article identifies the man as Brendan Sullivan, age fifty. I don't see that twelve-year-old I was introduced to last night inside the head shot. This Brendan Sullivan is bald, has jowls a Saint Bernard would envy, and thick glasses, thicker than Ellen's. Apparently, he put a handgun under his chin and pulled the trigger. He leaves behind his wife, Janice; no children. He was an upstanding citizen. Neighbors said he kept to himself, drove tractor trailers, and did a little gardening. Sad story. One that's impossible to believe.

I wish I had a shocked reaction at the ready for Ellen, something I kept like a pet and could let out on command. Instead, I give my honest reaction, a big sigh of relief. Yeah, my buffoonery in the DA's office probably killed this man, but now I have confirmation that Sullivan was the body I saw. And what I saw was what I saw, not a hallucination. That counts for something, right?

I say, "Isn't that odd." I've never been very smooth.

Ellen puts down the rest of her newspaper, the afterthought folded and stacked neatly. This might be her moment of epiphany, bells ringing and seraphim floating in her head. Ellen knows there's something going on. She might even think I know more than I know. I'll have to get her on her heels, put some questions out there, keep her from grilling me like a hot dog. I'd crack in record time under her interrogation lamp.

I say, "Did you know that Sullivan was living in Osterville?"

Ellen blinks, loses her train of thought, at least for the moment, and says, "What? No, no. I had no idea. The article says he'd bounced around the Cape, but I never ran into him."

"Strange."

"It gets stranger. I called Aunt Millie to tell her about poor Brendan, and she told me she saw him in Southie last week."

I squeeze the coffee mug and it doesn't squeeze back. "No kidding. Where?"

"She saw him in CVS on West Broadway. She said, 'Hi, Brendan,' and he just said a quick 'Hi' back, but he was in a hurry, left the store, and headed out into that terrible rain last week, remember? She said he started off toward East Broadway."

He was walking toward my office. He was coming to meet me

but got the narcoleptic me instead. The narcoleptic me accepted his pictures and wrote down notes on a yellow pad but didn't forward any other pertinent information, especially the promise to not show anyone the photos until I'd found *it*.

I make some toast. Ellen has an old two-slice toaster that burns the sides unevenly. The bell rings and the bread smokes. In the fridge is margarine instead of butter. I hate margarine.

Ellen says, "I'm actually leaving soon because I have a kiddie shoot at eleven. I was going to let you sleep, but now that you're awake, what do you want to do today? Feel like manning the antiques section for a while? I'll open it up if you want."

I haven't been here twenty-four hours and she's already trying to get me to work for her. At least these questions are ones I can answer. I say, "I'll pass on antiquing." Don't know if she noticed, but I have the Sullivan account folded under my arm. I'm taking it with me. "You can drop me at the library again. I've got work I can do there."

She says, "I didn't know you brought any work."

I down the rest of the coffee, scalding my gullet. A ball of warmth radiates in my stomach; it shifts and moves stuff around. "I'm not on vacation, Ellen, and this isn't Disney World. I do have clients who depend on me." I'm so earnest I almost believe it myself, at least until I drop the newspaper. It lands heads with the blazing headline facing up.

Ellen peers over the table. We both stare at the newspaper on the floor as if waiting for it to speak. Maybe it already has. She says, "I think you can take a few days off. Your clients would understand." It sounds angry, accusatory. She knows I'm keeping something from her.

"Sorry, the work—I just can't escape it." I take the toast on a tour of the bungalow. The tour ends where it should, with the photo of Tim, the DA, and Sullivan. Ellen is still inside her newspapers so she doesn't see me lift the photo, frame and all, and slide it inside my coat.

Finally, I have a plan. No more screwing around. The toast approves.

Twenty-four

I'm tired. I'm always tired; it's part of being me. But this tired is going radioactive. It's being down here in the Cape away from the city. Even when I'm doing nothing in Boston, there's the noise of action, of stuff happening, which helps me push through the tired. Down here, there's nothing but boxes and walls of lost memories.

I don't give Ellen a time to pick me up at the library. I tell her I'm a big boy and I'll make my way downtown eventually. She doesn't argue. Either the fight has momentarily left her or she's relieved to be free of my company. I have that effect on people.

I do an obligatory walk-and-yawn through the library stacks to make sure that I'm seen by the staff, all two of them. It's a weekday, and only moms and their preschoolers are here. The kids stare at me, but their moms won't look.

My cell phone feels like a baseball in my hand, all inert possibility. I have no messages; I knew that before I checked. Then I call Osterville's only off-season cabbie, Steve Brill. He's in the library parking lot two minutes later.

Brill is older than a sand dune and has been eroding for years. His knuckles are unrolled dice on his fuzzy steering wheel. The cab is an old white station wagon with brown panels and rust, I'm not sure which is which. Duct tape holds together the upholstery, and the interior smells like an egg and cheese sandwich, hold the cheese. A first-class ride.

I say, "Brill, I want you to drive like I'm a tourist."

Although Brill is a regular in Ellen's antiques store and he's met me on a couple of occasions, he isn't much for small talk and gives me nothing but a grunt. Maybe he doesn't like me. Don't know why, as I haven't done anything to him. Yet.

First, we make a quick trip to a florist. Brill waits in the cab with the meter running. I go small and purchase something called the At Peace Bouquet, which is yellow flowers mixed with greens, the sympathy concoction in a small purple vase I can hold in one hand. Me and the peace bouquet hop into the cab.

In the rearview mirror, Brill's eyes are rocks sitting inside a wrinkly bag of skin. The rocks disapprove of something. He says, "What, the big-city PI has a hot date tonight?" Then he cackles. His laughter shakes loose heavy gobs of phlegm in his chest, or maybe chunks of lung. Serves the old bastard right.

I'm nobody's joke. I say, "I have a hot date with your mother."

Brill shuts off the engine but doesn't turn around, just gives me those rocks in the rearview. He says, "I don't care who you think you are, I'm the only one allowed to be an asshole in my cab."

"You're doing a damn fine job of it, Brill. Kudos." I have a fistful of flowers in my hand and I'm talking tough to Rumpelstiltzkin. Who am I kidding? I'm everyone's joke.

He says, "I'll throw your ugly ass out of my cab. Don't think I won't. I don't need to give you a ride anywhere."

He's pissing me off, but at least he's getting my juices flowing. I stare at the back of his bald and liver-spotted head. There are wisps of white hair clinging to his scalp, pieces of elderly cotton candy.

I guess he's not going to apply for my personal-driver gig. I have to keep this from escalating. I need his wheels today. "Yeah, I know you can. But you'll give me a ride. Corner of Crystal Lake and Rambler, please."

Brill says nothing. I pull out two cigarettes and offer him one. His nicotine-stained hand snakes behind him, those dice knuckles shaking. He takes the stick and sets it aglow with the dash lighter. He inhales quietly, and the expelled smoke hangs around his head, stays personal.

I say, "Do you know how to get to where I want to go?" I pull out my lighter, flip open the top, and produce my one-inch flame.

Brill says, "I heard you the first time. And no smoking in my cab."

Brill starts up the cab and pulls out of the parking lot. I pocket my cigarette. I won't argue with him. I'm happy to be going somewhere.

Our ride from the florist to Sullivan's house should be short enough that falling asleep isn't really a worry. Knock on wood. The flowers are bothering my eyes and sinuses, though. I try to inhale the secondhand smoke instead. It's stale and spent, just like me and Brill.

He pulls over at the end of Rambler Road, the passenger side of the cab flush up against some bushes. I have to get out on the driver's side, which doesn't feel natural. The old man is screwing with me. He doesn't realize I don't need this shit.

Brill still doesn't turn around. He doesn't have to. He says, "Sad end for that Sullivan fella."

That's interesting. He could be just making small talk, but Brill doesn't do small talk. I'm going to play a hunch here. It sounds like Brill has something to say.

"Ends usually are sad. You know anything about Sullivan?"

Brill shrugs and says, "Maybe."

Even more interesting. I take out a twenty and throw it into the front seat. Brill picks it up quick and stuffs the bill into his front shirt pocket. The shirt is pink. I say, "Talk to me."

Brill says, "He was a quiet, normal guy. I gave him a ride a couple weeks ago to and from Lucky's Auto when his car was on the fritz. He tipped well." He stops. The silence is long enough to communicate some things.

"That's it? That's all you got?" I say it real slow for him, to let him try on the idea that I'm not amused.

He says, "Yeah, that's all I know," then laughs. "It's not my fault if you're playing Mickey Mouse detective."

There's no way this small-town pile of bones is pulling that on me. I may be amateur hour, but I'm not an easy mark. I reach over the bench seat and into his front pocket with my ham-sized fist. It comes back to me with my twenty and interest. I toss the interest back over the seat.

"You motherfucker, stealing from an old man." He still hasn't turned around.

"You know the language, but you wouldn't last a day driving a cab in Boston." It's mean, but it's also true. I add, "You can have the twenty back if you earn it."

He loses some air, deflates behind the wheel. He's a small, shrinking old man, and I don't care. He says, "The day before Sullivan killed himself, he had me pick him up and we just drove around town. I asked him about his car because it was sitting in his driveway, but he brushed me off, seemed agitated, spent most of the time looking out the windows and behind us."

Brill stops again, and he's staring at me. He needs another prompt. I'll provide. "Yeah, and where'd you go?"

"He had me drive by your mother's house. Twice. Second pass he told me to stop, so I did. He was talking low, mumbling stuff."

"What kind of stuff?"

" 'Gotta do it yourself, Sullivan,' that kind of thing. He always talked to himself so I didn't pay much attention. He never got out of the cab. I thought he was going to, though. Finally, he told me to take him home. He was all spooked and mumbling the whole way back."

I say, "Did you tell the police any of this?"

"No."

"How about Ellen?"

"No."

"Why not?"

"They didn't ask."

I say, "You mean they didn't gild your lily for the info."

He doesn't say anything. Looking for more bang from my buck, I say, "Kind of strange that he'd be casing her house the day before he offs himself."

Brill shrugs. "I figured Sullivan was cheating on his wife with Ellen. He was acting all paranoid, like a cheat. You know, the cheats are most of my off-season income. I cart them around to their secret lunches and goddamn by-the-hour motels."

Brill paints an alternate scenario in my head, one where Ellen did know Sullivan was living in Osterville and knew him well; secret lunches and other rendezvous. No. That isn't what happened. I dismiss it.

Ellen was genuine in her reaction this morning to the news of Sullivan's Osterville residency and suicide. She has had no contact with him. She wouldn't have shown me the picture of Tim, the DA, and Sullivan if she was playing the other woman with him. Right? I suppose her motivation behind showing me the photo could be a way to introduce me to her new fling, but that's not how it happened, did it? No.

No. The picture was part of her tour, coincidence only. Sullivan came by the bungalow to do his own looking for the fabled *it* because I hadn't come through yet. I have to go on that assumption. It's the only one that fits my case. I don't have the patience or time for curve balls and red herrings.

Still, Brill's cheats spiel shakes me up enough that I'll lie to him. I say, "Ellen doesn't know who Sullivan was. I promise you."

He says, "Maybe. Maybe not. It doesn't matter to me. I don't care what people are up to. I give rides wherever they want to go, and that's it, and everyone knows it. Now give me my twenty bucks, you motherfucker."

I give it to him. Twenty dollars very well spent. I say, "Don't go driving off too far, Brill. I might not be here all that long." I slide across the bench seat and get out. The road is narrow and I'm in its middle, exposed and unprotected.

Brill says, "Are you paying me to wait?"

"No." I pay the fare and add a tip. There's an insistent breeze coming off the nearby water. The individual flowers point in differing directions; they can't agree on anything.

Brill takes my money and doesn't stop to count it. He says, "Then call me later, fuzz face. Maybe I'll answer." Brill spins his rear tires and the station wagon cab speeds away, weaving down Rambler Road. Maybe I didn't tip him enough.

Sullivan's neighborhood is quiet. No one is out. The sun is shining, but it's cold and there are no signs of approaching spring. It's still the long cold winter here. I walk the one hundred feet to Sullivan's house. I have a plan, but I haven't decided what I'm going to do if his wife isn't home.

Looks like I don't have to worry about that. There are three cars in the driveway. One of them is the blue SUV I saw last time. The other two cars are small and of some Japanese make. Neither of them is red.

Okay, Sullivan's wife, Janice, is home but not alone. Alone would've been preferable, but I know such a state isn't likely, given hubby just died. I'm guessing the cars belong to members of the grief squad who swooped in to support her, friends in need and all that.

I walk down the gravel driveway and my feet sound woolly-mammoth heavy. Stones crunch and earth moves under my rumbling weight. I'm the last of some primitive line of prehistoric creatures on his final migration, the one where he dies at the end of the journey, that circle-of-life bullshit that's catchy as a Disney song but ultimately meaningless. Yeah, I'm in a mood.

The house is still white and needs a paint job. I'll try not to bring that up in conversation. I make it to the front door, which is red, and ring the bell. Two chimes. I hold the flowers tight to my chest, playing them close to the vest. This needs to be done right if I'm to learn anything.

When she opens the door, though, I won't take off my hat. No one wants to see that.

TWENTY-FIVE

An old woman answers the door. She might be the same age as Brill the happy cabbie. She's short and hunched, which maximizes her potential for shortness. Her hair is curly and white, so thick it could be a wig.

She says, "Can I help you?" After getting an eyeful of me, she closes the front door a bit, hiding behind the slab of wood. I don't blame her. I don't exactly have a face for the door-to-door gig.

I say, "Yes, hi—um, are you Mrs. Sullivan?"

"No, I'm her Aunt Patty." She wears a light blue dress with white quarter-sized polka dots, and a faux-pearl necklace hangs around her neck. I know the pearls are fake because they're almost as big as cue balls.

Aunt Patty. Doesn't everyone have an Aunty Patty? I give her my best opening statement. "My late father was an old friend of Brendan's. He grew up with Brendan in Southie. When I heard of his passing and the arrangements, saw I wouldn't be able to attend the wake or the funeral, I felt compelled to come down and give my family's condolences in person."

I hope that's enough to win over the jury. I look at her and see conflict. Aunt Patty doesn't know what to do. Aunt Patty keeps looking behind her but there's no one there to talk to, no one to make the decision for her. She's here to cook and clean and help keep the grieving widow safe from interlopers and unwanted distractions. She's here to make sure that grief happens correctly and according to schedule.

I know, because Ellen has been part of so many grief squads in Southie that she might as well register as a professional and rent herself out. Maybe Ellen does it to remember Tim and grieve for him all over again or she's trying to add distance, going through a bunch of little grievings to get over the big one.

I say, "I've come a long way. I won't stay too long, I promise."

That cinches it. Aunt Patty gives me a warm milk smile and says, "Oh, all right, come in. Thank you for coming." She opens the door wide behind her.

I'm in. I say, "You're welcome. Thanks for letting me in. Means a lot. Is Janice doing okay?"

"About as well as can be imagined. She's been very brave." Aunt Patty shuffle-leads me through the dining room, our feet making an odd rhythm on the hardwood floor.

It's dark in here. The shades are drawn over the bay windows.

The house is in mourning. It's something I can feel. Sullivan died somewhere in this house. Maybe even the front room. Gun under his chin, bullet into his brain. Coerced or set up or neither, this is serious stuff. I can't screw any of it up.

There are pictures and decorations on the walls, but it's too dark to see them. There are also cardboard boxes on the dining room table. The boxes are brown and sad, both temporary and final.

Aunt Patty limps, favoring her left side, probably a hip. When her hip breaks, she won't make it out of the hospital alive. Yeah, like I said, I'm in a mood.

She says, "What's your name?"

"Mark. Mark Genevich. Nice to meet you, Aunt Patty."

"What nationality?"

"Lithuanian." Maybe I should tell her what I really am: narcoleptic. We narcoleptics have no country and we don't participate in the Olympics. Our status supersedes all notion of nationality. We're neutral, like the Swiss, but they don't trust us with army knives.

She says, "That's nice." My cataloging is a comfort to her. I'm not a stranger anymore; I'm Lithuanian.

The kitchen is big and clean, and bright. The white wallpaper and tile trim has wattage. Flowers fill the island counter. I fight off a sneeze. There are voices, speaking softly to our right. Just off the kitchen is a four-season porch, modestly decorated with a table for four and a large swing seat. Two women sit on the swing seat. The hinges and springs creak faintly in time with the pendulum. One of the women looks just like Aunt Patty, same dress and pool-cue necklace. The other woman does not make three of a kind with the pair of queens.

Patty and I walk onto the porch. The swingers stop swinging; someone turns off the music. The vase of flowers is a dumbbell in my hand.

Aunt Patty says, "That's my twin sister Margaret and, of course, the other beautiful woman is Janice. This is Mark Genevich?" I'm a name and a question. She doesn't remember my opening statement or my purpose. I need to fill in the blanks and fast. I've never been good under pressure.

I open with, "I'm so very sorry for your loss." And then I tell Janice and Aunt Margaret what I told Aunt Patty. Janice is attentive but has a faraway smile. Aunt Margaret seems a bit rougher around the edges than her sister. She sits with her thick arms folded across her chest, nostrils flared. She smells something.

Janice is of medium build and has long straight hair, worn down, parted in the middle, a path through a forest. She looks younger than her front-page husband but has dark, almost purple circles under her eyes. Her recent sleeping habits leaving their scarlet letters. Most people don't like to think about how much damage sleep can do, evidence be damned.

Janice says, "Thank you for coming and for the flowers. It's very thoughtful of you." The dark circles shrink her nose and give it a point.

I give Janice the flowers and nod my head, going for the humble silent exchange of pleasantries. Immediately, I regret the choice. I want her to talk about Brendan but she's not saying anything. Everyone has gone statue and we sit and stare, waiting for the birds to come land on our shoulders and shit all over us.

My heart ratchets its rate up a notch and things are getting tingly, my not-so-subtle spider sense telling me that things aren't good and could quickly become worse. Then I remember I brought the picture, the picture of Brendan and the boys. I focus my forever-dwindling energies on it.

I ask, "Did Brendan ever talk about my father?" For a moment, I panic and think I said something about Brendan and my mother instead. But I didn't say that. I'm fine. I shake it off, rub dirt on it, stay in the game. I reach inside my coat and pull out the photo of Tim, the DA, and Sullivan on the stairs. It's still in the frame. Its spot on Ellen's windowsill is empty. "That's Brendan on the left, my father on the right."

Patty squeezes onto the swing seat, sitting on the outside of her sister. I'm the only one standing now. It's noticeable.

Janice says, "I don't remember your father's name coming up. Brendan and I had only been married for ten years, and he never really talked much about growing up in Southie."

It's getting harder not to be thinking about Ellen and Sullivan sitting in a tree as a slight and gaining maybe. Goddamn Brill. I say, "I understand," even if I don't. It's what I'm supposed to say; a nice-to-see-you after the hello.

Janice sighs heavily; it says, *What am I supposed to do now?* I feel terrible for her. I don't know exactly what happened here with Sullivan, but it was my fault. And this case is far from over. She doesn't know that things could get worse.

Janice fills herself up with air after the devastating sigh, which is admirable but just as sad, and says, "I wish Brendan kept more stuff like this around. Could I ask you for a copy of this picture?"

"Of course, consider it done," I say.

Janice smiles, but it's sad; goddamn it, everything is sad. We both know she's trying to regain something that has already been lost forever.

Aunt Margaret grabs the picture with both hands, and says, "Who's that boy in the middle?"

I say, "That's William Times. Currently he's the Suffolk County district attorney."

Patty clasps her hands together and says, "Oh, his daughter is the singer, right? She's very cute."

"Nah, she's a loser," Margaret says, waving her hand. Case dismissed.

Patty says, "She's not a loser. She sang on national TV. I thought she sang beautifully too."

"She stunk and she was a spoiled brat. That's why they voted her off the show," Margaret says.

Janice, who I assume has been acting as referee for the sisters for as long as they've been at her house, says, "She was a finalist on *American Star*. She's hardly a loser."

Margaret shrugs. "She lost, right? We'll never hear from her again."

The volley between family members is quick, ends quicker, and is more than a little disorienting. It also seems to be the end of the small talk. We're back to staring at each other, looking for an answer that isn't here.

I'm not leaving this house empty-handed, without knowing what the next step is, without having to grill Ellen about a tryst with Sullivan. Hopefully, the photo of the boys has bought me some familiarity chips that I can cash.

I say, "I'm sorry, there's no good way to say this, so I'm just going to come out with it."

Margaret says, "Come out with it already and be done then."

"Good advice." I pull out a business card and my PI ID and hand them to Janice, but Margaret takes them instead. "I'm a small-time, very small-time, private detective in South Boston."

Patty's eyes go saucer-wide and she says, "How exciting!"

It's not warm in here but my head sweats under my hat. I nod at Patty, acknowledging her enthusiasm. At least I'll have one of the three on my side. I say, "Last week your husband, Brendan, came to my office in Southie and hired me."

Janice sinks into her swing seat. Patty covers her mouth. Margaret still has her arms crossed. Janice says, "Hired you? Hired you for what?"

Christ, I probably could've come up with a better way to introduce the subject, but there's no turning back now. As uncomfortable as this is, asking the questions that will haunt Janice for years to come, I owe it to Sullivan to see this through. I owe it to myself too.

I say, "Mind if I sit?" No one says anything. I grab a fold-up chair that's leaning against a wall and wrestle with it for a bit; the wood clacks and bites my fingers. I'm sure I look clumsy, but I'm buying some time so I can figure out what I can and can't tell her. It doesn't work.

I say, "The hard part is that I don't think I can tell you much until I figure it all out for myself."

Margaret says, "He's a crock. This guy is a phony. He's trying to get something out of you, probably money. Let's call the police."

Patty says, "Stop it, he's a real detective."

"How do we know that? How do we know anything about this man? That picture doesn't prove anything. Might not even be Brendan in the picture," Margaret says, building up steam, and a convincing case against me.

Patty is horrified. She says, "Look at his card and ID. He's going to tell us something important, right?" Patty leans out toward me. To her I have the answers to life somewhere inside my coat. I only keep questions in here.

Margaret ignores her sister, points a worn-tree-branch finger at me, and says, "Shame on you, whatever it is you're up to. Janice is a good woman and doesn't deserve to be put through anything by the likes of you. I'm calling."

I say, "Whoa, take it easy, Auntie Margaret. I'm telling the truth and I'm not here to hide things from Janice, just the opposite. I don't know how everything fits together yet, and I don't have all the puzzle pieces either. What I'm hoping is that you"—I turn to Janice—"can help me."

The sisters argue with each other. They have their considerable arms folded over their chests and they bump into each other like rams battling over territory. The swing seat complains and sways side to side, not in the direction the swing was intended to go. I yawn and hope nobody sees it.

Janice says, "Wait, wait. Stop!" Her aunts stop. "Are you really the son of Brendan's friend?"

"Yes. And what I'm working on, what Brendan wanted me to figure out, is something from the past, the long past but not gone, and I think it involves both men in that picture, my father and the DA."

Janice says, "I already told you, I don't know anything about Brendan's past, never mind anything about your father and the DA."

I resist telling her that I know very little about my father's past and less about my own mother's present. I say, "That's okay. I think you'll still be able to help."

Margaret is shaking her head, silently *tsk-tsk*ing the proceedings. Patty has wide eyes and nods her head, yes. Janice is stoic, unreadable as a tabloid.

I say, "Janice, may I ask you some questions? Then I promise to tell you and show you what I know."

Janice nods. "Okay."

"How did you meet Brendan?" I start off with an easy question, get her used to talking about her and him, get her used to being honest and thinking about Brendan as past, maybe as something that can't hurt her, or can't hurt her much.

Janice cooperates. She gives a summary of their too-brief history. Her voice is low and calm, soothing, as if I'm the one who needs cheering up. Brendan was a truck driver and they met at a diner in New Hampshire. They sat next to each other at the counter. Janice worked at a local park, part of an environmental conservation and preservation team. They were married two months later, moved to Provincetown shortly thereafter, spent the last bunch of years bouncing around the Cape in accordance with Janice's varied environmental gigs. They loved the Cape and were going to stay forever, grow old, would you still need me, feed me, and the rest of the tune, happily ever after. . . .

Margaret is slapping me in the face, shouting. "What's wrong with you? Are you asleep? Wake up."

Patty hangs on her sister's arm, the nonslapping arm. "Stop it, Margaret, you'll hurt him!"

"I'm awake. I wasn't asleep. Jesus! Stop hitting me!" The old and familiar embarrassments swell, filling me with anger and hate for everyone, myself included. Makes me want to lash out, lie, share my poison with anyone around me. God help the person who finds my continued degradations and humiliations funny.

The twin aunts retreat to the kitchen, arm in arm, their cranky-hipped limps fitted together like the gears in a dying perpetual motion machine. Janice crouches at my feet. She says, "Are you okay? You just slumped in your chair. It looked like you passed out."

"I'm fine, I'm fine." I stand up, stumble a bit, but get my legs under me. I rub my face with my hands. If I could take my face off, I would.

Janice stands next to me, her hand on my elbow. It's a light touch, and comforting, but it's all I can do not to flinch and pull myself away. The twins come back. Margaret sits on the swing and has the cordless phone in her hand. Patty has a glass of water, which I assume is for me, until she takes a sip.

I swallow some air, willing the oxygen to do its goddamn job and keep me working right. "Sorry, I'm narcoleptic." I say it under my breath, the words cower and hide, and hope that only Janice hears my quick and unexpected confession.

Margaret says, "What?" Of course she heard me. She says it loud, like she's responding to a lie. This is not a lie.

I say, "I have narcolepsy." That's it. No explanation.

Patty appears at my left side like a spirit. "You poor dear. Drink this." There's lipstick on the glass. My job is so glamorous.

I say, "Please, everyone sit back down. I'm fine. It happens all the time and I know how to deal with it. I know how to live with it." I give back the community water. The women stare and investigate me. My status changing from potentially dangerous intruder to vulnerable afflicted person might just help my cause here.

I say, "Look. My narcolepsy is why I need to ask you questions, Janice. When Brendan came to my Southie office I fell asleep, like I did here, but not exactly like I did here because I probably looked awake to Brendan, did some sleep-talking and -walking like I do sometimes: automatic behavior, they call it." I stop talking and wave my hands in front of my own face, cleaning up the mess of words. "Anyway, I was out when he was in and all I've been able to piece together is that Brendan wanted me to find something, something that relates to my father and the DA." I pause and point at the picture again. It pays to have props. "I don't know what it is I'm supposed to find because I was asleep, and Brendan died before I could find out."

There. It's out. The truth as I know it and I feel fine. Everyone blinks at me a few times and I hear their eyelids opening and closing.

Margaret talks first. She says, "He's faking. Be careful, Janice."

Patty slaps her sister's hand.

Janice curls up her face and says, "Oh, be quiet, Margaret."

Margaret looks at me and shrugs, like we're commiserating, like I'm supposed to agree with her can-you-believe-these-knuckleheads-are-buying-what-you're-selling look. Can't say I'm all that fond of Aunt Margaret.

I say, "So, Janice, I assume you didn't know Brendan came to South Boston and hired me."

She says, "I knew he made a day trip to Boston, but I didn't know anything about you."

I nod. "I did talk with Brendan one other time. Is this a smoke-free house? Do you mind if I smoke?" My timing has always been impeccable.

Janice shakes her head and is now exasperated with me. "Yes. I mean, no, you can't smoke in here. When did you talk to Brendan?"

I can't tell her it was the day before he died. It won't help anyone, especially me. I say, "A couple of days after his visit he called to check on my progress. Because I'm stubborn, I didn't come right out and admit to him that I slept through our face-to-face. I didn't ask him what I was supposed to find. I hoped during our phone conversation that those details of the case would just, you know, present themselves."

Margaret says, "I take it back. He's not faking. He's just a buffoon." She sets off another family brouhaha. Yeah, all this because of little old me. Janice clears the room of the battling aunts, banishing them to the kitchen.

When Janice returns to her seat on the swing, I say, "The important or odd part of our phone conversation was that Brendan seemed agitated, even paranoid. Does that mean anything to you?"

Janice turns on me quick and says, "No, that's not the important part." She leans closer to me and enunciates her words, sharpening them to a cutting point. "Brendan, my husband, killed himself, shot himself in the face with a gun. He was downstairs, in our basement just a few days ago when he pulled the trigger. Your saying he was agitated and paranoid on the phone is not a surprise and certainly not the important part to me."

"I'm sorry. You're right. I'm sorry." I cannot say I'm sorry to her enough. I reach inside my coat and pull out the envelope. I'm careful to remove only one of the photos, the one with clothes. "While Brendan was there, the narcoleptic me managed to take some notes. Those are gone. Most of it was gibberish, but I'd written down South Shore Plaza. Do you know what that means? Brendan left me with this photograph, and I'm supposed to find something else, but obviously I haven't found it yet."

"South Shore Plaza means nothing to me. Brendan hated malls, wouldn't go in them if he could help it." Janice takes the picture, looks at it quick, and then looks away, like the photo might burn. "Who is she?"

"I don't know."

Janice looks at it again. "She looks a little like the *American Star* girl. The DA's daughter, right?"

I smile, and it doesn't feel right on my face. "It does look like her. But it's not her."

"No. I know. The photo is clearly older than she is."

I say, "Yes. Of course. Clearly. There was never any doubt."

"It does look a lot like her. Kind of spooky, in a way."

"Uncanny." I'm just going to agree with everything she says.

"Why did Brendan have this? Why did he give this to you?"

"I don't know, Janice. Like I said, he came to me to find something else. Not a person. An *it*."

She nods, even though I'm only answering her rhetorical questions, questions about her husband that will haunt her for the rest of her life because there might be no answers forthcoming. I don't know if she realizes that yet. Or maybe she does, and she's tolerating my presence with a staggering amount of dignity. Maybe she can share some dignity with me.

I say, "I'm sorry, but I have to ask this, Janice. Did Brendan act strangely, do anything out of character, say anything odd in the days before he died?"

"You mean besides going to South Boston and hiring a private investigator?"

I don't say anything or do anything. I know that much, at least.

Janice loses herself again in the photo, the piece of her husband's past that has no place here, even though I'm trying to find it.

Finally, Janice says, "That girl on *American Star*. What's her name?"

"Jennifer Times."

"Right. Jennifer Times." Another pause, drinking in more of the photo; then she gives it back. "Brendan and I both watched the show together when this season started, but he stopped watching once they started picking the finalists. I feel like I remember him leaving the room when that local girl, Jennifer, was performing." Janice isn't looking at me but off into some corner of the porch, seeing those final days she shared with her husband. She's not talking to me now, either. She's talking to herself, trying to find her own answers.

"There was a night when Brendan came into the room with two glasses of wine, sat down next to me on the couch, but stood up and left as soon as he saw the show was on. He said something about how dumb it was, and that was strange because up until a week or two before, he was watching with me. We liked to make fun of the really bad singers.

"But I remember when he left the room it was Jennifer on the TV; she was singing. Brendan went into the kitchen, still talking to himself. He talked to himself quite a bit. He was a truck driver, and he said truck drivers talked to themselves a lot, even when they were talking to other people. I never told him, but I loved that about him and eavesdropped on him whenever I could. I'd feel guilty after, like I was reading a diary, but I still did it.

"He was in the kitchen, talking away." Janice pauses. "Sorry, but this is hard. I've been thinking about nothing but him for days now, and it's not getting any easier."

"Perfectly understandable."

Janice nods. Her eyes are wide and she's still not here. She's back at that night with Brendan, listening to him in the kitchen. Maybe this is what it was like for Brendan that day in the office, when he was talking to me and I wasn't there.

I say, "Did you hear what Brendan was saying in the kitchen?" I keep still, don't move in my seat, not even a wiggled pinky.

Janice says, "He was muttering and wasn't very loud. I didn't hear much. I got up and tiptoed to the doorway, like I usually did when I caught him talking to himself." She stops and smiles, but it falls apart, and I think she might start crying and never stop but she doesn't. She goes on. "I didn't hear much, just snippets, nothing that made a whole lot of sense, so I walked into the kitchen. He was leaning on the kitchen island, talking and sipping his wine. When he saw me he smiled. I don't think he expected me to be there, but he smiled anyway. I walked over to him, gave him a kiss on the cheek, and thanked him for the wine. He said, 'Anytime,' squeezed my shoulder real quick, and I left him there, in the kitchen."

Janice sinks into the swing seat, slouching into the large green cushion. She's probably done, but I'm not moving. I won't move until I get what I need. I say, "When he was talking to himself, do you remember any phrases or words? Anything?"

Janice looks at me and covers her face with her hands. I know the feeling. She is done. She's going to tell me she doesn't remember anything else and that's it. She'll ask me, politely, to leave.

Then she sits upright again, her hands drop, and she says, "Yes. I think he said something about film, or more film."

My leg shakes, bobs up and down, tries to walk out of the room on its own. Is it more photos, then? An undeveloped roll, or more negatives, the rest of Tim's bedroom shoot? Maybe the rest of the pictorial includes more nudes, maybe the same girl, maybe a different girl, and I bet this missing portfolio includes some juicy eight-by-tens of Brendan and Billy Times, juicy enough to make the DA dangerously cranky. I say, "More film."

Janice nods. She wraps her arms around her chest, looks out the window, sits back in the swing seat, and sways. She says, "I have your card, Mark. I'll call you in a few days or a week. I need to know how this ends up."

I don't have to say anything, but I do. "Call me anytime. Thank you, Janice, you've been very helpful. And again, I'm so incredibly sorry about Brendan." I'm not going to tell her about the DA and his goons. I can't tell her it might be my fault that Brendan is dead. Not now, anyway. I need to finish this case first. There'll be time for the recriminations later.

Janice says, "Thanks. So am I."

It's past time to go. I get up and walk out of the porch, and I walk out fast, or as fast as I can handle. The twin aunts sit in the kitchen, huddled in two chairs they positioned near the breezeway entrance into the porch. They're whispering and they don't stop whispering as I walk by. Margaret has the phone in her hand, fingers hovering over buttons that spell 9-1-1. I'm sure they heard everything.

I say, "The pleasure was all mine. Don't get up, I can find the front door." I touch the brim of my hat for a faux tip, but the lid doesn't move, not for anyone.

Patty says, "Good luck." At least, I think it's Patty. I'm already out of the kitchen and through the dining room, where it's dark, so dark I can't really see, and I walk into the table shins first. Ow. The hutch and its china shakes. Nothing broken.

I right the ship, feel my way past the table, and find the front hallway and door. There are small curtained windows in the door-frame. My bull's charge through the dining room notwithstanding, I'm going to be as careful and cautious as I can the rest of the way. I know I'm close. I pull back the curtains for a little peek-a-boo.

The red car is outside. Can't say I'm surprised.

TWENTY-SIX

The red car idles in front of the gravel driveway. No, it's not idling, it's crawling, and it crawls by the house and down the road. They know I'm here. Maybe they planted some sort of homing device on me. I'm the endangered animal that needs to be tagged and tracked.

Or it's possible they don't know I'm here and they're just checking to see who's hanging at chez Sullivan. I didn't see the red car when I was in Brill's cab. Of course Brill could've spilled my beans for their twenty bucks. He strikes me as an equal opportunity kind of guy.

I take out my cell phone and dial. One ring and Brill answers. "Town Taxi, how can I help you?"

"Brill, it's me, Genevich. Can you pick me up on Rambler Road?"

He sighs. It doesn't sound nervous or guilty, just that he's pissed off to have to do his job. "Christ, where do you want to go now?"

The red car drives by again, in the opposite direction. It's moving faster, almost but not quite a normal, leisurely, obey-the-suburban-speed-limit pace. Then it's gone. I say with a mock British accent, "Home, James. Where else? Home."

Brill hangs up. I choose to believe that means he's coming to get me.

Voices from the kitchen: "Everything okay, Mark? Who are you talking to?"

I say, "I'm fine. Just calling a cab. He'll be here any minute. 'Bye and thanks." The weather is tolerable, it'd be hard to explain me standing inside, nose buried in the curtains by the front door, so I go outside, close the door gently behind me. Thinking better of sitting on the steps, in plain view of Rambler Road, I walk down the gravel driveway and conceal myself behind the blue SUV. Hopefully no one in the house is watching.

I go fishing for a cigarette and find one. It lights like it has been waiting for this moment all its life. I think about the red car and the goons. Are they planning another drive-by? Maybe they're getting the jump on my next destination. They'll be sitting in Ellen's kitchen when I get there, keeping the light on for me. They trashed my office and apartment, what's to say they won't do the same to the bungalow or to me? Nothing, far as I can tell.

Maybe I'm asking the wrong questions. I should be asking why haven't they ransacked the bungalow already? Would it look too fishy for break-ins and house-trashings to be following me around? Maybe they're not on such comfortable footing down here, away from the DA's stomping grounds. Didn't seem to bother them in Brendan's case, though. Maybe they're tired of looking for *it*, whether *it* is an undeveloped roll or a set of incriminating pictures, and they'll be happy just to deal with me after I do the grunt work for them.

Either or any way, doesn't matter to me anymore. What matters is that I have to find the goods before they find me again.

A car horn blasts two reports. That, or someone is trying to ride a goose sidesaddle. Brill's here. He beeps again. I step out from behind the SUV. He rolls down the passenger-side window and yells, "Come on, get in the goddamn car. We ain't got all day."

I say, "Ain't it the truth."

He says, "Did you get what you needed?"

"I was only offering my condolences and my flowers to the widow." I shouldn't be smug, but I am.

"Right. You didn't find shit."

I sit in Brill's backseat, and my ass picks up a strip of duct tape, which is just what my ass needs. I say, "The Genevich bungalow, Brill. You know where that is, right?"

He does. He drives down Rambler Road. According to my cell phone it's only 12:30. My cell phone doesn't tell lies. Ellen won't be home for another four hours, at least.

Brill pulls out onto the main drag. The library is just ahead. I try to turn around to see if anyone is tailing. I shift my weight in the seat and there's a loud and long ripping sound.

Brill says, "Goddamn it, you're tearing my seat apart!"

"Don't get your Depends in a bunch. It's your duct tape sticking to my ass like it's in love." I keep turning around, looking for the red car, and the duct tape keeps stripping off and clamping onto me.

He says, "Jesus Christ, stop moving around! What do you think you're doing back there anyway? It's going to take me the rest of the afternoon to fix that up right."

"Nothing. Just admiring the scenery." I stop moving, mostly because my legs are practically taped together. "Hey, did you see a red car today, earlier, when you were driving around?"

Brill's eyes get big. The wrinkles animate and release the hounds of his eyes. He says, "Yeah. It followed me to Rambler Road."

"No kidding." This isn't good. This—

Brill blows air through his lips, spitting laughter. Then it's out full. It's a belly laugh, a thigh-slapper. I'm not so amused. He says, "You are one sad sack, Genevich. Oooh, a red car, watch out for the red car! Ha! That's quite a gift for description you got there. You must solve all kinds of cases with those detailed detective powers of yours."

"All right, all right. Forget it."

"No, no, it's a good question. Except for holidays and a week off here and there, I've been driving around town ten hours a day, seven days a week for forty years, but I have never, ever, seen a red car on the road, not a one, until today. Man, I'm so glad you're on the case."

Brill laughs it up some more. I just might introduce my knuckles to the back of his head. He wheezes and chuckles until he drops me off at the bungalow. I don't tip. Let's see if he finds that funny.

He drives away. I'm here. I'm at the bungalow. And I know it's here. The rest of the film has to be here, if it's anywhere.

The sky has gone gray, the color of old newspapers. There's no red car in the driveway or anywhere on the block, but that doesn't mean the goons aren't inside. I have no weapon, no protection. I could grab something out of the shed, I suppose, but I don't know the finer points of Zen combat with pruning shears, and in the tale of the tape, trowels and shovels don't measure favorably when going against guns.

Play it straight, then. The front door is locked and intact. All the windows are closed. I peek inside a few, cupping my hands around my face. It's dark inside, but nothing seems out of place. I walk around to the backyard. It doesn't take me long. The house could fit inside my jacket. I hear the rain landing on my hat before I feel it.

I backdoor it into the kitchen. Everything is how we left it this morning: newspapers on the table, coffee mugs and toast crumbs on the counter. It's quiet, and I hope it stays that way. I won't turn on any lights, pretend I'm not here. It'll be easy.

Start at the beginning, the kitchen. I'll be thorough and check everything and everywhere: under the sink, between and behind pipes, the utensil and utility drawers. Maybe the film is hiding in plain view, just like Tim's photos on the walls, I don't know. There's a finite amount of space here in the old homestead; those family secrets can't stay hidden forever.

I look in the cabinets below the sink, past the pots and pans, the small pair of cabinets above the refrigerator that Ellen can't reach without a stool and neither can I. There's nothing but old phone books, a dusty bottle of whiskey, and books of matches, but I still push on the panels and wooden backings, seeing if anything will pop out or away, secret passages and hiding spots. I don't find any. The kitchen is clear.

The dining room and living room are next. Closets full of winter coats and dresses in plastic bags. No film. I move furniture and throw rugs, test for loose slats by rapping my foot on the floor. I go to my hands and knees and feel along the perimeters of the baseboards. Nothing and nothing. It's getting warm in here. My coat comes off, and the picture of Tim, Sullivan, and the DA goes back in its spot on the windowsill. It wasn't missed.

The guest room is next. There's only one closet and all it holds are two wooden tennis racquets, my old baseball glove—the one I pretend-signed with Carney Lansford's signature—four misshapen wire hangers, outdated board games that I open and rifle through, and empty luggage. The white suitcase and bag are as old as I am. I move the bed and bureau out, repeat my floor-and-baseboard checks, and find nothing.

It's all right. The nothing, that is. The first three rooms are only preludes, dry runs, practice searches for the real test. Ellen's room and the basement.

Ellen's room was their room. There are black-and-white photos on the walls, and they look to be half-and-half Tim pictures and antique finds. The Tim pictures are all of me, ranging in age from newborn to five years old. I'm in the pictures, but they're all someone else's memories, not mine. There's only one picture where Ellen shares the scene with me. It's a close-up and our faces are pressed together with Ellen in profile, hiding her smile behind one of my perfect chubby cheeks. My cheeks are still chubby.

No time for that. I do the bed and rug/floor check first, then the baseboard. I have a system, and I am systematically finding nothing. Then comes the nightstand, and I find her address book and flip through it. Nothing sinister, everything organized, all the numbers have a name. None of the names are Sullivan. Take that, Brill.

Next up, her antique wooden trunk that holds sweaters and sweatshirts, then her dresser, and, yes, I'm going through her dresser, and I have to admit that I fear finding personal items that I don't want to find, but I can't and won't stop now. Underwear drawer, shirt drawer, pants and slacks, bras, and all clear.

Her closet is a big one, the biggest one in the house. It must be in the closet somewhere. I remove all the hanging clothes and place them on the bed. Then I pull out all the shoes from the floor and the shelves, along with hatboxes and shoeboxes, most of them empty, some of them trapping belts and scarves, tacky lapel pins and brooches, general shit Ellen never wears. No clown pants in here.

The back of the closet is paneled and some of the panels hang loose. I pull up a few but find only plaster. To the left, the closet goes deeper, until the ceiling tapers down, into the floor. There are stacks of cardboard boxes and I pull those out. One box holds tax and financial information, the other boxes are assorted memorabilia: high school yearbook, plaques, track-meet ribbons, unframed pictures, postcards. No rolls of film, no pictures.

I put everything back. It's 2:25. My back hurts and my legs are stiffening up, revolting against further bending against their will.

On the way to the basement, I do a quick run through the bathroom. I look inside the toilet tank, leaving no porcelain cover unturned. Then back to the kitchen, and it's grab a flashlight and pound the stairs down into the basement.

The basement, like the house, is small, seemingly smaller than the bungalow's footprint, though I don't know how that's possible.

The furnace, washer, and dryer fill up an alcove. There's less clutter than I expected down here. There's a pair of rusty bed frames leaning against the foundation walls, a set of metal shelves that hold a mish-mash of forgotten tokens of home ownership, and an old hutch with empty drawers. It looks like Ellen was down here recently, organizing or cleaning. I check the exposed ceiling beams and struts; the take-home prizes are spiderwebs and dead bugs, but no film.

A tip, an edge, of panic is starting to poke me in the back of the head, now that I haven't found it yet. The bungalow doesn't want to let go of its secrets.

Back to the alcove. Behind and above the washer and dryer is a crawl space with a dirt floor. I climb up and inside I have to duck-walk. Not wild about this. Dark, dirt floor, enclosed space: there's a large creepiness factor, and it's very easy to imagine there are more than metaphorical skeletons stuffed or buried here.

I find a Christmas-tree stand, boxes of ornaments and table-cloths, and one of my old kiddie Halloween costumes, a pirate. Christ. Everywhere I turn in the damn house is stuff that doesn't need to be saved, but it's there, like a collection of regrets, jettisoned and almost but not quite forgotten.

I use the flashlight to trace the length of the dirt floor into the corners and then, above me, on the beams and pipes. The film is not here. Is it buried? I could check, get a shovel and move some dirt around, like some penny-ante archaeologist or grave robber. Indiana Jones, I'm not. Goddamn, that would take too long. Time is my enemy and always will be.

Maybe the missing film isn't here. Maybe the DA and his goons already found it in my apartment or the office with their quaint search-and-seizure operation; it would explain why they haven't torn this place apart. But that doesn't work. Ellen's parents were still alive and living in the building when Tim died. He wouldn't have hidden film at their place. Even if he did hide it there, too much work and change has happened to the interior of the building in the intervening years. The years always intervene. It would've been found.

It could be anywhere. It could've been destroyed long ago, purposefully or accidentally. It could be nowhere. Or it's here but it's lost, like me. Being lost isn't the same as being nowhere. Being lost is worse because there's the false hope that you might be found.

I crawl out onto the washing machine ass first. I'm a large load, wash in warm water. Brush myself off and back upstairs to the kitchen. I sit heavily at the table with the newspapers. I want a cigarette but the pack is in my coat and my coat is way over in the other room. My legs are too heavy. My arms and hands are too heavy. If I could only get around without them, conserve energy, throw the extra weight overboard so I could stay afloat. Can't get myself out of the chair. You never get used to the total fatigue that rules your narcoleptic life, and it only gets more difficult to overcome. Practice doesn't make perfect.

TWENTY-SEVEN

The sun shines bright, just like the ones in cartoons. Cartoon suns sing and wink and have toothy smiles. Do we really need to make an impossibly massive ball of fire and radiation into our cute little friend?

Tim and I are in our backyard. Everything is green. It's the week-end again. Tools go back in the shed, but he keeps the hand trowel, the special one. We've all done this before.

Tim is still in the shed putting things away. I take a peek inside. Along with the sharp and toothy tools are bottles of cleaners and chemical fertilizers, their labels have cartoon figures on them, and they wink at me, ask me to come play. I remember their commercials, the smiley-faced chemical suds that scrub and sing their way down a drain and into our groundwater. Oh, happy days.

Tim closes the shed doors and locks them, even though he'll just have to unlock them again later. A loop of inefficiency. The doors are newly white, like my baby teeth. I can't go inside. He tells me I'm too young, but maybe I just don't know the secret password. There are so many secrets we can't keep track of them. We forget them and shed them like dead skin.

I stand next to the doors. The doors are too white. Brown paper bag. Pat on my head. Good boy. It's time to clean up the yard, again and again and again.

The sky is such a light shade of blue, it looks like water, and it shimmers. I don't much feel like singing for Tim today, but I will. He'd be devastated if I didn't.

I sing the old standard, "Take Me Out to the Ball Game." Tim switches the lyrics around and I put them back where they belong. It makes me tired. It's hot and the poop bag gets full. Tim never runs out of names for the dogs, the sources of the poop. We never see the dogs, so he might as well be naming the dog shit, but that wouldn't be a fun or appropriate game.

We dump the poop in its designated and delineated area, over the cyclone fence and into the woods behind the shed. It smells back here. As he dumps the bag, Tim says, "Shoo, fly, shoo."

We walk around to the front of the shed and Tim opens the doors. It's dark inside and my eyes need time to adjust. Tim says, "So, kid, whaddaya think?"

My hands ball up into tiny fists, no bigger than hummingbirds' nests. The five-year-old me is pissed off and more than a little depressed that Tim was the photographer for those pictures, and for more pictures I can't find, some film that is a terrible secret and resulted in the death of his friend Brendan. Say it ain't so, Tim.

I say, "Where's the film? Who is she, Tim?"

Tim laughs, he loves to laugh, and he bends to one knee and chucks my chin with his fist, so fucking condescending. I should bite his knuckle or punch him in the groin, but I'm not strong enough.

Tim says, "I don't know and I don't know." He gets up and moves to lock the shed doors, but I make my own move. I jam my foot between the doors so they can't shut. I'm my own five-year-old goon, and my will is larger than the foot in the doors.

I say, "Who are you?"

Tim looks around, as if making sure the coast of our yard is clear, and says, "You don't know, and you never will."

He lifts me up when I'm not looking. I am all bluff and so very easy to remove from the doors. There's always next time. Tim puts me on his shoulders. I land roughly; my little body slams onto his stone figure. A sting runs up my spine and makes my extremities tingle. It hurts enough to bring tears.

I'm too high up, too close to that cartoon sun, which doesn't look or feel all that friendly anymore. My skin burns and my eyes hide in a squint that isn't getting the job done. The five-year-old has an epiphany. The cartoon sun is why everything sucks.

Tim walks with me on his shoulders. I'm still too high up. I wonder if he knows that I could fall and die from up here.

Twenty-eight

Full body twitch. A spasm sends my foot into the kitchen table leg. The table disapproves of being treated so shabbily and groans as it slides a few inches along the linoleum. My toes aren't crazy about the treatment either. Can't please anyone.

I'm in the kitchen and I'm awake. Two states of being that are not constant and should probably not be taken for granted. As a kid, I thought the expression was *taken for granite*, as in the rock. I still think that makes more sense.

All right. Get up. I go to the fridge and keep my head down because I do not want to look out the kitchen window, out in the backyard. I need to let the murk clear from my latest and greatest little sleep, to burn the murk away like morning fog before I'll allow a eureka moment. I don't want to jinx anything, not just yet. It's 3:36.

I make a ham and cheese on some whole-grain bread that looks like cardboard with poppy seeds. Tastes like it too. Everything sticks to the roof of my mouth. I eat one half of the sandwich and start the other half before I let myself look out into the backyard.

There it is, the answer as plain as my crooked face. Down at the bottom of the slanted yard: the shed. The missing film is hidden in the shed. It has to be.

I finish the sandwich and gulp some soda straight from the two-liter bottle. What Ellen doesn't know won't gross her out. Then I go into the living room for my jacket, my trusty exterior skin, and then to the great outdoors.

The sun is shining. I won't look at it because it might be the cartoon sun. I light a cigarette instead. Take that, cartoon sun. I ease down the backyard's pitch.

The shed has gone to seed. It's falling apart. Because of the uneven and pitched land, the shed, at each corner, sits on four stacks of cinder blocks of varying heights. The back end is up a couple of feet off the ground. The shed sags and tilts to the left. A mosquito fart could knock it to the ground. My ham-and-cheese sandwich rearranges itself in my stomach.

The roof is missing shingles, a diseased dragon losing its scales, tar paper and plywood exposed in spots. The walls need to be painted. The doors are yellowed, no longer newly white, just like my teeth. Looks like the doors took up smoking. The one window is covered with dust and spiderwebs. It's all still standing, though. Something to be said for that.

The shed was solely Tim's domain. Ellen is a stubborn city dweller with no interest in dirt or growing things, other than the cosmetic value live grass supposedly gives to her property. Ellen does not mow or rake or dig or plant. Even when I was a kid and we had no money, she hired landscapers to take care of the yard and they used their own equipment, not the stuff that has been locked in the shed for twenty-five years. After Tim died, the shed stayed locked. It was always just a part of the yard, a quirk of property that you overlooked, like some mound left by the long-ago glacial retreat.

The shed doors have a rusted padlock as their neglected sentinel. It has done the job and now it's time to retire. I wrap my hand around the padlock and it paints my hand with orange, dead metal. The lock itself is tight, but the latch mechanism that holds the doors closed hangs by loose and rusted screws. Two quick yanks and it all comes apart in my hand. The doors open and their hinges complain loudly. Crybabies.

Might as well be opening a sarcophagus, with all the dust and decay billowing into my face. One who dares disturb this tomb is cursed with a lungful of the stuff. I stagger back and cough a cough that I refuse to blame on my cigarettes.

I take a step inside. The floorboards are warped, forming wooden waves, but they feel solid enough to hold me. There's clutter. The years have gathered here. Time to empty the sucker. Like I said before, I'm not screwing around anymore.

I pull out rakes and a push mower, which seems to be in decent shape despite the long layoff. Ellen could probably sell it in her antiques store. Shovels, a charcoal grill, a wheelbarrow with a flat tire, extra cyclone fencing, bags of seed, fertilizer, beach toys, a toddler-sized sled, a metal gas can, an extra water hose, empty paint cans and brushes. Everything comes off the floor and into the yard. There's a lot of stuff, but it doesn't take long to carry it outside. The debris is spread over the grass; it looks like someone is reconstructing a Tim airplane after it crashed.

Shelves on the side walls hold coffee cans full of oily rags, old nails, washers, and screws. There's nothing taped underneath those shelves. The shed has no ceiling struts like the basement did, but I do check the frame, the beams above the door. Empty.

The rear of the shed has one long shelf with all but empty bottles of windshield washer fluid, antifreeze, and motor oil. Underneath the long plank of wood is a section of the rear wall that was reinforced with a big piece of plywood. There are nails and hooks in the plywood. The nails and hooks are empty, nothing hangs, but it looks like there's some space or a buffer between the plywood and the actual rear wall of the shed, certainly room enough for a little roll of film, says me.

How much space is there? I knock hard on the plywood, wanting to hear a hollow sound, and my fist punches through its rotten surface, out the rear wall of the shed, and into the sunlight. Whoops. I pull my bullying fist back inside unscathed. There's less space between the plywood and wall than I thought, and it's all wet and rotted back there, the wall as soft as a pancake from L Street Diner.

Ellen won't notice the fist hole in the wall, I don't think. When does she ever go behind the shed? I try to pry off more of the plywood, but another chunk of the back wall comes with it.

Dammit. I'll demolish the shed looking for the film, if I have to. Can't say I have any ready-made excuses to explain such a home improvement project to Ellen, though.

Take a step back. The floorboards squeak and rattle. Something is loose somewhere. I back up some more, pressing my feet down hard, and in the rear left corner of the shed, where I was just standing and punching a second ago, the flooring rises up and off the frame a little bit and bites into the crumbling plywood above it. Maybe X marks the spot.

I go back out onto the lawn and fetch a hand trowel. It might be the poop-scooping shovel of yore, it might not. It ain't Excalibur. I use the thing like a crowbar and pry up that rear corner until I can grab it with my hands. The floorboard isn't rotted; the wood is tougher and fights back. I have a tight grip on the corner, and I pull and yank and lean all my weight into it. There's a clank and the hand trowel is gone, falling into the gap and beneath the floor, making a suitable time capsule.

The wood snaps and I fall on my ass. The shed shakes and groans, and for a second I think it's going to come down on my head, and maybe that wouldn't be a bad thing. Maybe another knock on my head will set me straight, fix me up as good as new.

The shed doesn't come down. The shaking and groaning stops and everything settles back. My fingers are red, raw, and screaming, but no splinters. I squeeze my hands in and out of fists and walk toward the hole in the floor. The sun goes behind a cloud and everything gets dark in the shed.

I go into snake mode, crawl on my belly, and hover my face above the hole. I look down and see the ground and the hand shovel. Fuck it. Leave the shovel under the shed where it belongs. I don't need it to tear up more of the floorboards. My hands will do just fine.

Wait. There's a dark lump attached to one floor joint, a black barnacle, adjacent to the corner. I reach out a hand. I touch it: plastic. Two different kinds of plastic; parts feel like a bag and other parts feel more solid but still malleable. I jack my knees underneath my weight and the floorboard buckles and bows out toward the ground under the pressure, but I don't care. I need the leverage and both hands.

I lean over the dark lump; it's something wrapped in a garbage bag and duct-taped to the frame. My fingers get underneath, and it comes off with a quick yank. On cue, the sun comes out again. Maybe that cartoon sun is my friend after all.

Things get brighter and hotter in the shed. I move away from the hole and stand up. There's duct tape wound all around the plastic bag. I apply some even pressure and the inside of the package feels hard, maybe metal. Jesus Christ, my heart is beating, and—yeah, I'll say it—I am goddamn Indiana Jones, only I'm not afraid of snakes. If this thing were a football I'd spike it and do a little dance, make a little love. But I'm a professional. It's all about composure.

Through the plastic, I trace its perimeter. I'm Helen Keller, begging my fingers to give me the answers. It's shaped like a wheel, and it's too big to be a roll of film. It's a tin, or a canister, or a reel of film. A movie.

It gets darker inside the shed again, but the sunlight is still coming in through the punched-out hole in the back wall. My back is to the door and I feel their shadows brushing up against my legs. I've been able to feel their shadows on me since the first trip to Sullivan's house.

"Whaddaya say, Genevich?" says one goon.

"Jackpot!" says the other.

TWENTY-NINE

Looks like I was right about them choosing to wait me out, let me do all the heavy lifting. Seems to have worked out for them too. They get the gold stars, but I can't let them have the parting gift.

I turn around slowly, a shadow moving around a sundial. The two goons fill the doorway. They replace the open doors. They are mobile walls. The sun might as well be setting right behind them, or maybe one of them has the sun in his back pocket. I can't see their faces. They are shadows too.

One of them is holding a handgun, a handgun in silhouette, which doesn't make it look any prettier or any less dangerous. Its barrel is the proboscis of some giant bloodsucking insect. Its bite will do more than leave an itchy welt, and baking soda won't help.

I say, "If you're a couple of Jehovah's Witnesses, God isn't in the shed and I'm a druid."

"Looks like you're having a little yard sale. We thought we'd drop by, see what hunk of worthless junk I can get for two bucks," says Redhead. "Whaddaya say, Genevich? What can I get for my two bucks?" He's on the right. He's the one with the gun and it threatens to overload my overloaded systems. Things are getting fuzzy at the edges, sounds are getting tinny. Or it could be just the echoes and shadows in a small empty shed.

Even in silhouette, Redhead's freckles are visible, glowing future melanomas. Maybe if I keep him talking long enough he'll die of skin cancer. A man can hope.

Baldy joins in, he always does, the punch line to a joke that everyone sees coming. He says, "Two bucks? Nah, he'll ask for ten. He looks like a price gouger. Or maybe he's selling his stuff to raise money for charity, for other retards like him."

I'm not sure what to do with the plastic-wrapped package in my hands. They've seen it already. Hell, I'm holding it in front of my stomach, so I nonchalantly put it and my hands behind my back. Nothing up my sleeves.

I say, "What, you two pieces of shit can't read the KEEP OFF THE GRASS sign out there?"

They take a step inside the shed and have to duck under the doorframe to enter. The wood complains under their feet. I empathize with the wood. I did say I was a druid.

The goons take up all the space and air and light in the shed. Redhead says, "We're gonna cut the banter short, Genevich. You have two choices: we shoot you and take the movie or we just take the movie."

"And maybe we shoot you anyway," Baldy says.

I do register that they're confirming my find is in fact a movie, which is a plus, but I'm getting tingly again and the dark spots in my vision are growing bigger, ink leaking into a white shirt pocket. Come on, Genevich. Keep it together. I can't go out now, not now.

I shake my head and say, "That's no way to treat the gracious host. Bringing over a bottle of wine would've sufficed."

Redhead says, "We don't have manners. Sometimes I'm embarrassed for us. This isn't one of those times."

I say, "There's no way I'm giving you the flick. You two would just blab-blab-blab and ruin the ending for me." I don't think they appreciate how honest I'm being with them. I'm baring my soul here.

Baldy says, "Sorry, Genevich. We get the private screening."

They take another step forward; I go backward. We're doing a shed dance. I go back until the rear wall shelf hits me across the shoulders.

Redhead raises the gun to between-my-eyes level and says, "We do appreciate you clearing out a nice, clean, private space for your body. The way I see it, we shoot you, put all that crap back inside the shed, and no one will find you for days. Maybe even a week, depending on how bad the smell gets."

I say, "I didn't shower this morning and I sweat a lot."

Baldy says, "Give us the movie. Now."

That's right, I have the film, and until they get it, I have the upper hand. At least, that's what I have to fool myself into believing. I am a fool.

I can't move any farther backward, so I slide toward the right, to the corner, to where I found my prize and to the hole I punched through the back wall. The rotted plywood and wall are right behind me.

I say, "All right, all right. No need for hostilities, gentlemen. I'll give it to you." I pretend to slip into the floorboard hole, flail my arms around like I'm getting electrocuted. Save me, somebody save me! The movement and action feels good and clears my head some. I might be hamming it up too much, hopefully not enough to get me shot, but I don't want them watching my sleight of hand with the package, so I scuff and bang my feet on the floor, the sounds are percussive and hard, and then, as I fall to my knees in a heap, I jam the film inside my jacket, right next to the manila envelope. The photos and film reunited and it feels so good.

Redhead traces my lack of progress with his gun. He says, "Knock off whatever it is you're doing, Genevich, and stand up."

I say, "Sorry. Tripped. Always been clumsy, you know?" I hold out my empty hands. "Shit, I dropped the movie. I'll get it." I turn around slowly. I'm that shadow on the sundial again.

Baldy says, "Get away from there, I'll get it," but it sounds tired, has no muscle or threat behind it because I'm trapped in the corner of the shed with nowhere to go, right? Redhead hesitates, doesn't say anything, doesn't do anything to stop me from turning around.

My legs coil under me. My knees have one good spring in them. I'm aimed at the fist-sized hole in the wall and ready to be fired. I'm a piston. I'm a catapult.

I jump and launch shoulder first toward the plywood and the rear wall underneath the shelf, but my knees don't have one good spring in them. My feet fall into in the hole, lodge between the floor and the frame, and then I hit the plywood face first. The plywood is soft, but it's still strong enough to give me a good shot to the chops. There's enough momentum behind me and I bust through the shed and into the fading afternoon light. I'm a semisuccessful battering ram.

There's a gunshot and the bullet passes overhead; its sound is ugly and could never be confused with the buzz of a wasp or any living thing. The grass is more than a couple of feet below me. I tuck my chin into my chest, my hat falls off, and I dip a shoulder, hoping to land in some kind of roll. While dipping my shoulder, my body twists and turns, putting a tremendous amount of pressure on my feet and ankles; they're going to be yanked out of their respective sockets, but they come out of the corner. Upon release I snap forward, and land awkwardly on my right shoulder, planting it into the ground. There's no roll, no tens from the judges. My bottom half comes up and over my head into a half-assed headstand, only I'm standing on my shoulder and neck. I slide on the grass in this position, then fall.

There are two loud snaps, one right after the other. Breaking wood. I'm on my stomach and I chance a look back at the shed, instead of getting up and fleeing for my life. Most of the rear wall is gone, punched through, and the hole is a mouth that's closing. The roof is falling, Chicken Little says so. Yet despite the sagging roof, the shed is growing bigger, a deflating balloon somehow taking in more air and taking up more of my view. Wait, it's moving, coming right at me. The cinder blocks are toppling, and so is the propped-up shed.

The goons. They're yelling and there's a burst of frantic footsteps but those end suddenly. The curtain drops on their show. I might meet a similarly sudden fate if I don't move. The shed falls and roars and aims for me. I roll left, out of the way, but I go back for my hat. I reach out and grab the brim right as that mass of rotted wood and rusty nails crash-lands on the hat and my fingers are flea lengths away from being crushed. More stale dust billows into my face. All four walls have collapsed, the doors broken and unhinged. Just like that, the shed that stood forever is no more.

I yank my hat out from beneath the rubble. It has nine lives. I stand up and put the hat on. It's still good.

Most of my body parts seem to be functioning, though my face is wet. My fingers report back from the bridge of my nose; they're red with blood. No biggie. Just a scratch, a ding, otherwise good to go.

I have the film. The goons don't and they're under a pile of sub-urban rubble. I step over the cyclone fence and remake myself into a woodland creature. I give one last look behind me.

The backyard of the Genevich family plot has the appearance of utter devastation and calamity, the debris of Tim's life destroyed and strewn everywhere, spread out for everyone to see, should they care to. Secrets no more. Tim's stuff, the stuff that defined Tim for the entirety of my life, is nothing but so much rusted and collapsed junk, those memories made material are asleep or dead, powerless and meaningless, but not harmless.

I walk away from the damage into the woods, thinking that Ellen won't be pleased when she finds the shed. Hopefully, I'll be around long enough to improvise a story.

Thirty

I walk a mile, maybe two. Keep to the woods when I can, stay off the streets. When there aren't any woods, I cut through people's yards, stomp through bushes, trample on lawns, cross over driveways. I hide behind fences meant to keep riffraff like me out. I walk past their pools and swing sets. People are home, or coming home from work. They yell at me and threaten to call the police. But they don't, and I keep walking. Small children run away; the older ones point and laugh. I don't care. I wave them off, shooing away flies. I'm carrying the big secret. It gives me provenance to go where I need to go.

I'm hungry, thirsty, and tired. Not the same tired as usual, but more, with a little extra spice, a little kick. Buffalo tired, General

Gao tired. I can't do much more walking. The aches and minor injuries from the rumble and tumble with the shed are building, combining into a larger pain. They aren't inert.

I have no immediate destination in mind other than away from the goons and my house, just to go somewhere they won't find me. That's it. No more walking. I find two homes that have an acre or more of woods between them. I go back into hiding, but get the street name and address numbers first.

I call Brill, tell him where to pick me up. He says he'll be there in ten minutes. That's a good Brill.

Being the only cab in town during the off-season, this is a risk. Assuming the goons have emerged from the woodpile, they'll do all they can to get back on my trail. They'll figure out he's the only way around town for me, if they don't know that already. I have to chance it. I need one more ride from him.

I sit on a tree stump. The street is twenty yards away, far enough away that I can see the road, but I'll only be seen if someone stops and searches for me. I won't be seen from a quick drive-by.

I take the film—what I presume to be the film—out of my coat. The wrap job is tight. After an initial struggle to get the unraveling started, the layers of tape and plastic come off easy and fast, the way I like it. It's a canister of film, maybe six inches in diameter. I open the canister and there's a reel of celluloid. I lift it out like a doctor extracting shrapnel, or like I'm playing OPERATION, careful with that funny bone, can't touch the sides.

The film is tan and silky and beautiful, and probably horrible. It holds thousands of pictures, thousands of moments in time that fit together like the points in a line. It's getting dark in the woods and I try holding the film up to the vanishing light. There are shapes, but I can't make out much of anything.

I need equipment. Luckily, I know a film expert. She wears clown pants sometimes.

My cell rings. I dig it out of my pocket. I don't recognize the number, but it's the Boston area code.

"Hello."

"Hi, Mr. Genevich? It's me, Jennifer."

I look around the woods like she might pop out from behind a maple. I say, "What's wrong? Daddy doesn't know where I am?"

There's a beat or two of silence on the phone, long enough to make me think the call was dropped or she hung up. She says, "I'm sorry about what happened. I just thought my father was going to watch you, make sure you weren't dangerous or up to some crazy blackmail scam. That's all. I got your message and today I saw the break-in of your office and apartment in the paper. And I'm sorry, Mr. Genevich. Really, I didn't know he was going to do anything like that."

I'm in the middle of the woods, and I'm too tired to breathe. I want to sit down but I'm already sitting down. Not sure what to believe or who to believe, not sure if I should believe in myself.

I say, "On the obscure chance you're telling it straight, thanks."

"Why would my father do that?"

"No *would* about it. Did. He did it."

"Why did he break into your apartment? Was he looking for those pictures?"

I say, "Your father was looking for a film to go along with those pictures I showed you. The pictures are meaningless; they can't hurt anyone. But the film. The film is dangerous. The film can do damage."

"Do you have it?"

"Oh, yeah. I have it. I'm getting copies made right now. Going to send them to the local stations as soon as I get off the phone with you." Dressing up the truth with some bluff can't hurt, especially if she's trying to play me on behalf of DA Daddy again.

"Oh, my God! Seriously, what's on it?"

"Bad stuff. It's no Sesame Street video."

"Is it that girl who looks like me?"

"What do you think, Jennifer?"

"How bad is it?"

"One man is already dead because of it."

There's a beat of silence. "What? Who's dead?" Her voice is a funeral, and I know she believes me, every word.

"Brendan Sullivan. Police report says he shot himself in his Osterville home. He was the one who hired me, sent me the pictures, and wanted me to find the film. I found the film. Sullivan was a childhood friend of my father and your father. We're all in this together. We should all hold hands and sing songs about buying the world a Coke."

More silence. Then: "Mr. Genevich, I want to see it. Will you meet me and show it to me?"

"Now that sounds like crazy talk. Even assuming that I don't think you're trying to set me up again, I don't know why I would show you the film."

"I know and I'm sorry. Just listen to me for a sec. After our dinner, I couldn't stop thinking about those photos, and then when I heard about your apartment, it got worse, and I have such a bad feeling about all this, you know? I just need to know what happened. I promise I'll help you in any way I can. I need to see this. I'll come to your office and watch it. I can come right now. It won't take me long to get there."

Jennifer talks fast, begging and pleading. She might be sincere, but probably not. With the goons having lost my trail, the timing of her call just plain sucks. That said, the DA can't go to her well too often. She'll know too much.

How about I keep the possibilities open? I say, "We'll see. Need to finish getting copies made. Maybe I can offer you a late-night showing. I'll call you later." I hang up.

The cell phone goes back in my pocket. I need to chew on this for a bit. For such a simple action, watching a film, there are suddenly too many forks and branches and off-ramps and roadblocks and . . .

Three loud beeps shake me off my tree stump. I land in a crouch. A white car crawls along my stretch of woods, stops, then beeps again. It's my man Brill.

I try to gather myself quickly, but it's like chasing a dropped bundle of papers in a windy parking lot. I come crashing through the woods. The film is back inside my coat pocket. There's a moment of panic when I expect the goons to be in the backseat waiting for me, but it's empty. I open the door and slide in. The seat's been retaped, just for me.

Brill says, "I'm not even gonna ask how you got out here."

"That's mighty fine of you."

"I won't ask what happened to your face, either. But I hope it hurt like hell because it's killing me."

"Just a scratch. The perils of hiking through the woods, my man."

"All right. Where to, Sasquatch?"

I say, "That's actually funny. Congrats."

Let's try a change of destinations. I can't rely on Brill anymore, too risky. I say, "Take me to the nearest and dearest car rental agency. One that's open."

THIRTY-ONE

I'm leaned back into the seat, relaxed. I feel magnanimous in my latest small victory. Let Brill have his cheap shots. Let the people have cake. At least I feel magnanimous until I wake up, not on a sleepy Osterville road but in the parking lot of a car rental agency.

Brill is turned around. The old bastard has been watching me. His skeleton arm is looped around the back of his seat, and he shows me his wooden teeth. I suppose it's a smile. I didn't need to see that. I'll have nightmares the next time I pass out.

I say, "What are you smiling at?"

He says, "Your little nap made me an extra ten bucks. If I had any kids, you'd be putting them through college one *z* at a time."

I say, "I wasn't asleep. Making sure the lot and inside was all clear. Sitting here thinking. You should try it."

"You must've been doing some hard thinking with all that twitching and snoring." He laughs and coughs. Can't imagine he has much lung left.

I don't have a comeback for him, so I change the thrust of our departure conversation. "Nice tape job on the seats, Brill. You're first class all the way." I'm running low on cash. I have just enough to pay the grinning bag of bones.

Brill takes the bills. He says, "You here to rent a car?"

"No, I'm going to get my shoes shined and then maybe a foot massage. All that walking and my dogs are barking."

Brill turns back around, faces front, assumes the cabbie position. "You driving on my roads, any roads? That can't be legal."

I open my door. I don't have to explain anything to him, but I do. I say, "I have a driver's license and a credit card. I can drive a car. I'm sure the transaction will be quite easy. Wait for me here, we'll drag-race out of the lot. I'll let you be James Dean. You got the looks."

"No, thanks. I'm turning in early if you're going to be on the road." He revs the tiny four-cylinder engine. My cue to leave.

I get out. The lot is small and practically empty. The sun-bleached pavement is cracked and the same color as the overcast sky. Brill drives away. He's no fun.

Inside the rental agency, everything is bright yellow and shitty brown. There are cheery poster-sized ads hanging on the walls featuring madly grinning rental agents. Those madly grinning rental agents are at their desks but outside with a bright blue sky as their background. Apparently renting a car should be some sort of conversion experience for me. We'll see.

Before docking my weary ass at the service counter, I make a side trip to a small ATM tucked away between two mini–palm trees. I need to replenish the cash supply. First I do a balance check: $35.16. Been spending too much and it's been weeks since I had a paying client. I'll take out twenty. While patiently waiting to add the exorbitant transaction fee to my ledger, I check my reflection in the handy-dandy mirror above the ATM. There's dried blood on the right side of my nose and cheek. The shed hit me with a pretty good shot but I won by TKO in the fifth.

No other customers in the joint, so I'm up next at the counter.

The agent says, "Can I help you?" He's a kid, skinnier than a junkie. Greasy hair parted all wrong, shadow of a mustache under his nose.

I say, "I need a car. Nothing fancy. But if you have something that has bumpers, real bumpers with rubber and reinforced, I don't know, metal. Not those cheap plastic panels they put on the front and back of most cars now. Real bumpers."

The kid stares at me. I know, I'm pretty. The dried blood adds character to a face already overburdened with character. He probably thinks I'm drunk with my slow, deep voice and my sudden bumper obsession. I suppose I should've cleaned myself up in the bathroom first. Can't do much about my voice, though. I am what I am.

He snaps out of his trance and types fast, too fast. There's no way he's hitting the keys in any sort of correct order. He says, "The only vehicles we have with what you described are a couple of small pickup trucks and three SUVs."

"Nah, I hate trucks and SUVs. Too big." I don't want to hurt anyone more than I already might. "I want something compact, easy to drive." I know enough not to add, *Won't cause a lot of collateral damage.*

"Okay. We have plenty of compacts." He types again at warp speed. It's actually kind of impressive. Good for him for finding his niche at such a young age.

I say, "A compact, but something safe. Air bags and all that stuff, and maybe with bumpers."

"I'm sorry, sir, but we don't have any compacts or sedans with the bumpers you described."

"Right, right, you already told me that. Sorry. Oh, and it should have one of those GPS thingies for directions."

"Our vehicles all come equipped with GPS."

Fantastic. I give him my license and credit card. All is well. We will complete our vehicular transaction and there will be joy.

I look outside the bay windows. No sign of the goons. There's a slowly creeping thought, bubbling its way up through the murk, the remnants of my cab nap. And here it is: I forgot to ask Brill where he dumped me. I was asleep and have no idea if we're still in Osterville or not. There's a nondescript strip mall across the street from the agency. It looks like every strip mall on the Cape. It has a pharmacy, bank, breakfast joint, gift shop, and water sports store. Maybe we're in Hyannis.

Wait. I find a life jacket. There's a stack of business cards on the counter; I paw at a couple and spy the address. Okay, still in Osterville, at its edge, but I know where I am now.

I say, "Oh, if you haven't picked me a car already, can I get one that has a lot of distracting stuff going on inside?"

He doesn't look up from his computer. He knows that won't help him. "You mean like a CD player?"

I say, "That's okay too, but I'm thinking more along the lines of a car that has a busy dashboard, tons of digital readings, lights, and blinking stuff."

"You want to be distracted?"

"When you say it like that, it sounds a little silly, but yeah, that'd be swell."

"I think we can accommodate you, Mr. Genevich."

"You're a pro's pro, kid."

I relax. I know I'm making a fool of myself, but the looming situation of me behind a steering wheel has me all hot and bothered. I know it's irresponsible and dangerous, reckless, and selfish. Me behind the wheel of a car is putting Mr. and Mrs. Q. Public and their extended families in danger. But I'm doing it anyway. I can't wait to drive again.

I'm done with Brill. Renting a car is the only way I'm going to get around without further endangering Ellen, and hopefully it'll be less likely the goons will pick up my scent again. They know my condition, they've been following me around; they won't be expecting me to rent a car.

I tell the kid I want the car for two days. He quotes me the price and terms. I cross my fingers and hope there's enough room on my credit card. Then he says, "Will you be buying renter's insurance for the vehicle?"

I laugh. Can't remember the last time I laughed like this. This could be a problem. For many narcoleptics, laughter is a trigger for the Godzilla symptoms, the ones that flatten Tokyo. But I know where I am and I know what I'm doing and I know where to go next. I feel damn good even if my contorted face reopens the cut along my nose.

I say, "Oh, yeah, kid. I'll take as much insurance as you'll give me. Then double the order."

Thirty-two

My car is blue and looks like a space car. Meet George Jetson.

The kid has to show me how to start the thing, as it has no ignition key. Insert the black keyless lock/alarm box into a portal in the dash, push another dash button, and we're ready to go. Simple. The car is one of those gas-electric hybrids. At least I'll be helping out the environment as I'm crashing into shit. Hopefully I don't damage any wetlands or run over endangered owls or something similarly cute and near extinction.

Okay, I start the car up. My hands grip the wheel hard enough to remold the plastic, turn it into clay. White knuckles, dry mouth, the whole bit. I wonder what the air bag tastes like. Probably not marshmallow fluff.

I roll to the edge of the lot and onto the street, and I don't hit anything, don't pass out asleep, and the wheels don't fall off, so I relax a little bit. I join the flow of traffic, become part of the mass, the great unending migration, the river of vehicles, everyone anonymous but for a set of numbers and letters on their plates. My foot is a little heavy on the brake pedal, otherwise I'm doing fine. If millions of privileged stunted American lunkheads can operate heavy machinery, I can too. Driving is the easy part. It's staying awake that'll take some doing.

Yeah, I'm an accident waiting to happen, but I should be all right on a short jaunt into town. This first trip is only to downtown Osterville. It's the later excursion back to Southie that'll be my gauntlet.

I'm driving at the speed limit. I check all my mirrors, creating a little rotation of left sideview, rearview, right sideview, while sprinkling in the eyes-on-the-road bit. The OCD pattern might lull me to sleep so I change it up, go from right to left. I forgot how much you have to look at while driving, the proverbial everywhere-at-once. It's making me tired.

Of course, the roads are congested all of a sudden and out of nowhere. Did I run over a hive or something? Cars swarming and stopping and going and stopping. The town has been deader than the dinosaurs since I've been here, and all of a sudden it's downtown LA.

No signs of the red car, or at least one particular red car and its goons. I should've asked for a car with tinted windows so nobody could see me. I wasn't thinking. My windshield is a big bubble and I'm on display, behind glass; don't break in case of emergency.

Traffic stretches the ride out to fifteen minutes before I penetrate the downtown area. There's Ellen's photography studio/antiques store. The antiques side is dark. During the off-season, she only opens on Fridays and weekends. There are lights on in her studio, though, so she's still here. Not sure if that's a good thing or bad thing. I take a left onto a one-lane strip of pavement that runs between Ellen's building and the clothing boutique next door, and I tuck me and my rental behind the building. There's no public parking back here, only Ellen's car, a Dumpster, and the back doors.

I get out and try the antiques shop first. There are two large wooden doors that when open serve as a mini-bay for larger deliveries. The doors are loose and bang around in the frame as I yank on them, but they're locked. Damn. It's where I need to go and I don't have any keys.

Door number 2, then, the one I wanted to avoid. Up three wooden stairs to a small landing and a single door, a composite and newer than the antique doors, which is how nature intended. That's locked too. I'm not walking around out front on the off-chance the goons do a drive-by. I ring the bell. It doesn't ring. It buzzes like I just gave the wrong answer to the hundred-dollar question.

Footsteps approach the door and I panic. Ellen can't know that I drove here. I'm parked behind the Dumpster, my shiny space car in plain view. Crap. I try to fill the doorway with my bulk, but Ellen will be half a step above me, elevated. The door opens.

Ellen's wearing her clown pants again. She says, "Hey. What are you doing back here?"

I yawn and stretch my arms over my head, trying to block her view. For once, me being tired is schtick. I say, "I don't know. There

was a lot of traffic out front and Brill came back here to drop me off.
He's kind of a surly guy."

"Stop it. He's a sweetheart." Ellen is whispering and throwing
looks over her shoulder. "I've got a client and I'm in the middle of a
shoot. Go around front."

I say, "Come on, I'm here, my knees have rusted up, and I'm
dead tired. Let me in. Your client won't even notice me limp through."
I lay it on thick but leave out the pretty please.

She says, "Yeah, right," but steps aside, holds the door open, and
adds, "Just be quick."

"Like a bunny," I say. I shimmy inside the door, crowding her
space purposefully so she has a harder time seeing over me and into
the lot. I compress and crumple her clown pants. It's not easy being a
clown.

She says, "What the hell is that car doing back here?"

My hands go into my pockets. Instead of balls of lint and thread,
maybe I'll find a plausible excuse. I say, "Oh, some guy asked if he
could park there real quick. Said he was just returning something
next door. I told him it was fine." Lame story, but should be good
enough for now.

Ellen lets out an exasperated sigh. "If he's not out in five
minutes, I'm calling a tow truck. I can't have people parking back
here." She's all talk. She'll forget about the car as soon as the door is
shut. I bet.

Ellen leads me through a small back hallway and into the studio.
The background overlay is a desert and tumbleweeds, huge ones,
bigger than my car. A little kid is dressed up as a cowboy with hat,
vest, chaps, six-shooters, spurs, the whole bit. He must've just heard

the saddest campfire song ever because he's bawling his eyes out while rocking on a plastic horse.

Those UFO-sized photographer spot lamps are everywhere, warming the kid up like he's a fast-food burger that's been sitting out since the joint opened. I don't blame him for being a little cranky.

His mom yaks on her cell phone, sniping at someone, wears sunglasses and lip gloss shinier than mica, and has a purse bigger than Ellen's mural tumbleweed. It ain't the OK Corral in here.

I say, "Sorry to interrupt. As you were."

The little kid jumps at the sound of my voice, cries harder, and rocks the wooden pony faster, like he's trying to make a break for it.

I say, "Remember the Alamo, kid."

Ellen apologizes, puts on a happy face like it's part of her professional garb, something that hangs on a coatrack after work is over. She ducks behind her camera. "Come on, Danny boy, you can smile for me, right? Look at my pants!"

Yikes. I'm out of the studio, door closed behind me, and into her nondescript reception area. Ellen has a desk with a phone, computer, printer, and a buzzer. Next to that is a door to the antiques store. That's locked too. The doorknob turns but there's a dead bolt about chest high. I need me some keys. Don't want to have to see the clown pants and cowboy-tantrum show again. I go behind her desk and let my fingers do the walking through her drawers. I find a ring of ten or so keys.

Guess and check, and eventually the right key. I don't turn on the lights, as the store's bay window is large and I could easily be seen from outside. The afternoon is dying, but there's enough light in here that I can see where I'm going.

The antiques store is packed tight with weekend treasures: wooden barrels filled with barely recognizable tools that might've come from the dawn of the Bronze Age, or at least the 1940s; home and lawn furniture; kitschy lamps, one shaped like a hula girl with the shade as the grass skirt; fishing gear; a shelf full of dusty hardcover books; tin advertising placards. Piles of useless junk everywhere. If it's old, it's in here somewhere. I never understood the appeal of antiques. Some things are meant to be thrown away and forgotten.

The photography and film stuff has its own corner in the rear of the store. There's a display counter with three projectors under glass. Short stacks of film reels separate the projectors. Nice presentation. No price tags, but the specs and names of the projectors are written on pieces of masking tape that are stuck to the counters. The curling and peeling tape is in much worse condition than the projectors, which look to be mint.

All right. I assume the film is 8 millimeter, but I'm not exactly sure what projector I need to play it, and even if I had the right projector I don't know how to use it. I need Ellen's help. Again.

Out of the dusty store and back into the reception area, I stick my head inside the studio. Glamour Mom is still on the phone, talking directly to a Prada handbag maybe. The kid continues to wail. Ellen dances some crazed jig that pendulums back and forth behind her tripod. She makes odd noises with her mouth. A professional at work.

I say, "Hey, Bozo. I need your expertise for a second."

Under normal circumstances (maybe these are her normal circumstances, I don't know), I'd assume she'd be pissed at me for interrupting. She mumbles something under her breath that I don't quite hear, but it might be *Thank Christ.*

Ellen has to say, "Excuse me," three times before the woman puts down her phone. "Maybe we should try something else. I don't think Danny likes being a cowboy. Why don't we change him, let him pick something else out of that bin over there, and I'll be right back?"

The brat has worked her over pretty good, softened her up, and hopefully made her head mushy enough so she can't add one and one together. I need to take advantage and throw stuff at her quick.

Ellen has only one foot in the reception area and I'm sticking the film canister in her face. I say, "I just need a little help. This is eight-millimeter film, right? Or super eight? Or something else?"

Ellen blinks a few times, clearly stunned after trying to wrangle Danny the Kid into an image. She says, "Let me see."

I open the can and let a six-inch tail grow from the spool. She reaches for it. I say, "Don't get your grubby fingerprints on it."

"I need to see the damn thing if I'm going to tell you what it is." I give it to her, ready to snatch it back out of her hands should she hold it up to the light and see something bad. "This isn't super eight, it's too dark. Eight millimeter." She gives it back, yawns, and stretches. "My back is killing me. Where'd you get that?"

I don't answer. I say, "I need a projector. I need to watch this. Got anything I can borrow?"

"Yeah, I have projectors. Silent or sound?"

"I don't know. Do you have one that plays both?"

I take her by the arm and lead her into the store. She doesn't turn on the lights. What a good clown.

Small key goes into small lock, and the glass slides open to the left. "This one will play your movie, sound or no sound. It's easy to use too."

I read the tape: Eumig Mark-S Zoom 8mm magnetic sound projector.

She picks it up, shuts the glass case, and rests it on the counter. It's a mini-robot out of a 1950s sci-fi flick, only the earth isn't standing still.

She says, "Let me finish up the shoot and I can set up the projector in here. I've got a screen in the closet."

"No, I can't watch it here. This film, it's for a client. Just need to make sure what's in the can is the real deal, that it's what I think it is. No one else but me can see it."

"Why? Where did you get it?"

"Sorry. Secrets of state. I can't tell you."

"Wait. What client? How have you had any contact with a client since we've been down here?"

I think about the backyard and demolished shed. She'll know where I found it.

I hold out my cell phone, wave it around like it's Wonka's golden ticket. "I've been on the phone with my clients all day. I'm not gonna just sit on my ass the whole time I'm down here. That wouldn't be very professional, would it? Don't worry. It's no big deal. I watch the flick for simple verification, then stick it in a FedEx box, case closed. You go. Go finish up with that little cherub in there. I'm all set."

Ellen folds her arms across her chest. She's not having any of it. She digs in, entrenches, a tick in a mutt's ear. She says, "I think you're lying to me."

"Frankly, I'm nonplussed. Would I lie to you, Clowny?"

"Yes. You do, all the time."

"True. But this time everything is kosher." I spread the word *everything* out like it's smooth peanut butter.

Ellen sighs and throws up her hands. "I don't know what to do with you, and I don't have time to argue. I'll set up the projector, then go back into the studio, and you can watch it in here by yourself."

Okay, I'm by one hurdle, now on to the next. I talk as fast as I can, which isn't very. "No good. I need someplace private. Not rush-hour downtown Osterville in an antiques store with a huge bay friggin' window. Let me borrow it. I promise to return it in one piece. I'll set it up and watch it at the house before you come home."

"You're a giant pain in my butt, you know that, right?"

I say, "I'll have a bowl of popcorn ready for you when you get back. Extra butter."

"Fine. Let me see if the bulbs still work." Ellen plugs it in, turns it on. A beam of light shines out of the projection bulb and onto a bearskin rug and its matted fur. I resist the urge for a shadow puppet show. She turns off the projection bulb and two small lights come on within the body of the projector.

I say, "What are those lights?"

"You could thread the film in the dark, if you needed to."

"Good to know."

"This projector will automatically thread through the film gate, which is nice. If you think it's a sound film, you'll have to thread it manually through the sound head and then to the take-up reel. It's easy, though." Ellen points out the heads, loops, and hot spots. I should be taking notes, drawing diagrams.

She says, "The instruction manual is taped underneath the projector if you want to mess around with it. If you can figure out how to do it yourself, great, or just wait until I get home. I won't be long. This kid is my last shoot of the day." She shuts off the projector and unplugs it.

I say, "Thanks. I think I can handle it from here."

Ellen walks to the other side of the counter, then ducks down and disappears. Momentarily inspired, I take one of the display case's stacked film reels and tuck it inside my coat. The reel is black, not gray, but about the same size as the one I found. I'm a collector now.

Ellen emerges with a carrying case. "This was Tim's projector. If you break it, you're a dead man." The little robot disappears into the case. I hope it won't be lonely, separated from its friends.

Tim's projector for Tim's film that was in Tim's shed. I've opened one of those sets of nested Russian dolls, and I don't know when the dolls will stop coming out or how to stop them. I grab the case by the handle and let the projector hang by my hip. It's heavy. It's all heavy.

"How come you don't sell these projectors, or the cameras on the wall?"

"What? We don't have time for this."

"You're right, we don't, but I want to know. Maybe the answer is important. Give me your gut-shot answer. Quick. Don't think about it. Don't think about what I'd want to hear or don't want to hear. Just tell me."

She says, "Because no one else should be using Tim's stuff."

I want to take the question back because she can't answer it. It wasn't fair to try and distill something as complex as her twenty-five-plus years of being a widow into a reaction. She gave it an honest try. Don't know what I was expecting, maybe something that would make Tim seem like a real person, not a collection of secrets, clues, and consequences. Something that helps me to get through tonight.

I say, "Fair enough. There will be no breaking of the projector. I'm a gentle soul."

Ellen puts her hands in her hair. "You've got me all frazzled. I need to go back. There's a stand-alone screen in that closet over there. Take it with you."

I scoot down to the end of the display cabinet, boxing her in while I root through the closet for the screen. I hold up a long heavy cardboard box. "Is it in the box?"

"Yes! Now get out of the way. Shoo!"

I hustle after Ellen, my arms full of film equipment. Let's all go to the lobby. I follow her into the reception area, to the studio. Ellen stops at the door.

"Where are you going?"

I say, "I'm going out the way I came in. Brill is going to meet me out back. He went to get a coffee and a pack of smokes and a *Playboy*. I'm telling you, he's a sick old man."

Ellen ignores me and walks into the studio. "Okay, so sorry for the interruption. He's leaving, finally."

It's true.

Ellen breaks into a fake-cheery voice. She's a pro at it, which makes me wonder how many years she used that voice on the kid me: everything is great and happy and there's nothing wrong here, nothing can hurt you.

She says, "How's Danny doing? Is he ready? You're going to look so cool in the pictures, Danny. Picture time!"

The movie-show equipment is cumbersome. I flip the screen up onto my left shoulder, lugging it like a log. Balancing and carrying it is not easy.

Glamour Mom couldn't care less about the goings-on and continues to talk on the phone. Danny is still crying, and is now dressed like a duck; yellow feathers and orange bill split wide open over his face, the suit swallows him. His wings flap around as Ellen changes the desert scene to a sunset lake.

I'm no duck. I am the guy waddling out, away from the sunset lake and into a back alley.

Thirty-three

The sun is setting but there's no lake back here. I buckle the projector into the passenger seat. It could be a bumpy ride and I don't want it rolling around the trunk or backseat. It needs to survive the trip.

Before I climb behind the wheel, I take out the cell phone. No messages. I consider calling Brill, but I won't. There's no way he'd give me a ride to Southie, even if I did have enough cash, which I don't. I turn off the cell phone. I'm sure Ellen will be calling me as soon as she gets home.

Yeah, Southie. I've made a decision. Don't know if I'm going to call Jennifer, but I'm going back to Southie and my apartment. This is the only way to finish the case. My case. I don't think I have the cash or credit card balance left to hole up in a local motel, or any motel on the way to Southie, and watch the film. Besides, this isn't about hiding anymore. That skulking-around shit I went through today is not for me. It makes me irritable and fatigued. This is about doing it my way. I'm going to go back to my office and my apartment, where I will watch this film and solve this case. It's going to end there, one way or the other, because I say so.

Okay, the drive. The downtown traffic has decreased considerably. The townies are all home, eating dinner, watching the local news. I wonder what Janice Sullivan is doing tonight. I don't remember if Brendan's wake was today or not. I wonder how long her twin aunts are staying at the house. I think about Janice's first day alone, and then the next one, and the next one. Will I be able to tell her, when all this is over, about the death of her husband?

Stop. I can't lose myself in runaway trains of thought. Those are nonstop bullets to Sleep Town.

Motoring through the outskirts of Osterville and I need to make a pit stop before the big ride. I pull into a convenience store. Mine is the only car in the lot. If this was Southie, the townie kids would be hanging out here, driving around and buzzing the lot because there's no other place to go. They'd spike their slurpies and drink hidden beers. But this isn't Southie. I'm not there yet, not even close.

Inside, a quick supply run: supersized black coffee, a box of powdered donuts, and a pack of smokes. Dinner of champions. Let's hope it brings on a spell of insomnia.

Back behind the wheel with my supplies, I check the seat belt rig on my copilot. I apologize for not getting it a Danish. I'm so inconsiderate.

I turn on the space car. The dashboard is a touch-screen computer with settings for the radio, CD player, climate control, fuel efficiency ratings for the trip, and a screen that displays an animated diagram of the hybrid engine and when the power shifts from gas to electric. Have to hand it to the rental agent, I wanted distracting and the kid gave it to me.

Next is the GPS. I plug in the convenience store's address, then the destination, my apartment. I choose AVOID HIGHWAYS instead of FASTEST TRIP. Driving on the highway, especially the expressway when I get closer to Boston, would be too dangerous for everyone. I know the drive, normally ninety minutes, will take twice, maybe even three times as long by sticking to back roads, but there's always congestion on the highways and the likelihood of me killing myself and someone else with my car at highway speeds is too great. I'll take it slow and steady and win the race on the back roads.

The GPS estimates driving time to be three hours and twenty-two minutes. I pat the projector, say, "Road trip," and pull out of the lot. The GPS has a female voice. She tells me to turn left.

"You're the boss."

I drive. Osterville becomes Centerville becomes Barnstable becomes Sandwich. My coffee is hot enough to burn enamel, the way I like it. The combination of excitement, fear, and caffeine has me wired. I feel awake. I know it's the calm before the storm. I still could go out at any minute, but I feel good. That's until I remember there's only two ways off the Cape. Both include a spot of highway driving and a huge bridge.

It's past dusk and there's no turning back. The sun is gone-daddy-gone and might never come up again if I'm not careful, as if careful ever has anything to do with narcolepsy. I'm in Sandwich when the GPS tells me to get on Route 6. She's too calm. She doesn't realize what she's telling me to do.

The on-ramp to the highway winds around itself and spits me onto a too-small runway to merge into the two-lane traffic. I jump on with both feet and all four tires, eyes forward, afraid to check my mirror. A hulking SUV comes right up my behind and beeps. The horn is loud enough to be an air raid siren. I jerk and swerve right but keep space car on the road. Goddamn highway, got to get off sooner than soon.

The Sagamore Bridge is ahead, a behemoth, seventy-plus years old. That can't be safe for anyone. It spans the Cape Cod Canal and is at least 150 feet above the water. Its slope is too steep, the two northbound lanes too narrow. No cement dividers, just double yellow lines keep northbound and southbound separated. They need more than lines. North and south don't like each other and don't play well together. Doesn't anyone know their history anymore?

There are too many cars and trucks squeezing over the towering Cape entrance and exit. I stay in the right lane. I'm so scared I'm literally shaking. White powder from a donut I stuff in my mouth sprinkles all over my pants. I probably shouldn't be eating now, but I'm trying for some sort of harmless everyday action while driving, just like the other slob motorists on the death bridge.

The steel girders whisper at my car doors. I'm on an old rickety roller coaster. The car is ticking its way up the big hill, still going up, and I'm anticipating the drop. My hands are empty of donut and back on the wheel, still shaking. This is a mistake. I can't manage my narcolepsy and I can't manage who or what I'll hit with the space car when I go to sleep. No if. When. I don't know when an attack will happen. There's no pattern. There's no reason.

I try to drink the coffee but my tremors are too violent and I get my lips and chin scalded for the trouble. The swell of traffic moves at a steady 45 miles per hour. There are other vehicles on the front, back, and left of me. I can't slow down and can't switch lanes. I won't look right and down, to the water. I'm not afraid of the bridge or the fall. I'm afraid of me, of that curtain that'll just go down over my eyes.

I crest the top of the bridge. A blast of wind voices its displeasure and pushes me left a few inches. I correct course, but it's not a smooth correction. The car jerks. The wind keeps blowing, whistling around the car's frame. My hands want to cry on the steering wheel. They're doing their best. They need a drink and a cigarette.

After the crest is down. The down is as steep as the up, and almost worse. The speed of the surrounding traffic increases. We have this incredible group forward momentum and nothing at the bottom of the hill to slow us down. I tap my brakes for no reason. I chance a look in the rearview mirror and the bulk of the bridge is behind me. Thank Christ. I'm over the canal and off the Cape. I breathe for the first time since Sandwich. The breath is too clean. Need a smoke, but that will have to wait until I get off the highway.

I'm finally off the bridge. Ms. GPS says she wants world peace and Route 6 is now Route 3 north, and I need to take the first exit to get with the back-roads plan again. Easy for her to say. I still have some highway to traverse.

I'm putting along Route 3 in the right lane, going fifty while everyone else passes me. The flat two lanes of highway stretch out into darkness, and the red taillights of the passing cars fade out of sight. I think about staying on the highway, taking it slow, pulling over when I get real tired and getting to Southie quicker, but I can't chance it. I crash here, I'm a dead man, and I'll probably take someone with me.

I'm already yawning by the time the first Plymouth exit shows up on my radar screen. Maybe I'll show my movie on Plymouth Rock. I take the exit and pull over in a gully soon after the off-ramp. Need to reset my bearings, take a breather. My hands and fingers are sore from vise-gripping the wheel.

I light a cigarette and turn on my cell phone. It rings and vibrates as soon as it powers up. It's Ellen. I let it ring out, then I call her back. My timing is good. She's still leaving a message for me so my call is directly shuffled off to her voice mail.

Talk after the beep. "I'm okay, Ellen. No worries. Just so you know, the DA is crooked, can't be trusted. You stay put and call the police if you see a couple of mountain-sized goons on your doorstep, or if any red cars pull into the driveway. Or if that doesn't make you feel safe, go to a motel. I'm being serious. I'd offer to treat but I'm just about out of cash. I've almost solved my case. I'll call you back later, when it's over."

It is possible the goons are in the house, have Ellen tied to a chair, gun to her head, the whole mustache-twisting bit, and are making her call me under the threat of pain. Possible but not likely. Sure, it's getting late and the DA and his squad are desperate to get the film, but they also have to be careful about how many people know what they're doing. They start harassing too many folks, the cleanup gets too big and messy. Then again, maybe I shouldn't underestimate their desperation.

I can't turn back now. If the goons want me, they can call from their own phone.

The cell rings. It's Ellen and I don't answer it. She must've heard my message. I'll make it up to her later, if there is a later. I turn on the car, and it's back on the road again for me.

Plymouth is its own state. The biggest city in Massachusetts by square mileage, and I'm feeling it. Drive, drive, drive. Lefts and rights. Quiet back roads that range from the heart of suburbia to the heart of darkness, country roads with no streetlamps and houses that don't have any neighbors.

It's a weeknight and it's cold, so no one is out walking or riding their bikes. Mostly, it's just me and the road. When another car approaches in the opposite lane, I tense up, a microwave panic; it's instant and the same feeling I had on the highway. I think about what would happen if I suddenly veered into that lane, into those headlights, and I'm the Tin Man with no heart and everything starts to rust. Then the car passes me and I relax a little, but the whole process is draining.

I pull over and eat a few donuts. I pull over and take a leak, stretch my legs. I pull over and light another fire in my mouth. I pull over and try to take a quick nap, but as soon as I park the car, shut everything off, I'm awake again. The almost-asleep feeling is gone. I close my eyes, it's lost, and for once I can't find it.

Drive, drive, drive. The GPS says I'm in Kingston, but I don't remember leaving Plymouth. That's not good. My stomach fills with acid, but that's what I get for medicating with black coffee and powdered donuts.

I think about calling someone, just to shoot the shit. Talking can help keep me awake, but there's no one to call. I try to focus on the GPS, its voice, maps, and beeps. I learn the digital pattern, how soon before a turn she'll tell me to turn. This isn't good either. The whole trip is becoming a routine. I've been in the car long enough that driving is once again automatic behavior.

I sing. I play with the touch screen, changing the background colors. Kingston becomes Pembroke. Pembroke becomes Hanover.

More than ninety minutes have passed since the start. I'd be in Southie by now if I could've driven on the highway. That kind thinking isn't helping. Stay on the sunny side of the street, Genevich.

The road. The road is in Hanover, for now. I flick the projector's latches up and down. The projector doesn't complain. The road. How many roads are there in Massachusetts? Truth is, you can get they-uh from hee-uh. You can even find roads to the past. Everything and everyone is connected. It's more than a little depressing. I flick the latches harder; apparently I'm sadistic when it comes to inanimate objects. The road. Flick. Then everything is noise. The engine revs and the space car fills a ditch. My teeth knock and jam into each other with the jolt. The car careens left into bushes and woods. Budding branches scratch the windshield and side panels. I cut the wheel hard right and stomp on the brake pedal. The car slows some, but the back end skids out, and it wants to roll. I know the feeling. The car goes up and I'm pitched toward the passenger seat and the projector. The space car is going to go over and just ahead is the trunk of a huge tree.

Then the car stops. Everything is quiet. The GPS beeps, tells me to turn right.

I climb out. The car is beached on a swale, a foot away from the big tree. It's pitch dark and I can't see all that much, but the driver's-side door feels dented and scratched. I crossed over the right lane and into some woods. There's a house maybe two hundred yards ahead. I walk around to the passenger side and check the projector, and it seems to be in one piece.

"Now that we've got that out of the way."

I climb back in the car and roll off the hill; the frame and wheel wells groan but I make it back to the road and go a half mile before I pull over again. The space car's wounds seem superficial. Tires still inflated. No cracked glass, and I have no cracked bones.

The GPS and distracting dashboard aren't enough to keep me conscious. I need another stay-awake strategy. I dig a notepad and pencil out of my coat and put it in the passenger seat. It's worth a shot.

Hanover becomes Norwell. I'm keeping a running tally of yellow street signs. Whenever I pass one, I make a slash on the notepad, a little task to keep me focused and awake. Norwell becomes Hingham. I'm driving with more confidence. I know it's a false confidence, the belief that the disaster has already happened, lightning struck once, and it won't happen again. I know that isn't true but after a night spent in a car, by myself, it's easy to cling to my own lies.

I keep up with the tally marks. I play with the dashboard some more. I still get sleepy. I push on. Hingham becomes Weymouth. I pull over twice and try to sleep. Again, no dice. I walk around, take deep breaths, alternating filling up my lungs with hot smoke and with the cold March air. I pee on someone's rosebushes.

It's almost midnight, but as I creep closer to the city there are more lights, a neon and halogen path. Things are getting brighter. Weymouth becomes Quincy. Despite the late hour, there are more cars around. I let them box me in and go where the currents take me. Quincy becomes the outskirts of Dorchester. I pass the JFK library and UMass Boston and BC High School. Dorchester becomes Southie.

I've made it. Bumped and bruised, scratched, damaged, more than a little weary, but I'm here.

Thirty-four

I drive by my building three times, approaching it from different angles and streets. I'm circling, only I'm not the buzzard. I watch the local traffic and eyeball the parked cars. No sign of the goon car. My office and apartment windows are darkened. No one left the light on for me.

Time to end the magical mystery tour. I park on West Broadway, a block away from my building, across from an empty bank parking lot. I wait and watch the corner, my corner. There's nothing happening around my apartment. Cabs trolling the streets, homeless sinking inside their upturned collars and sitting on benches, and pub crawlers are the only ones out.

I take out my cell and flip it around in my hands, giving the fingers something to hold besides the steering wheel. I'm not going to call Jennifer right now. Maybe later. Maybe after I watch the film. Maybe not at all. I don't care all that much about what happens after the film. I just need to see it before everything falls apart and on top of me.

Phone goes back inside the jacket and the manila envelope comes out. I check that the photos are still inside, that they haven't run and hid anywhere. The photos are still there, so are the young woman and those three letters. LIT, Tim's signature. I tuck the envelope under the driver's seat, a pirate hiding his booty. I don't know if I'll be able to reclaim the pictures later, but I want to keep the film and the photos separate, just in case.

I get out of the car and remove a small branch that was pinned under a wiper blade. That's better. Here, under the streetlights, the damage to the space car looks severe and permanent, more a bite from a pit bull than a bee sting. Bumpers wouldn't have helped, either.

I unload the screen and projector, the precious cargo. My muscles are stiff and the joints ache from the drive. They don't want to move and they liked it in the car. Sorry, fellas. There's work to do.

Screen lying across my shoulders and the projector dangling from my left hand, I hike up the street. I'm some limping and bent documentary director about to see my life's work for the first time. I have no idea what kind of story, what kind of truth I've discovered, documented, even created. I'm afraid of that truth and wish I could hide from it, but I can't. Won't. Yeah, I'm a kind of hero, but the

worst kind; the one acting heroic only by accident and because of circumstance.

There's a cold breeze coming off the bay. It's insistent and gets
trapped and passed between the rows of buildings, bouncing around
like a ricocheting bullet, hitting me with multiple shots. No tumbleweeds, but wisps of paper wrappers and crushed cans roll on the side-
walks. West Broadway isn't deserted, but it might as well be. There's
a distinct last-person-on-earth vibe going on. I'm alone and have
been for a long time.

I make it to my front door and put my burdens down on the
welcome mat. The door is locked, both knob and dead bolt. I feel
so protected. My keys fit into their assigned slots and Open Sesame.
I should have a flashlight. I should have a lot of things. I lump
the equipment inside and I turn on the hall and office lights for a
quick peek.

The office and hallway have been cleared and cleaned out, the
carcass picked over and stripped. Only the file cabinet and the desk
remain in the office. The desk is missing a leg and leans crookedly
toward a corner of the room. It's almost like I was never there. I'm a
ghost in a ghost office. I don't bother to check if any of my files sur-
vived the purge. I don't want to advertise my triumphant return, the
not-so-prodigal son, so I shut the lights off. The darkness comes back,
slides right in, settles over everything, a favorite blanket.

The ascent up the stairs to the second-floor landing isn't quite
blind, since leftover streetlight spills through the landing window. I
huff and puff up the stairs, then put down the equipment next to my
door. It's shut. Ellen's peeps have already fixed it. I take out my
lighter and the half-inch flame is enough to guide my entry into the

apartment. Unlike the office, my apartment has yet to be cleaned or even touched. The shambles and wreckage of my personal life are right where I left them, which is nice. Seems an appropriate scene as any for this little movie.

I scavenge some scraps of paper, find an ashtray, and light a small fire. The fire burns long enough for me to find two small candles in the kitchen. I light those. Don't know if their orange glow can be seen from the street, so I get a couple of wool blankets out of my bedroom and hang them over the windows, tucking and tying their corners into the curtain framing. A makeshift darkroom.

I set the screen up in front of my bedroom door, which is opposite the blanket-covered windows. Next up, quietly as I can, because anyone could be listening, I clear out some space and bring in the kitchen table. Two legs are broken. I experiment with varied hunks of the living room flotsam and jetsam and manage to jury-rig a flat stable surface for the projector. It'll hold the weight even if I can't.

I take the projector out of its case, careful, reverential, a jeweler plucking a diamond from the setting of an antique ring. The projector goes on the table. Its dual arms are stubby and upright. I plug it in, turn it on. Out spits a ray of blinding light, a spotlight that enlarges to a rectangle that's half on and half off the screen. I shut off the projection bulb and small pilot lights glow around the feeds. I read the manual. It has directions in English and French. It seems like straightforward stuff, but then I think I should try the other film I nabbed from Ellen's store first, just a little film-threading practice. Never mind. I don't have the time. I make adjustments to the height of the projector. I place the film on the front reel and thread it through the sound head like Ellen showed me. It's working.

I fear I might do something to tear or snap the tape, this collection of lost memories is so fragile its impossible thinness passes between my fingers, but the film feeds smooth and the take-up reel gathers frames. A quick adjustment to the lens and everything is in focus. I stand next to the projector and the table with its two legs. The projector is doing its projecting. I'm standing and watching. The film is playing.

THIRTY-FIVE

White empty frames are accompanied by a loud hiss, a loud nothingness. Then the white explodes into sound and color. The projector's speaker crackles with off-camera laughter, laughter that momentarily precedes any clear images. It's the laughter of boys, full of bravado and mischief and oh-shit-what-have-we-got-ourselves-into? The bedroom is drab with its green bedspread and off-white paint-chipped walls; nightstand and bookcase are splintering and warped. A neglected, dying bedroom in a Southie project. The scene is fixed; the camera is on a tripod.

She sits on the bed wearing her white T-shirt and short denim skirt, but also wearing big purple bruises and rusty scrapes. In color, she looks even more like Jennifer, but an anorexic version. Her arms are thinner than the film running past the projector's lens, skin washed with bleach. Her eyes are half open, or half closed. I want her to have a name because she doesn't have one yet. She sways on her knees and pitches in her own two cents of laughter. It's slurred and messy, a spilled drink, a broken cigarette. She's not Jennifer.

Off camera, the boys speak. Their voices are boxed in, tinny, trapped in the projector's speaker.

"Let me take a couple of quick shots."

"What the fuck for?"

"So he can beat off to 'em later."

"Fuck off. For cover shots, or promos. It'll help sell the movie, find buyers. What, am I the only one here with any business sense?"

"You ain't got no fuckin' sense."

"And you ain't got no fuckin' dick."

More of that boy laughter, plus the clinking of bottles, then Tim appears on-screen, backside first. He turns around, sticks his mug into the camera and travels through decades. He fills the frame, fills the screen in my apartment. He's a kid. Fifteen tops. Dark hair, pinched eyes, a crooked smile.

Ellen was right. He does look like me, like I used to look. No, that isn't it. He looks like how I imagined my own appearance, my old appearance in all the daydreams I've had of the pre-accident me. He is the idealized Mark Genevich, the one lost forever, if he ever existed in the first place. He's young, whole, not broken. He's not the monster me on that screen. He's there just for a second, but he's there. I could spend the next month wearing this scene out, rewinding and watching and rewinding, staring into that broken mirror.

Then Tim winks and says, "Sorry. I'll be quick, just like the boys will."

Off camera: a round of *fuck yous* and *you pussys* mixes in with laughter. Tim turns away from the camera and snaps a picture. He says, "One more. How 'bout a money shot. Take the shirt and skirt off." The chorus shouts their approval this time. The camera only sees Tim's back. He completely obscures her. She mumbles something and then the sound of clothes being removed, cloth rubbing against itself and against skin. T-shirt flutters off the bed, a flag falling to the ground. Tim snaps a second picture, then hides behind the movie camera.

No one says anything and the camera just stares. She's shirtless and skirtless. She opens her eyes, or at least tries to, and says, "Someone gimme a drink."

Off camera. "When are we gonna start this shit?"

Tim says, "Whenever you're ready. Start now. I'll edit out your fuckups later."

Two bare-chested teens enter the scene, both wearing jeans. Their skin is painfully white and spotted with freckles and pimples. These guys are only a couple of years removed from Ellen's keepsake picture on the stairs, boys in men's bodies. Sullivan is on the right and Times on the left; both have wide eyes and cocksure sneers. Unlike in the stair picture from Ellen's house, Sullivan is now the bigger of the two, thick arms and broad shoulders. He's the muscle, the heavy lifter, the mover, the shaker. Times has a wiry build, looks leaner, quicker, and meaner. Here's your leader. He's holding a bottle of clear liquid, takes a swig.

Times kneels on the bed beside the woman and says, "You ready for a good time?" No one responds to or laughs at the porn cliché, which probably isn't a cliché to them yet. It's painfully earnest in this flick.

The new silence in the room is another character. Times looks around to his boys, and it's a moment when the whole thing could get called off, shut down. Sullivan and Tim would be all right with a last-second cancellation of this pilot. I can't know this but I do. The moment passes, like all moments must pass, and it makes everything worse, implicates them further, because they had a chance to stop and they didn't.

Times says, "Here." He gives her the bottle and she drinks deep, so deep I'm not sure she'll be able to come back up for a breath. But she does, and hands back the bottle and melts out of her sitting position and onto her back. Sullivan grabs a handful of her left breast and frantically works at the button and fly of his pants with his free hand.

Her right hand and arm float up in front her face slowly, like an old cobra going through the motions for some two-bit snake charmer, and her hand eventually lands on Times's thigh. She's like them, only a kid. And she's a junkie. I wonder if those three amigos could see that and were banking on it, or if they were too busy with their collective tough-guy routine to see anything.

Times says, "Lights, camera, action."

The sex is fast, rough, and clumsy. With its grim and bleak bedroom setting, drunk, high, and uninterested female star, and two boys who are awkward but feral and relentless, it's a scene that is both pathetic and frightening at the same time. The vibe has flipped

180 degrees, from should-we-do-this to where the potential for violence is an ogre in the room. Like someone watching a scary movie through his fingers, I cringe because I know the violence is coming.

The camera stays in one spot and only pans and scans. There's never a good clear shot of the woman's face. We see her collection of body parts in assorted states of motion but never her face. She's not supposed to matter, and even if nothing else were to happen, this is enough to make me hate the boy behind the camera and the man he became. Tim says nothing throughout the carnal gymnastics. He's the silent but complicit eye.

Sullivan finishes first and stumbles out of the scene. He gives Tim—not the camera—a look, one that might haunt me for the rest of my little sleeps and short days. When that kid's middle-aged version killed himself in the basement of his Cape house, I imagine he had the same look on his face when he pulled the trigger. A look one might have when the truth, the hidden and ugly truth of the world, that we're all complicit, has been revealed.

Times is still going at her. He's on top and he speeds up his thrusts for the big finish. Then there's a horrible choking cough. It's wet and desperate and loud, practically tears through the projector's speaker, and makes Brill's lung-ejecting hacks sound like a prim and proper clearing of the throat.

"Jesus, fuck!" Times jumps off the bed like it's electrified.

It's her. She's choking. I still can't see enough of her face; she's lying down and the camera isn't up high enough. She coughs but isn't breathing in. Out with the bad but no in with the good. Yellow vomit leaks out of her nose and mouth and into her hair. Her hands try to cover her face but fall back onto the bed. She shakes all over, the convulsions increasing in speed and violence. I think maybe I accidentally sped up the film but I didn't; it's all her. Maybe the bed is electrified.

From behind the camera, and it sounds like he's behind me, talking over my shoulder, Tim says, "What's fuckin' happening?" He doesn't lose the shot, though, that son of a bitch. The camera stays focused on her.

"Oh, fuck, her fucking eyes, they're all white. Fuck! Fuck!"

Sullivan says, "She's freaking out. What do we do?"

The camera gets knocked to the floor, but it still runs, records its images. A skewed, tilted shot of under the bed fills the screen. There's nothing there but dust and cobwebs and darkness.

The bed shakes and the springs complain. The choking noises are gone. The boys are all shouting at the same time. I can only make out snippets, swears, phrases. It's a mess. I lean closer to the screen, trying to hide under that bed, trying to hear what they're saying. Their voices are one voice, high-pitched and scared.

Then the three voices become only two. One is screaming. I think it's Times. He's says, "Shut the fucking camera off!" He shouts it repeatedly, his increased mania exploding in the room.

And I hear Tim—I think it's Tim. He's whispering and getting closer to the camera. He's going to shut it off, taking orders like a good little boy. He's repeating himself too, has his own mantra. Tim is saying, "Is she dead? Is she dead?"

The screen goes white. The End. *Fin.*

The take-up reel rattles with a lose piece of film slapping against the projector. My hands are sweating and I'm breathing heavy. I shut off the projector, the screen goes black, the take-up reel slows, and I stop it with my hand. The used engine gives a whiff of ozone and waves of dying heat. Everything should be quiet, but it isn't.

"Who is she?" A voice from my left, from the front door.

I say, "Don't you mean, who was she?"

THIRTY-SIX

Jennifer Times stands in the front doorway. She looks like she did at the mall autograph session. Sweatpants, jean jacket over a Red Sox T, hair tied up into a tight ponytail. It might be the weak candlelight, shadows dampening her cheekbones and eyes, but she looks a generation older than when we were at the restaurant. We're both older now.

I say, "I don't remember calling and inviting you over. I would've cleaned up a bit first. Maybe even baked a cake."

She walks in, shuts the door behind her. Someone raised her right. She says, "Who was she? Do you know?"

I say, "No idea. No clue, as it was. How much did you see?"

"Enough."

I nod. It was enough.

She says, "What are you going to do now?"

"Me? I'm done. I'm taking myself out of the game, making my own call to the bullpen. I'm wrapping this all up in a pretty red bow and dumping into the state police's lap. Or the FBI. No local cops, no one who knows your dad, no offense. I was hired to find it. I found it."

Jennifer carefully steps over the rubble and crouches next to me, next to the projector. She stares at it like she might lay hands on it, wanting to heal or be healed, I don't know. "What do you think happened to her after?"

I say, "How did you get in here?"

"I checked the welcome mat and there were keys duct-taped underneath."

Keys? I never left any keys. I don't even have spares. Ellen wouldn't do that either. Yeah, she's the de facto mayor of Southie, friends with everyone, but she's also a pragmatist. She knows better than to leave keys under a welcome mat on one of the busiest corners of South Boston. All of which means Jennifer is lying and also means I'm screwed, as I'm sure other unexpected guests are likely to arrive shortly.

Jennifer holds up a ring of two keys on a Lithuanian-flag key chain.

Shit. Those are Ellen's keys. I say, "How did you know I was here?"

"Why are you interrogating me?"

"I'm only asking simple questions, and here you go trying to rush everything to the interrogation level."

She says, "I was parked outside of your apartment and saw you. I waited a few minutes and let myself in, then I sat outside your door listening. I came in when I heard them yelling."

I fold up and break down the projector as she talks. I don't rewind the film but, instead, slip the take-up reel into my coat pocket, next to the other film. I wrap up the cord and slide the projector into its case, latch the latches twice for luck. I say, "Why are you here?" and walk past her to the screen.

"I needed to see if you were telling me the truth on the phone. I had to know."

The screen recoils quickly and slides into its box nice and easy. I say, "And now that you know, what are you going to do?"

Jennifer walks past the table and sits on the couch. "How about answering my question?"

"What question was that? I tend to lose track of things, you know?"

"What do you think happened after? After the movie? What did they do?"

My turn to play the strong silent type. I lean on the screen, thinking about giving an answer, my theory on everything, life, death, the ever-expanding doomed universe. Then there's a short bang downstairs. Not loud enough to wake up neighbors, a newspaper hitting the door.

Jennifer whispers, "What was that?"

"It ain't no newspaper," I say. "Expecting company, Jennifer? It's awful rude to invite your friends over without asking me."

"I didn't tell anyone where I was going or what I was doing." She gets up off the couch, calm as a kiddie pool, and tiptoes into my bedroom. She gestures and I lean in close to hear. She whispers, "See if you can find out who that woman was and what they did with her after. You know, do your job. And if things get hairy, I'll come out and save you." Jennifer shuts the door.

No way. I'm going to pull her out of the room and use her as a human shield should the need arise. I turn the knob but it's locked. Didn't know it had a lock.

If things get hairy. I'm already hairy and so are the things. Yeah, another goddamn setup, but a bizarre one that makes no sense. Doesn't matter. Prioritize. I need to hide the equipment, or at least bury it in junk so it doesn't look like I'd just watched the film for the first time. I lay the screen behind the couch, unzip a cushion and stuff the film inside, then go to work with the projector and case, putting it under the kitchen table, incorporating it into one of the makeshift legs. I move the candles to the center of the table.

Maybe my priorities are all out of whack. I give thought to the back exit and the fire escape off the kitchen, but the front door to my apartment is currently under assault. I'm not much of a runner or climber, and I'd need one hell of a head start. I could call the police, but they'd be the DA's police, and even if they weren't, they wouldn't get here in time. No sense in prolonging this. I walk over to the front windows and pull down the blankets. I lean against the wall between the windows, light a cigarette, shine the tops of my Doc Martens on the backs of my calves, adjust my hat, pretend I have style.

The door flies open and crashes into the wall. The knob sinks into the plaster. The insurance bill just got a little bigger. As inevitable as the tides, the two goons are in my doorway.

I say, "That ain't the secret knock, so I'm going to have to ask you gentlemen to leave."

Redhead says, "Candles. How romantic."

Yeah, even with the added ambience of streetlamps and assorted background neon, the light quality isn't great, but it's enough to see a hell of a shiner under his right eye, scratches on his face, and the gun in his hand. He holds it like he's King Kong clutching a Fay Wray imposter and can't wait to squeeze.

Can't focus on the gun. It gets my panic juices flowing. This time with the goons, it feels different already, like how the air smells different before a thunderstorm, before all the action. My legs get a jump on the jellification process.

Baldy says, "Romancing yourself there, retard? You're fuckin' ugly enough that your right hand would reject you."

I blow some smoke, don't say anything, and try to give them smug, give them confidence. My bluff will work only if I get the attitude right. And even then, it still might not work.

Redhead is a totem to violence. He wears threat like cologne. He says, "I wouldn't be standing there fucking smiling like you know something. Smiling like you aren't never gonna feel pain again, Genevich."

I say, "Can't help myself, boys. I'm a happy guy. Don't mean to rub your noses in it."

Baldy says, "We're gonna rub your nose all over our fists and the fuckin' walls." He cracks his knuckles, grinding bone against bone.

They walk toward me, necks retracted into their shoulders, and I can just about hear their muscles bulging against their dress shirts and suit coats. Dust and sparks fall out of their mouths. Oh, and the gun is still pointed at me.

Can't say I've thought my Hail Mary bluff all the way through, but I'm going with it. I open my jacket and pull out the dummy film, the black one, the one from Ellen's store. Only what I'm holding isn't the dummy film. Apparently I put that one inside the couch cushion. What I'm waving around in front of the goons is the take-up reel, half full with Tim's film.

Oh, boy. Need to regroup, and fast. I say, "Have you boys seen this yet? Some of the performances are uneven, but two thumbs way up. You know, you two fellas remind me of the shit-talking boys that star in the movie. Same intensity and all that. I'm sure the reviews will be just as good when it gets a wide release. Twelve thousand theaters, red-carpet premiere somewhere, Golden Globes, then the Oscars, the works."

The goons stop their advance, share a look. My cigarette is almost dead. I know the feeling well.

Redhead laughs, a car's engine dying. He says, "You trying to tell us you made a copy?"

Baldy's head is black with stubble. I guess, with all the *mishegas*, he hasn't had time for a shave. He should lighten his schedule. He says, "You haven't had time to make any copies."

"Says you. I had it digitized. Didn't take long, boys. Didn't even cost that much. Oh, I tipped well for the rush and all. But it got done, and done quick. Even made a few hard copies for the hell of it. You know, for the retro-vibe. The kids love all the old stuff."

Baldy breaks from formation and takes a jab step toward me. I think he's grown bigger since he first walked into the room. His nostrils flare out, the openings as wide as exhaust pipes. I'm in big trouble. He says, "You're fuckin' lying."

I don't know if that's just a standard reply, maybe Baldy's default setting. The goons creep closer. My heart does laps around my chest cavity and its pace is too fast, it'll never make it to the end of the race. Appearing calm is going to be as easy as looking pretty.

I say, "Nope. This one here is one of the copies. You don't think I'd wave the original around, do you? I figure I can make a quick buck or two by putting that puppy on eBay."

It's their turn to talk, to give me a break, a chance to catch my breath, but my breath won't be caught. It's going too fast and hard, a dog with a broken leash sprinting after a squirrel. Black spots in my vision now. They're not buying any of this, and I'm in a barrel full of shit. I move back, away from the window. My legs have gone cold spaghetti on me and I almost go down, stumbling on my twisted and bent CD tower. Muscles tingle and my skin suddenly gets very heavy.

I say, "If my video guy doesn't see me on his doorstep tomorrow morning, alone and in one piece, he uploads the video onto YouTube and drops a couple of DVDs into FedEx boxes, and the boxes have addresses, important addresses, on them, just in case you were wondering."

The goons laugh, split up, and circle me, one goon on each side. I'll be the meat in the goon sandwich. Looks like I should've gone with a frantic fire-escape escape. There isn't always a next time.

Redhead scratches his nose with the gun barrel and says, "You're bullshitting the wrong guys, Genevich. We don't believe you, and we don't really care. We're getting paid to find the film, take that film, copy or not, and then knock the snot out of you."

Things are getting more than hairy. Things are going black and fuzzy and not just at the edges. I say, "Don't make me drop another shed on your asses."

Baldy lunges, his coat billowing behind him like giant bat wings. The wings beat once, twice, he hangs in the air, and I feel the wind, it's hot and humid, an exhaled breath on glass that lifts the hat off my head. Then he takes a swing, but he doesn't land the blow because I'm already falling, already going down.

Thirty-seven

I open my eyes and everything is wrong. Cataplexy. My waking coma. The wires are all crossed, the circuit breakers flipped. I can't move and won't be able to for a while.

DA Times sits in front of me. He's wearing black gloves and holds a gun. Maybe I should get me one of those; seems like everyone else is buying. I'm always the last one in the latest trends. I'm the rotten egg.

"Mark? You there?"

I try to say, "Yeah," but it's only loosened air, don't know if he hears it so I blink a few times. Yeah, I'm here, and here is wrong. Here is my couch. The projector is on the kitchen table, the take-up reel and the film hang off the rear arm. The candles are two fingers from burning out, white melted wax pools around the holders. The screen is set up in front of my bedroom door. The blankets are over the windows.

The DA is dressed all in black: tight turtleneck and pants. He says, "I never realized how awful narcolepsy was, Mark. Are you currently experiencing cataplexy?" He shakes his head, his faux pity the answer to his own question. "These symptoms of yours are just dreadful. I feel for you, I really do. I don't know how you make it through the day."

"Positive thinking," I say. "I'm fine. I could get up and pin your nose to the back of your head if I wanted to, but it'd be rude." The murk is still in my head and wants me to go back under, back down. It'd be so easy just to close my eyes.

He frowns and talks real quiet. He's a dad talking to a screwup kid, the one he still loves despite everything. "From what Ellen tells me, you've had a real tough go of it."

"Ellen likes to worry." Luckily, I'm in no condition to present a state of shock or agitation at the mention of Ellen's name.

"I'd say she has reason to. Look at the couch you're sitting on, Mark. It's absolutely riddled with cigarette holes. Ellen mentioned the couch to me, but I thought she was exaggerating. It's a minor miracle you haven't burned this place to the ground. Yet."

I say, "Those aren't cigarette burns. I have a moth problem." My voice is weak, watery. It usually takes me twenty minutes to fully recover from cataplexy. I need to keep the chatter going. Despite his daddy-knows-best schtick, the gun and black gloves broadcast loud and clear what his real plan is for the evening.

The DA gets up and fishes around in my pockets. I could breathe on him real heavy, but that's about the only resistance I can offer. The DA takes my lighter out. No fair, I didn't say he could have it. Then he finds my pack of smokes, pulls one out, sticks it in my mouth, and lights it. It tastes good even though I know it's going to kill me.

Time to talk. Just talk. Talking as currency to buy me time. I hate time. I say, "Don't know why you and the goons bothered setting the equipment back up. But who am I to critique your work?" The cigarette falls out of my mouth, rolls down my chest and onto the floor between my feet. I hope it's on the hardwood floor, not on rug or debris.

The DA pulls out another cigarette and fills my mouth with it. He says, "Goons?"

I concentrate on the balancing act of talking and keeping the butt in my mouth. I'll smoke this one down to the filter if I have to. "Yeah, your boys, your goons. Redhead and Baldy. I'd like to make an official complaint to their supervisor when all this is over."

The DA leans in and hovers the gun's snub nose between my eyes. It's close enough that I smell the gun oil. The DA waving that thing in my face isn't going to speed up my recovery any.

He says, "Are these the same imaginary goons you warned Ellen about in a voice mail? You said something about a red car and a crooked DA too."

An upper cut to my glass chin. He really did talk to Ellen. I say, "If you did anything to Ellen, I'll—"

"She called me, Mark. Tonight. She was distraught, didn't know where you were. She said you had destroyed the shed today, emptied your bank account, and maxed out your credit cards in the last week.

She told me how strangely you'd been behaving and said your symptoms seemed to have been worsening.

"We had a nice long chat. Ellen is a wonderful and brave person. She told me everything about you and your narcolepsy, Mark. She told me that stress triggers the worst of your symptoms." He moves the gun all around my face, tracing the damaged features but not touching me. "I told her I'd check up on you. And here I am." He switches hands with the gun.

I can't think about Ellen and her motivations for calling the DA despite my pointed instructions to the contrary. It would ruin what little resolve I have left.

I say, "Gee, thanks. You're like a warm blanket and cup of hot chocolate, even if you are lying about the goons through your capped and whitened teeth." Despite my apartment being made to appear that I didn't break down all the film equipment before everyone showed up, I know he's lying.

He leans in and says, "For what it's worth, and that's not much because it has no bearing on what will happen here tonight, I'm telling the truth. No goons. You hallucinated or dreamed them up. This is all about me and you." His voice goes completely cold, can be measured only in the Kelvin scale.

I say, "And a woman. You know, the one who looks like your daughter? Except dead."

The DA doesn't say anything but leans back into his chair.

Need to keep the chatter going. I say, "What about your old pal Brendan? He's dead too."

The DA pushes the gun into my face again and says, "Are you

stressed, Mark?" He looks down toward the floor, to something between my feet. "That cigarette has already caught on something. Can you smell the smoke? You need to be more careful and take care of yourself. No one else will."

He's bluffing about a fire, I hope. The paranoid part of me feels the temperature rising around my ankles, a fledgling fire starting right under my feet, a hotfoot joke that isn't so funny. I try to move the feet—and nothing. Might as well be trying to move the kitchen table with my mind.

I wiggle my fingers a little bit but can't make a fist, wouldn't even be able to hitchhike. But they'll be back soon. My legs are another matter. Those won't be able to hold me up for at least fifteen minutes, maybe longer. My second cigarette is burning away like lost time.

I say, "Jennifer is here."

"Mark, I really am sorry about all of this. I know you don't want to hear it, but at least your suffering will be over. You won't be a burden to Ellen or yourself anymore. It's really going to be for the best."

Now I'm getting mad. The fucker is talking to me like I'm some drooling vegetable and should pull my own plug.

I say, "Jennifer is hiding in my bedroom. Go take a look. I apologize if my bed isn't made. I've been a little busy." My cigarette jumps up and down, performing carcinogenic calisthenics as my volume rises. This is desperation time. I need him to go into that bedroom.

He says, "Mark, enough, really."

"Listen to me! If she isn't in there, you win, and I'll close my eyes and you can burn me up and stub me out like the rest of my cigarettes. But go fucking look, right now!" My voice breaks on the last line.

The DA stands up, puts his gun down on the projector table and his hands in his pockets. Then he leans forward, sticking his face in mine, our noses a fly hair away from touching. His eyes line up with mine and I don't see anything there that I recognize or understand. Anyone who tells you they can read someone's eyes is lying.

I blow smoke in his face and say, "Be careful, that secondhand smoke is a killer."

He hits me in the arms, chest, stomach, and the groin, looking for reactions, movement. I'm the dead snake and he's poking me with a stick.

I feel it all, but I don't move. I say, "Stop it, I'm ticklish."

He backs off, picks up the gun. "All right, Mark, but only because you're Tim's kid. I shouldn't be an enabler, but I'll go look in your bedroom, and then we'll be done."

"Say hi to Jennifer for me."

The DA backs away from the couch, moves the screen out from the front of my bedroom door. Still watching me, he turns the knob and pushes the door open. Yeah, I know now that Jennifer and the goons were a hallucination, but part of me is still surprised that the door is unlocked. Times ducks inside my bedroom.

My right hand is heavier than a mountain and moves like a continent, but it moves, aiming inside my jacket pocket. I don't need more smokes, but I do need my cell phone. I'm moving too slow. I have only moments, moments that can't be defined or measured in seconds, not by me anyway. My fingers are clumsy and thick, but they find the hunk of plastic, hold on, and pull it out. I can't hold the phone up in front of my face, so I flip it open and rest my hand, arm, and phone on my stomach. The LCD screen glows brightly in the dark room.

The DA says, "Drop the phone, Mark." Gun held out like he means it, but he won't shoot me unless he absolutely has to. I'm banking that it would be too messy to cover up. Here's hoping there isn't a run on the bank.

I say, "No need to get your tassels in a twirl, DA, I just wanted to show you I had a little phone chat of my own, earlier."

Goddamn it, the buttons are so small and my thumb isn't ready for the minute motor coordination test. I hit the wrong buttons. The DA lunges across the room. My thumb cooperates, I select INCOM-ING CALLS from the main menu, scroll down, and there it is. The magic number. Phew. It's actually there.

The DA grabs the cell phone, but he's too late.

I'm breathing heavy. Ash floats onto my chest. Cigarette two is getting low. I say, "Take a gander at the screen. That's a list of incom-ing calls, not outgoing. See that menu heading, DA? Tell me, what does it say?"

He complies without looking up. Good DA. "Incoming calls."

I say, "Oh, I lied about Jennifer being here. Sorry about that. If I had told you to check the incoming calls of my cell phone, you either wouldn't have or would've lied about what you saw. That, and it was nice to have a few seconds of me time."

The DA doesn't say anything, just stares at the phone and then up at me.

I say, "I think you recognize Jennifer's number, unless that's some secret line you don't know about. Nah, you know that number. I can tell. Note the time too. She called me this afternoon. Hours and hours ago. And now I'm wondering: have you talked to her since she called me? I'm guessing not. I'm guessing that if she was home, she avoided you like herpes."

He says, "Why would she call you?"

I say, "I'm also guessing she didn't really tell you about our date at Amrheins either. Did she tell you I showed her the pictures? No? Fancy that. Tell me, are you stressed now, Billy?"

He yells, "What did you tell her?"

Cigarette number two is a bullet between my teeth, and I'm chomping the hell out of it. I say, "I told her everything. I told her that once upon a time there were three musketeers, you, my father, and Brendan Sullivan, the lords of Southie—or lords of their project at least—and they decided to try their hand at an amateur porno. Tim was the director, Brendan an actor, and everyone's local hero, Billy, was costar and producer. They found and bribed some young barely-there junkie, and a star was born. Only she OD'd, or was just so drunk she choked on her own vomit, and died on camera as you guys just sat and watched with your thumbs up your asses.

"Some bad luck there, I guess, but you three of Southie's finest never reported the death. No. You see, Billy Times used to go around bragging about mob and Whitey Bulger contacts to whoever would listen. Yeah, you had a big mouth and it was always running, but maybe it wasn't all talk, maybe you weren't just full of shit. So the junkie died in your bedroom, you called in a favor, and the body magically disappeared. But what you weren't expecting was that two of your musketeers, your pals, Tim especially, didn't trust you. Not one goddamn bit. He didn't destroy the pictures or the film. He split them up with Brendan, a two-man tontine of your former musketeers. That's gotta hurt a little, eh, DA?"

While I'm talking, the DA drops my cell phone and it disappears into the rubble. He jams the gun in his waistband, by his left hip, and slumps over to the projector. He plucks the take-up reel and film from the rear arm.

I say, "Fast forward to last week. Brendan saw Jennifer performing on *American Star*, and she looked so much like the junkie, like the dead girl, and your name was being bandied about on fluff news pieces all over the state, Brendan had a belated attack of conscience. He brought me the photos and hired me to find the film. Of course I was, shall we say, indisposed when he was in my office and I thought it was Jennifer who gave me the pics. This is where you come in again. Yeah, this Monday morning quarterback knows taking the pictures to you was a full ten on the Richter scale of mistakes, which resulted in my apartment and office being torn apart and your goons putting the lean on me and making sure Brendan Sullivan was out of the picture, so to speak, or dead if you prefer I speak plainly. But I found the film.

"Oh—and this last bit is pure conjecture, but Jennifer thought it sounded plausible—the narcoleptic me had taken some notes when Brendan was here. The only piece of automatic writing that wasn't gibberish was *South Shore Plaza*, and that notepad was stolen from my office. Haven't had a chance to check dates yet, but I'll bet more than two bits there was some heavy construction going on at that mall back in your day, and Dead Girl has herself a cement plot, maybe parking-garage Level Three?

"That's what I told Jennifer. All of it. She found it to be riveting stuff. Begged me to show her the film and told me she'd help me if I needed it. So, Billy boy, what do you think? How'd I do? Did I get it right?"

He says, "Not perfect. But you're more right than wrong."

He doesn't accuse me of bluffing, doesn't deny the goons, either. I nailed it. Perfect dismount. I broke him down. I'm the one with all the hand. In the midst of the mental back pat, cigarette number two falls out of my mouth and onto my chest. My arms are tree trunks, but I slowly manage to brush the glowing stub off onto the couch— but still too close to me. Wasn't thinking right. Should've flicked it across the room with my fingers.

I still smell smoke, and now I see it. It's coming up from the floor, from between my legs. Unless my floor has taken up smoking, there's a fire down below. I try to move my legs; still no go. I don't have much time.

The DA has gone all quiet. He's the secret that everyone knows. He passes the film from hand to hand. He says, "Jennifer wouldn't believe you."

I try to move, but all I manage is some feeble twisting of my torso and some hip movement. It's not the Twist and I'm no Chubby Checker. The dummy film inside the couch cushion digs into my ass as I move. It's not helping. I say, "Why wouldn't she believe me? Especially after I wind up quote *accidentally dead* unquote."

The DA looks at me, his wheels turning, but they aren't taking him anywhere. He says, "She'll believe me over you. Time will pass, and she'll believe me." He says it, but I don't think he buys it, not even at discount. He stands in the dark of my ruined apartment.

Need to keep those wheels a-spinnin'. I say, "Who was Dead Girl? Tell me."

He says, "I don't know, Mark. I really don't."

The couch on my too-close left is smoking now. Maybe it's my imagination but the apartment is getting brighter. The heat down by my feet is no longer a phantom heat. It's real.

I say, "Come on. It's over, Times. Just cross the Ts for me."

The DA pulls his gun out. I might've pushed him too far into desperation mode. "I can't tell you what I don't know. We found her in Dorchester. Tim had seen her wandering the streets for days, bumming smokes and offering five-dollar blowjobs. We didn't even know her name, and after—after, no one missed her. No one asked about her."

I say, "That's not good enough—" and then a searing pain wraps around my left ankle, worse then anything I've ever felt, worse than anything I've ever imagined. I scream and it's enough of a jolt to bend me in half, send my arms down to the emergency scene. My left pant leg is engulfed in flame; so is most of the floor beneath my feet. I beat frantically at my pant leg, each swipe of my paw like mashing a nest full of yellow jackets into my ankle. I quickly and without thinking or planning try to stand, and manage a somewhat upright position but fall immediately to the left, crash-landing on shards of broken coffee table. That hurts too. The high-intense pain of my actively burning flesh is gone, replaced by a slow, throbbing, and building ache. I belly-crawl away from the flames, but things are getting hotter and brighter in the apartment.

I look up. Times is still there, looking down, watching me, gun in one hand, film in the other. I say, "Burning me up isn't gonna solve anything. You'll still have questions to answer." The flames are speaking now, the greedy crackle of its expanding mouth.

He says, "I'm sorry it has to be this way. I'm not a good guy." He bends down, knocks my hat off, grabs a handful of my hair, and yanks my head up. Can't say I'm thrilled with this by-the-scruff treatment. He says, "Your father wasn't a good guy either, Mark. But I liked him anyway."

The pain in my leg starts to subside and this isn't a good sign, because it likely means I'm going out again, and this time the sleep won't be a little one. I yell, and scream, and bang my forehead on the floor, anything to keep myself awake.

The fire races up the blankets over the windows, throwing an orange spotlight on the room and waves of powerful heat. The DA stands up, coughs, and takes a step toward the front door.

I reach out with my right hand and clamp down on his ankle. I'm a leech, a barnacle, and I'm not letting go. I yell, "Go ahead, shoot me!" He won't. If he's careful, he won't even step on my hand to break it, or mark me up with bruises. He can't chance ruining his quaint narcoleptic-burned-himself-up-smoking setup.

The DA halfheartedly tries to pull his leg out of my hand, and it gives me time and an opening to pull my torso close and wrap myself around his leg. Now I'm an anchor, a tree root, and he isn't going anywhere.

Apparently my apartment isn't very flame retardant, because a full-on blaze is roaring now. I curl up into a tighter ball, trying to keep my assorted parts out of the fire. The DA is yelling, getting more violent and desperate.

I turn my head and pin my face to his leg, trying to protect it. I close my eyes, waiting for a bullet that doesn't come. Instead, he kicks me in the back of the head and kicks me in the ribs, but I'm not letting go. No way.

The DA drags me and his leg behind him, toward the front door. He gives me a few more kicks, then pulls us out into the hallway. My legs are weak, but they have something in them, they have to.

He sticks the gun barrel in my ear, jams it inside, trying to poke at my brain. The pain is like that pressure-point pain where your whole body involuntary gives up. He yells, "Fucking let go! Right now!"

I twist and load my legs under my weight, like I did in preparation for my ill-fated shed leap. Then I lift his leg off the ground and I'm in a crouch. The gun hand goes away with the sudden shift and he stands and waves his arms like a kid on a balance beam. I throw his leg left, which spins the DA around, away from me and facing the stairs.

I jump up, my burned leg erupting into new pain, but I get into a standing position right behind the DA. I grab handfuls of his turtleneck first, fixing to twist his gun arm and pin it behind his back, disarm him, and be the hero, but my legs go out like they were never there. My momentum takes me forward into the DA's back and my legs tangle and twine in his, knocking out his knees. He can't hold us and we pitch down the wooden stairs.

The DA lands almost halfway down the flight, face first, with me on his back, clinging, hands still full of turtleneck, and I'm driving, forcing all my weight down, not that I have a choice. We land hard. There's a crack and I bounce up and manage to stay on his back, riding him like a sled, until we hit the first-floor landing. I involuntarily roll off him, crashing back first into the outside door. The glass window rattles hard in the frame but holds together.

The DA comes to a stop at my feet, sprawled and boneless, his head bent back, too far back, a broken doll. The gun is still in one gloved hand. The take-up reel of film sits on the bottom step, between the DA's feet.

I think about sitting here and just closing my eyes, letting that orange warmth above rock me to sleep. I think about crawling into my office, maybe that bottle of whiskey is still in the bottom drawer of my file cabinet. Those scenarios have a nice captain-going-down-with-the-ship appeal to them, but that's not me.

I grab the film, open the front door, and crawl out onto the sidewalk, the gritty and cold sidewalk, and the door shuts behind me. Everything goes quiet, but below the quiet, if my ears dig hard enough, is the not-so-subtle rumble of flames doing their thing inside the building.

I crawl the first fifty feet down the street, then struggle onto unsteady feet. I use the facades of apartment buildings and pizza joints and convenience stores to rappel down West Broadway and to my rental car.

Inside. I start the car. The dash lights up and I have plenty of gas, enough for another road trip. Beneath my seat, the manila envelope is still there, the pictures still inside, the girl still dead and anonymous. The film goes inside the envelope. It fits.

The sound of flames has disappeared but there are sirens now. One fire truck roars up Broadway past me. I watch it go by; its sound and fury stops at the corner, my corner. Maybe they're in time to save the building and some of my stuff, like the projector. I know better. They won't be able to save anything or anyone.

It's the wee hours of someone's morning. I'm all out of cigarettes, but my leg feels like a used one. Hands on the wheel at two and ten. I check my mirrors. No one is double-parked. My U-turn is legal and easy, and I drive away.

Thirty-eight

I'm back at the bungalow. Ellen isn't home and she didn't leave the lights on for me. I'm used to it. I limp inside the back door and into the kitchen. First I grab that dusty bottle of whiskey from the cabinets above the refrigerator, take a couple of pulls, and then head to the bathroom to check out my leg. Priorities, man, priorities.

I took the back roads to the Cape, made a pit stop or two, pulled over and napped a couple of times. The sun was coming up as I white-knuckled it over the Sagamore Bridge again, but I made it here. And I made it here without another car accident, although I think I ran over a squirrel when I found myself two-wheeling it up a sidewalk. Sorry, fella.

Bathroom. I roll my pants up and the burned parts stick to my leg. I clean it up best as I can in the tub, but the water hurts. The whiskey doesn't help as much as it should. The skin on my ankle and about halfway up my calf is burned pretty good. I have no idea of the degree scale, but the skin is red and has oozing blisters. I squeeze some Vaseline onto gauze pads and wrap things up tight, but not too tight. It's a bad wrap job, gauze coming undone and sticking out, Christmas presents wrapped in old tissue paper. But it'll have to do.

Me and the bottle of whiskey, we hobble into the living room and I sit on the couch like a dropped piano. I take out the manila envelope and one of the pictures, the picture of Dead Girl wearing the white T-shirt and skirt. The photo is black-and-white but I'll remember her in color, like in the film. She seems a little more alive in this picture, as if the second picture, taken moments later, wears that spent time instead of clothes. The girl in the second photo is that much closer to death, and you can see it.

The living room is getting brighter and my eyes are getting heavier, but I can't go to sleep just yet. I walk to the front windowsill and grab the picture of the old fisherman holding whatever it is next to his head, and I still think it looks like a gun. I also take the picture of the three musketeers: Tim, Billy, and Brendan, those clean-looking carefree preteens sitting on the stairs. I escort the pictures back to the couch and put them on the coffee table, whiskey bottle between them.

I pick up the old fisherman, flip it around to the back, undo the golden clasp, and remove the photo from the frame. I put the picture facedown on the table. Don't mean any disrespect to the guy.

I stick the first picture of the girl into the frame. Don't need to trim the edges or margins. It's a perfect fit. I spit-polish the glass. Looks good as new. I put her down next to the boys. LIT in the lower left of both pictures.

The boys. Those goddamn buzz cuts and soda-pop smiles. That picture might as well be of anyone. I don't know them, any of them, never did, never will, and don't really want to, but I know their lies.

I think about taking down all the photos off the walls, making a pile, mixing these two in, then reshuffling the deck and hanging everything back up. Maybe I could forget that way and no one would ever find them again.

I think about Jennifer, Ellen, Janice, and me and of how, because of them, our lives will always be about lies and lost time, just like my little sleeps. I think about the dead girl, the stubborn memory that everyone has forgotten. Maybe tomorrow someone will remember.

I gather up my cargo and walk into the hallway. Framed black-and-white pictures hang on the walls on both sides of my bedroom doorway. Faux-lantern lamps hang on either side of the doorway and beneath the lamps are two pictures. I take those two frames down and stack them on the floor.

I double-check that the manila envelope with the other photo and the film is still inside my jacket. It is. I'm holding on to that sucker like a mama bird with a wing around her egg.

The other photos, those I hang on the wall. The girl and the boys fit the nails and fill those glowing empty spots on the walls, one picture on each side of my door for all the world to see.

I open the bedroom door. Unlike the hallway, it's dark inside. I won't open the curtains or pull the shade. I won't turn on the light. I know where I am and I know where I'm going.

Tomorrow, if there is one, will be for remembering. Now? I'm going to sleep, even if it's just a little one.

Thirty-nine

The sun shines bright and hot, too hot. It's a remorseless desert sun, a sun completely indifferent to the effect of its heat and radiation. It's the real sun, not a cartoon. Can't even be bothered to say *fuck you*.

It's the weekend. Tim and I are in our backyard. I'm five years old. Not everything is green. Debris and old equipment cover the yard. Someone's life has exploded. The shed has been destroyed and is nothing but a pile of sharp and splintered pieces. All the king's men can't put it back together again. The shed is dead.

Tim and I stand in front of the fallen shed, hand in hand. His big hand sweats around my little one and I want to let go. I really want to let go, but I can't.

He pats me on the head, hands me the brown paper bag, and says, "Come on. Let's clean up all this shit."

I follow Tim around the yard. He picks up his old lawn mower along with the sharp and toothy tools that used to wink and gleam at me from inside the shed. They go inside my little brown paper bag. Next into the bag are the bottles of cleaners and bags of fertilizer. There's no game today and Tim doesn't name dogs after the stuff we pick up.

He says, "You can still sing your song, buddy."

I don't. And I won't.

Some of the stuff we find lying on the grass is charred and smoking. He picks up a projector, a screen, and a film can, all empty secrets, and they go into the bag. There are other bits and pieces burned beyond recognition, and I get the sense that this is a good thing. Everything goes into the bag. The bag is getting heavy.

We still have much more to pick up, haven't made a dent with our cleanup effort, but Tim leads me behind the fallen shed, takes the brown bag, and tips it upside down behind the fence. Nothing comes out. Tim says, "Goodbye," as he shakes out the empty bag.

We walk around to where the front of the shed used to be. He kicks at the fallen cinder blocks, gray as tombstones, and paces in the rectangular dirt spot left by the shed. I stay where the shed's front doors used to be, like a good boy.

Tim stops walking and stands in the middle of the dirt spot. He says, "So, kid, whaddaya think?"

The five-year-old me is tired, tired of the cleanup and the questions, tired of everything. I say, "I think you're a coward." It has no ring of authenticity to it, not one bit, because I think I'm a coward too. Like father, like son.

Tim doesn't offer me any apologies, recriminations, or excuses. He doesn't tell me what I know already, that I have to clean up the mess by myself. He doesn't even say goodbye. He turns, walks over the pile of wood and glass and tar, and disappears into the woods behind our house.

FORTY

The real sun shines bright and hot. It has some bite to it.
Spring has become summer. I guess there was a tomorrow after all.
Fancy that.

Ellen and I are in the bungalow's backyard. It's my first time in
Osterville since I was allowed back into my apartment and office just
over a week ago.

Ellen cooks chicken and hot dogs on the small charcoal grill,
the grill from the old shed. I think it's the only piece of the lost trea-
sure she kept. The shed is long gone and she hasn't put up a new
one. Landscapers spread topsoil and planted grass over the site. Grass
grows, but the footprint of the shed is still visible. It's the backyard's scar.

Ellen wears black gym shorts that go past her knees and a green sleeveless T-shirt that's too small. She has a cigarette in one hand, spatula in the other.

She says, "The hot dogs will be ready first." It might be the longest sentence offered to me since arriving at the bungalow.

"Great. I'm starving." A cigarette rolls over my teeth. I'm sitting on a chaise longue, protected by the shade of the house while I wrestle with a newspaper. There are cigarette ashes in my coffee cup. I don't mind.

Almost four full months have passed since the night of the fire in my apartment. Newspaper articles and TV exposés about the DA and the repercussions of my case are still almost a daily occurrence. Today's page 2 of the *Boston Globe* details the complexities associated with the planned exhumation of the body from the foundation of the South Shore Plaza's parking garage.

We know her name now too. Kelly Bishop. An octogenarian aunt, her only living relative, recognized Kelly in the photos, but very little is known or has been reported about Kelly's life. Other than the photos and film, the evidence of their shared time, no further link between Kelly and the boys from Southie has been unearthed.

I don't think the DA was lying to me when he said they didn't know who she was. She was already an anonymous victim, which is why the press drops her story and sticks with the headliners, the DA and his daughter. Kelly's story is too sad and all too real. No glamour or intrigue in the death of the unwanted and anonymous. I remember her name, though, and I'll make it a point not to forget.

I flip through the paper. There's a bit about Jennifer Times in the entertainment section.

I say, "Looks like somebody is cashing in, and it isn't me."

Ellen gives me a hot dog and bun, no ketchup or mustard. She says, "Who are you talking about?"

I say, "Jennifer Times is forging an alternate path back to celebrity land. She's due to be interviewed on national TV again. Tonight and prime time. She has plans to announce that a book and a CD are in the works."

Ellen shrugs, finishes her cigarette, and grinds it under her heel. Her heel means business. It's the exclamation point on the months of stilted conversations and awkward silences. I probably shouldn't be mentioning Times around her. She clearly doesn't want to talk about that.

Then Ellen hits me with a knockout punch. She says, "I saw Tim with her."

I drop the hot dog and ash-filled coffee cup to the grass. I say, "Who?" but I know the answer.

Ellen says, "Kelly Bishop."

I struggle out of the chaise longue. I need to stand and pace or run away. I need to do something with the adrenaline dump into my system. I'm still in the shade but everything is hot again. I repeat what Ellen said, just to get the facts straight like a good detective should. "You saw Kelly with Tim."

Ellen opens the grill's lid, and gray smoke escapes and makes a run for it. She crosses her arms, knotting them into a life jacket. Then she takes off her glasses and hides her eyes. I might not be able to find them.

She says, "It was early evening, and it was already dark. I was leaving Harbor Point to meet my friends on Carson Beach. I'd stolen a quarter bottle of gin from the top of our refrigerator. I got busted later, when I came home drunk.

"I was fourteen. I remember running down the front steps, hiding the bottle in my fat winter coat even though it was summer. I was so proud of myself and thought I was so smart. Well, there was Tim and the girl, arm in arm, walking through the parking lot. He was holding her up, really. She was obviously drunk or high and couldn't walk. I had no idea who she was. She was so skinny and pale.

"Tim said, 'Hey, Ellen.' Then he smiled. It wasn't a good smile. It was a smile I used to get from the boys who snapped my bra strap or grabbed my ass when I wasn't looking. I didn't say anything back to him. That Kelly looked at me but she couldn't focus. She giggled and rested her head on Tim's shoulder. Then they just stumbled away, into the building.

"I invited you down today to tell you this, Mark." Ellen closes the lid on the grill and the smoke goes back into hiding.

I don't know what to think, but I'm angry. I probably shouldn't be. "Why didn't you tell anybody else?"

"I told the police. I told them as soon as I saw the pictures of her. I just didn't tell you."

My anger evaporates instantly and leaves only sadness. Sadness for us and for everything. The truth is sadness. I walk over toward Ellen and the grill and say, "Why didn't you tell me?"

Ellen isn't hiding her eyes anymore. I get the double barrel. "You kept that case a secret from me. You kept everything he did from me."

"I told you everything I knew once I'd solved the case."

"Only because you had to, Mark. Would you have told me

anything if you managed to solve your case without destroying the shed and setting my building on fire?"

I take off my hat and scratch my head. "Yeah, Ellen. Of course I would've told you."

Ellen turns away and opens the grill again. The chicken hisses and steams. It's done. She plucks the meat off the grill with tongs, then dumps on the barbecue sauce. She says, "I know, Mark. I'm sorry. I'm not being fair. But I'm still so angry. I wish you'd told me about what was going on earlier."

"I didn't want to say anything until I knew exactly what had happened. There was no guarantee I was going to figure it all out. Giving you the bits and pieces and then living with the doubt would've been worse."

Ellen breathes in sharp, ready to go on offense again, but then she exhales slowly and shakes her head. She says, "I've tried telling myself that it wasn't Kelly I saw with Tim that night. Maybe I'm just putting that face from those pictures onto someone else's body. It's possible, right?" She pauses and fiddles with the burner knobs. "I do know that just a few days after I saw him with that girl, Tim stopped hanging around with Times and Sullivan and started chasing after me. He was a different kid. He wasn't obnoxious and loud and cocky like the rest of them. He got real quiet, listened way more than he talked. At the time, I thought it was because of some puppy-love crush he had on me. Jesus Christ, I thought he was acting like that because of me. Ridiculous, right?"

Ellen talks just above a whisper but waves the spatula over her head and scrapes the blue sky. "Now, I don't know what to think. Did he only start pursuing me and dating me because of what happened, because of what he did? Was he using me to hide his guilt, to try and somehow make up for that night, to try and become some person that he wasn't? What do you think, Mark? I want to know. I have to know. Can you answer any of those questions for me, Mr. Private Detective?"

I could tell her that maybe it was her and that she somehow saved Tim, redeemed him. But she knows the truth; I can't answer any of those questions. No one can. I don't even try.

I say, "I'm sorry, Ellen," and I give her a hug. She accepts it grudgingly. It's the best I can do.

Ellen releases me quick. "Let's eat before the flies and yellow jackets find us."

So we sit outside, next to each other on adjacent chaise longues, and eat our barbecued chicken and hot dogs. We don't talk because we don't know what to say anymore. When we finish eating we each smoke a cigarette. The filters are pinched tight between our fingers. We're afraid to let go.

Eventually, I get up and say, "Thanks for dinner, Ellen. It was great. I'm getting tired. Should probably move around a bit or I'm gonna go out." I get up and gather the dirty dishes and makeshift ashtrays.

Ellen says, "Thank you, Mark." She doesn't look up at me. She starts in on another cigarette and stares out to where the shed used to be, to where the grass isn't growing fast enough.

I say, "You're welcome."

I walk through the back door, dump the dishes in the sink, then mosey down the hallway and into the living room. I dock myself on the couch as the murk and fatigue come rolling in.

My eyelids are as heavy and thick as Dostoyevsky novels and my world is getting dim again, but I see all the black-and-white pictures are still on the walls. Ellen hasn't taken any of them down. Not a one. Maybe it means that, despite everything, Ellen is determined not to forget, determined to keep her collected memories exactly where they were before, determined to fight against her very own version of the little sleep.

I don't think she'll succeed, but I admire the effort.

ACKNOWLEDGMENTS

There are so many people who need proper thanks that I won't be able to thank them all, but I'll give it a try. If I've forgotten anyone, it wasn't intentional and mea culpa.

Gargantuan thanks to Lisa, Cole, Emma, Rascal, Kathleen M., Paul N. T., Erin, Dan, Jennifer, the Carroll and Genevich clan, and to the rest of my family and friends for their love and support and for putting up with my panics, mood swings, and egotistical ramblings. Special acknowledgment to Michael, Rob, and Mary (along with the tireless and wonderful Lisa and Dad) for acting enthusiastically as my first readers way back when I wrote just awful, terrible stuff.

Giant, sloppy, and unending thanks and admiration to Poppy Z.

"I love Steve Nash, really" Brite, Steve "Big Brother" Eller, and Stewart "Don't hate me because I root for the Raiders" O'Nan. They have been and continue to be invaluable mentors, supporters, and friends. I will never be able to thank them enough.

Big, aw-shucks, punch-you-in-the-shoulder thanks to the following who have shared their talent and helped me along the way: assorted Arrows, Laird "Imago" Barron, Mairi "seismic" Beacon, Hannah Wolf "da Bulls" Bowen, Michael "The Kid" Cisco, Brett "They call me F" Cox, JoAnn "He's not related to me" Cox, Ellen "Owned by cats" Datlow, dgk "kelly" goldberg (you are missed), Jack "I know Chandler better than you" Haringa, John "Don't call me Paul" Harvey, and the rest of the Providence critique crew, Brian "bah" Hopkins, Nick "I hate TV" Kaufmann, Mike "Blame Canada" Kelly, Dan "Samurai" Keohane, Greg "Hardest working man in horrah" Lamberson, John "Purple flower" Langan, Sarah "He's not related to me" Langan, Seth "I'm taller than you" Lindberg, Simon "IO" Logan, Louis "A guy called me Louie . . . once" Maistros and his family, Nick "nihilistic kid" Mamatas, Dallas "They call me . . ." Mayr, Sandra "I can whup Chuck Norris" McDonald, Kris "Mudd" Meyer, Kurt "Fig" Newton, Brett "el Presidente" Savory, Kathy "I played Mafia before you" Sedia, Jeffrey and Scott "But not Kristen" Thomas, M. "Not related to them" Thomas, and Sean "Cower as I crush you" Wallace.

Special thanks to my agent, Stephen "They're coming to get you" Barbara, who understands my work and tolerates my occasional tantrums and delusions.

More special thanks to the entire Henry Holt team, and especially to Sarah "The Dark" Knight for her thousand-watt enthusiasm and for believing in *The Little Sleep* and in Mark Genevich.

Thanks to (give yourself a nickname) for reading *The Little Sleep*. Now, go tell your friends and neighbors or blog about it. Blogging would be good.

Cheers!

About the Author

PAUL TREMBLAY was born in Aurora, Colorado, but raised in Massachusetts. He graduated from Providence College in 1993, and then the University of Vermont in 1995, earning a master's degree in mathematics. During those college and postgrad years he spent his summers working at the Parker Brothers factory in Salem, Massachusetts, unloading tractor trailers, driving the occasional forklift, manning the Monopoly and Ouija board assembly lines, and once beta testing a Nintendo game. After graduation, Paul taught high school mathematics and coached junior varsity basketball at a private school outside of Boston.

He has sold over fifty short stories to markets such as *Razor Magazine*, *Weird Tales*, *Last Pentacle of the Sun: Writings in Support of the West Memphis Three*, and *Horror: The Year's Best 2007*. He is the author of the short speculative fiction collection *Compositions for the Young and Old* and the hard-boiled/dark fantasy novella *City Pier: Above and Below*. He is a two-time Bram Stoker Award finalist and a juror for the Shirley Jackson Awards. *The Little Sleep* is his first novel.

Other fun facts: Paul once gained three inches of height in a single twelve-hour period, and he does not have a uvula. He is an insufferable Boston sports fan, and can shoot the three. He enjoys reading *The Tale of Mr. Jeremy Fisher* aloud in a faux British accent to his children. He plays the guitar adequately, mainly Bob Mould and Ramones tunes. He once purposefully ate a student's homework assignment. Paul still lives in Massachusetts with his wife, two children, a hairy dog, and a soggy basement. *www.paultremblay.net*.